The Town Park
and Other Stories

The Town Park
and Other Stories

HERMANN GRAB

Translated by
Quintin Hoare

With an Introduction by
Theodor Adorno

VERSO
London · New York

Original publication details: 'Der Stadtpark', Zeitbild Verlag, Vienna and Leipzig 1935; 'Hochzeit in Brooklyn. Sieben Erzählungen', Bergland Verlag, Vienna 1957, in the series *Neue Dichtung aus Österreich*, edited by Rudolf Felmayer, vol. 34/5 ('Ruhe auf der Flucht' first published in *Neue Rundschau*, Stockholm 1949, p. 594); 'Der Taxichauffeur' in *Das Silberboot*, vol. 2, no. 2, Salzburg 1946, pp. 79–80; 'Der Mörder' and 'Gespräch des Toten' in K. Hobi, 'Hermann Grab, Leben und Werk' (Dissertation), Freiburg/Schweiz 1969, annexes pp. 134–9.

This collection first published as 'Der Stadtpark und andere Erzählungen', Fischer Taschenbuch Verlag GmbH, Frankfurt am Main 1985. English translation published by Verso 1988. © this translation Quintin Hoare 1988.

Verso
UK: 6 Meard Street, London W1V 3HR
USA: 29 West 35th Street, New York, NY 10001 2291

Verso is the imprint of New Left Books

British Library Cataloguing in Publication Data
Grab, Hermann, 1903–1949.
  The town park and other stories.—
  Verso fiction.
  1. Short stories in German, 1900–1945 –
  English texts.
  I. Title
  833'.912 [F]

ISBN 0–860911–89–6

US Library of Congress Cataloging in Publication Data
Grab, Hermann, 1903–1949.
  [Stadtpark und andere Erzählungen. English]
  The town park and other stories/Hermann Grab: translated by
  Quintin Hoare: foreword by Theodor Adorno and an afterword by
  Peter Staengle.
  p. cm.
  Translation of: Der Stadtpark und andere Erzählungen.
  Bibliography: p.
  ISBN 0–86091–189–6
  1. Grab, Hermann, 1903–1949 — Translations, English. I. Title.
  PT2613.R13A24   1988
  833'.912–dc19   87–34999 CIP

Printed in Great Britain by Bookcraft (Bath) Ltd,
Midsomer Norton, Avon.
Typeset by Columns of Reading

Contents

On Hermann Grab

by Theodor Adorno

The aesthetic nerves no longer serve to register truth. Whosoever still retains sensibility must alloy artistic expression, for the sake of its own truth, with an alien, corrosive kind. The stuff of an artist may almost be told these days by whether he is capable of anything other than what was crooned over his cradle. Hermann Grab had such a carefully sheltered upbringing that Austrian impressionism still came naturally to him when the smooth, shining surface of society had long lain shattered. He lived out the poetic conflict between the tender subject and the entrenched bourgeois world at a time when Kafka was already writing his black parables, in which the subject by now appeared only at its last gasp. Yet, with a toughness equalling his tenderness, he fashioned from anachronism a means of alienation. Terror of the cold, grown-up world became the medium whereby he attributed monstrosity to human experience deprived of it. Just as he did not rebel against the conformist pressure of his milieu, but defended himself with graceful scorn and Jewish jokes, so as a refined and modulated writer he yielded hesitantly to the inorganic, the fragile and the inhuman. The author of lyrical prose submitted to the burden of horror, without a care for his own disposition and prehistory. His strength was the consciousness of weakness.

1

Acquaintance with Marcel Proust marked a turning-point in his literary existence. He shared with him, apart from the imaginary world of wondering childhood, the hypochondria through which he trained himself as a measuring instrument and the genius of remembrance. *The Town Park*, his only published book, still exhibits the influence of Proust and Thomas Mann, with its psychological portrait of the dubious friend and the unsuspecting mother. Later he began to write methodically damaged novellas, like the one about the clerk who – at the very moment when the National Socialist terror is settling over her home town – takes a trip to Italy during which she experiences nothing but the lifeless decantation of approved culture. Finally, he was thinking about a big novel that was to portray the hectic ascent of a Jewish banking family and its destruction in Poland, providing a kind of archetype of society between the two wars.

Its execution was denied him. He spent three years struggling against the incurable illness whose existence he heroically concealed from himself. His luminous consciousness appeared to mock all brute misfortune. The fact that he died without accomplishing what he might have done indicates something about the impotence of the spirit itself.

Words spoken at Hermann Grab's funeral
New York, August 1949

The Town Park

The Town Park

I

When they left the meal table, Renato would always go back to his room for a while. On fencing-lesson days, mind you, he had actually said he would be going out. But even from the next-door room Miss Florence would notice that he was still there. 'Come along', she would call, 'why are you still dawdling?' 'Yes, I'm just going', Renato would say and then sit there a little longer.

Even in autumn it would sometimes happen that a shaft of sunlight spilled through the window-panes. It would reach the hand-basin and cause the taps to shine a little more brightly. These would then be mirrored on the wardrobe and the panes of glass covering the pictures Miss Florence had sent for from England, back in prewar days. She said that the pictures represented Mr Pickwick. But on another occasion she said that the fat gentlemen with red faces were simply Englishmen at sport. They were playing golf, driving carriages and playing at curling. This last activity involved pushing objects before them over the ice with large brooms – objects which Mama maintained were hot-water bottles.

When Renato had stepped out onto the street, he had nevertheless not altered his corporeal state. For what would now have been termed the movement of his feet differed not at all from the repose in which he had been sitting in his chair at home just before; it was the same repose, just as two melodies were the same of which Fräulein Konrad maintained that one was simply transposed into another key. And he would seek to re-establish this selfsame repose even in the fencing lesson. When Herr Kvapny requested him to practise the same thrusts several times, a pleasant electric current would run through his limbs together with the sensation of repose.

In the breaks Herr Kvapny would take off his mask and gloves and look down at the street. The fencing school was on the fifth floor. 'Like ants', said Herr Kvapny, then nodded contentedly. Renato asked him what still had to be covered. 'For now, just the double feint', he said, 'and next year there'll be sabre'. He saw pupils come and go, he knew that some were not yet very far advanced with foils, while others were already registering very fine results with sabres. That was how he ordered his world – in terms of proficiency with the foils and with Italian or German sabres – just as the Creator's world was divided into water and earth, into evil and good spirits and perhaps also into great and petty ones.

On the way back, Renato would notice how one or other of the shop windows would already be illuminated at that hour, thereby transplanting an interior into the midst of the cold streets. In the gateway he would always encounter Herr Knobloch the caretaker, who would be standing chatting to the footman from the second floor, to the greengrocer or to some stranger. It would already be time to switch on the lights on the landings, but Herr Knobloch would have no thought of relinquishing his meditations. He would speak of the times and now and again he would sigh. But since between whiles his face would break into a smile as wide as his gold-rimmed glasses, it had to be concluded that he was not really so dissatisfied with the times, the misery or that year of war, since it all gave him the opportunity to stand here and sigh, in this twilight which had slowly settled upon the streets and which, even inside the building, had soundlessly emerged from the recesses to accumulate with the afternoon coffee-aroma on the stairs.

At home Miss Florence would just be announcing tea-time. Taking tea was a sacred business for her and Renato soon found the ritual with which tea was served and drunk here in the nursery a little ridiculous and wearisome. But Miss Florence attached great importance to this hour. Sometimes one could not even disturb her by speaking during it. If she raised her cup and gazed over it without drinking, then one had to be silent. 'She's thinking about England now', Renato would say to himself. And he saw how she was busy comparing the country in which she now sat at the tea table, and of which she used to say 'People are terrible here, they have no idea of the proper way to do things' – how she was busy comparing that country with her own island. In England, Renato thought, the people are all kindly, noble, valiant and sensitive, though admittedly also rather unjust and limited like Miss Florence herself. But Renato knew that this must be tolerated: this small measure of stupidity which made the ways and purposes of the higher powers so great and inscrutable.

To be sure, there was a contrast between this picture, the picture of Miss Florence's good country, and the views which now, in the second year of war, were presented at school and could be read in the newspapers, of the evil, perfidious Albion, the cunning, insidious enemy (Renato too thought he hated it when, after the announcement of a victory, he went over to the wall to shift the drawing pins with the little black-white-and-red flags on the Ordnance Survey map of the Western Front which hung in his room). But how at that age should a person be presumed to have any thought of bringing things into accord with one another? Even later on, when we may perhaps have succeeded in drawing a little closer to the truth, even then we are certainly still a long way from possessing the full truth which causes all things to harmonize with one another. The world is obviously presented to human vision only in sections and only insofar as these sections are at variance with one another. And if, in the years we call the years of maturity, problems are resolved and the world begins to fall into place, we should not deceive ourselves about this: we have probably reached superficial compromises, while the true harmony remains concealed from us.

Well, so far as Miss Florence was concerned, it could be that she would come to Renato's room just to tell him extra editions were to be distributed on the streets, carrying reports of a victory by the German and Austrian armies. She would be happy then and say it was important to make sure Knobloch did not forget to hoist the flag. But things could also go quite differently. If Renato asked her whether she had already heard about the new victory, it could be that she would give him a long look. 'You're a big boy', she would say, 'you'll soon be thirteen, you ought to know the proper way to behave.' And if she had then made up her mind not to say a word to him, she would stick to that for the rest of the afternoon.

Whatever he tried would then be of no avail. 'Miss Florence', he would say – and he would say it so gently that he could not help thinking himself how fine and touching it sounded – 'Miss Florence, it was really marvellous what we read together yesterday in *Oliver Twist*'; or else he would say: 'Miss Florence, I can't stop thinking about the way those two dogs were fighting in the Town Park today.' But Miss Florence would stare wordlessly before her – her gaze seeming to embrace anew the coast of England, Hyde Park with its children who rode so prettily, the lawns with their broad trees and her dear father sitting on a bench with his big, uptwirled moustache and one hand holding his cane (that was how the photograph showed him) – and Renato could not help saying to himself: 'I'm low and despicable' ('low-minded', Miss Florence was wont to call it).

Sometimes Mama too would come for tea. But she mostly lay on the sofa. Mama was always ill and if Dr Wanka came by, looking hurried and gloomy and holding in one hand the valise in which, instead of slippers, toothbrush and hard-boiled eggs, he carried that silvery something he called his instrumentarium, and if Cook then said to Miss Florence: 'Forever the doctor and nothing but the doctor, the quantity of money it must cost!', Renato would never be quite sure against whom the complaint was directed – against the physician, against the universal scheme of things or against his Mama. 'Your mother is ill', his Papa would say, then fall silent. Renato would look at him, would see the sparse hairs of his moustache and sense that he was angry with his son for not managing to transmit visibly from his heart the substance of his sadness, that sadness which should be felt at his Mama's illness, while in Papa's own case this grief had grown inwards in such an entirely natural manner, he carried the grief so thoroughly ingrained within himself and already knew how to handle it with such assurance, that he could take fruit at table, then read the newspapers and eventually even smile, without thereby violating the rite of his sadness in the slightest (just as an artist at the wheel will take a cigarette and chat, while simultaneously being able to control the swift and tricky ride with the utmost nonchalance).

'It's dreadful that Mama is ill', Renato would think as he stood beside her in her room. And then he would wait for some object to detach itself in the middle of his chest – a small plate to shift perhaps – so that the resulting friction would make his grief over Mama's illness perceptible. It was that same occurrence that he used to expect at chamber-music recitals, when in the darkened concert hall only the little lamps on the stage were burning and they had begun to play a Beethoven quartet. Then he would always think: 'That's Beethoven, that's the most beautiful music ever written, it must be a great experience.' But when the expected failed to materialize, he would give it no further thought.

His Mama always used to ask: 'Have you been tested by Miss Florence?' Then Renato would tell himself that obviously certain words – like the hateful expression 'tested' – possessed the power to summon a situation into existence and equip it with all particulars. When Miss Florence put on her spectacles and sat before him with the Latin grammar in her hand, and when she wanted to hear the sentences from the textbook repeated word for word and asked about things that one did not have to know at all in school – all this obviously came about only because they used that term 'tested'. They probably said: 'A boy must be tested' and just with that word 'boy', moreover, caused a pupil to rise from the earth, who would stand before Miss Florence with head cocked to one side and whose clothes she would inspect – the grey jacket and grey trousers of which Mama always said at the time of 'purchase' that they were 'respectable', then adding: 'It's just the right thing for a boy like him' – whose suit, that is, Miss Florence would want to 'cast an eye over' in order to see whether it was 'in order', while she would already have taken up position with her Latin book and spectacles as if behind some new-fangled machinery of war.

'Transporto equitatum Rhenum', Renato would say when he stood before Miss Florence, 'I take the cavalry across the Rhine.' But Miss Florence would interrupt him at once: 'Whatever possesses you to say: "*I* take the cavalry across the Rhine", here it simply reads: "*take* the cavalry across the Rhine"! You don't have the faintest idea again.'

Renato could, of course, have attempted to explain Latin grammar to her. But Miss Florence understood only what she wanted to understand. For instance, she had not even allowed Hauff's Tales to be explained to her. When Renato had come to her with the book in his hand, to read her the beginning of the tale that started so wonderfully with the description of the evening at the opera and the white-and-gold auditorium, she had always found some reason to postpone the matter. She would be just about to settle up with Cook, or she would be busy with her sewing box. She would have placed the wooden box before her on the table; its yellow colour had changed to grey since the time when it had contained sweets, and Miss Florence would now extract from it, instead of pieces of chocolate, little sewing needles – which, though, she would now and again, perhaps according to the rules of that box, take in her mouth and hold tightly between her teeth like pieces of candy. 'Not now', she would tell Renato when she had taken the needle from her mouth. 'As you can see, I've no time for your Hauff stories.' But Renato knew then that she would persist in her wrong idea of the Tales. If, for instance, he made a remark in front of a stranger about the theatre or about some event or other, Miss Florence would invariably interrupt him. 'Oh, pay no attention to him and his clever talk', she would tell the other party, 'you should know he has read the Hauff stories, that's all.'

Visiting Mama in her bedroom, Renato would look at the elongated glass drops which were always just on the point of falling from the chandelier (but without this ever happening or being able to occur). He would also listen to the ticking of the French clock. A creature rose from its flank – the nether half a fish, the upper a person – a woman who gazed into the distance and shaded the dial with her great bronze summer hat. Renato would think then: 'I could mention something about Miss Florence now.' Miss Florence used to say a great many bad things about Mama in the kitchen. And Renato knew what would happen if Mama were to learn about it. He knew that with this communication – in other words, with certain little movements he could make with his lips – he would execute one of those infinitesimal lever-shifts through which sometimes a complicated piece of equipment, a great industrial plant or a magic theatre, was instantly set in operation. And he also saw what he would trigger off with this little movement: the indignation of his parents at Miss Florence – she would already be packing her cases – a running through the apartment, a slamming of doors and a telephoning and, eventually, also the indignation of the servants at his parents ('It's terrible', they would say, 'she's being put out on the streets in the middle of wartime.'). It would perhaps already be late in the evening. But Knobloch would at once carry her trunk down. He would carry the wide, low trunk on his back as he went down the stairs. Once down, he would place the trunk on the pavement, right under the gas-lamp. And then Miss Florence would sit on the trunk. – But none of all this ever happened. Renato would sit by his Mama and the bronze lady would continue to listen out, there in the motionless air of the bedroom: she would listen, over the slow ticking of her clock, and hear nothing save occasionally perhaps a low gurgle in the central-heating pipes.

Why he could say nothing to Mama – Renato did certainly sometimes ask himself that question. But if he then came to the conclusion: 'I cannot do anything because I love Miss Florence', it would be as if instantaneously – like an instrument in an orchestra which hands over the melody to another: to another, though, which does not wait until the former falls silent to proceed, but already makes its entry heard during the first instrument's final phrase – it would be as if instantaneously that explanation were superseded by a voice that seemed to say: 'No, you don't love her, you've just heard talk of love and you think you must experience it too.' In reality, he thought, it was humiliating just to love her. But if, on some other occasion, he should happen to have to tell himself: 'She's stupid, she's nasty', then the voice would instantaneously be awake again: 'How can you even think like that, you love her really!'

One thing was certain, though. She was quite unlike ordinary people – the teachers at school, the members of his family, the visitors who came to the house. The lives, the words, the opinions of those people were transparent, boring and of no consequence, whereas the figure of Miss Florence seemed, like a priceless tabernacle, to conceal within it a piece of the mystery that kept the world in motion. Sometimes it even seemed as though the mystery itself were brought to the surface for a moment. When she stared in front of her, when she gave no answer, it would suddenly be there; and long afterwards the room would still remain filled with the sadness it had left behind. Often she would not even have to do anything and yet, all of a sudden, one would be standing before it. One might perhaps see her name – two syllables fashioned for everyday use, unheeded like the mechanics of our ambulatory system or like the purpose of the controls for the experienced motorist – might perhaps see this name abruptly lit up and totally transparent, as though illuminated by a lamp placed behind it. And the word Florence – Renato even then connected it with the image of a generously laid out hill town, of beautiful women in red velvet robes, of an impassioned youth and secret passages of arms – this word Florence was so very incongruous in relation to the poor English girl with her pale skin, her pointed nose and her small, lame figure, that it was impossible to restrain one's tears. Her good parents had concentrated all their pride and hope in the name. They had given her the name Florence, whose English pronunciation seemed to transplant the wonders of the fairy town into the fresh green of the North; the image of a young lily could be distinguished in its delicate severity behind the frosted window-pane. But life had decided otherwise and the name, which would have shone appropriately like a lodestar over a happy existence, now had no other function than to expose her physical ugliness to pitiless illumination. 'I love you', Renato would sometimes say to himself and he would think love and pity were one. Should it ever happen that he was unable to recite his history task by heart and she entered his room once more, late at night, to unleash her fury afresh with blazing eyes – he would be lying in bed already and she too would be dressed only in her nightgown – he could not be angry with her even so, for he would see her pitiful, scrawny arms and her small, black plait only just reaching down to the neck of her shift.

Then he had to think of other days too. As they entered the house of an afternoon after a cold walk, she would sometimes say: 'Come along, we'll make ourselves a nice fire in the grate.' He would have to help her with it, pile up the logs and lay newspaper underneath. And when it began to burn, she would say: 'Now we can sit in front of it.' Then he would pull up his chair beside hers, let the warmth climb slowly from his feet through his body and be moved at the thought of Miss Florence, who understood how to savour such an hour.

Though she was always ready to take up the cudgels with relentless criticism against his parents, against the whole family – if Papa had perhaps neglected to introduce her to some stranger accompanying him through the room – it seemed as if she had reserved all her humility in order to bestow her love upon another circle, the circle of the nannies whom they encountered in the Town Park.

Above all Miss Harrison, the little Gérard girl's governess, enjoyed her unbounded respect. Before Frau Gérard had engaged her, Miss Harrison had had a 'situation' in England, in the house of the Duke of Teck, and the children's uncle, King Edward the Seventh, had often honoured her with a friendly handshake. If before falling asleep Renato let the day's images pass through his mind, if he saw Miss Harrison coming with little Marianne along the main avenue in the Town Park, then simultaneously in the background there would always surface that little scene in which the King would hold Miss Harrison's hand in his and shake it for a few seconds in a vigorous, comradely fashion. His bearded face would meanwhile be lit up by a jovial laugh, while Miss Harrison would probably display nothing but that silent smile which she still wore today, when her gentle figure with its mop of blonde hair came gliding very slowly across the gravel from the other end of the Town Park. But the setting of the royal handshake – once the nursery in the Teck residence, another time a room at Buckingham Palace when Miss Harrison had just dropped in with the children to visit their uncle – this setting was so familiar to Renato (it was his own nursery or Aunt Melanie's room with the green plush armchairs) that it took all the frivolity and dissipation of kingship to make the image glow in its painful splendour.

Renato would reflect about this dissipation of kingship and think that precisely only one who scorned dismal principles – those principles which Herr and Frau Martin, his parents, adhered to in pursuit of their boring lives – could manage it: that it was possible only with bad, disorderly finances, only on the basis of a dubious existence, to cause that kingship – saluting in so ingenuous and otherworldly a manner from a blue baronial hall – that kingship in its sombre and yet so tender youthful splendour to rise into flesh anew, here beside the central heating and the water closet. The kings of England could figure in Renato's eyes only as frauds, as frauds just like the great minds and famous artists who knew how to rise above a life such as was lived at home. That was why Marianne Gérard too was such an enviable being, for her mother – so people maintained – was a woman of bad reputation. And since someone had once said it was unclear how Frau Gérard managed to support herself, Renato had concluded that it was necessary to be in unsettled financial circumstances in order to wear such a beautiful red coat as Marianne, in order to have a skin that was transparent at the temples and lustrous eyes.

Miss Florence always used to have a great deal to talk about with Miss Harrison, so Renato and Marianne would be urged to walk ahead of them. These outings took place four times a week, on the days when there was no fencing lesson. Already in the morning Renato would be thinking of the coming meeting with Marianne and even endeavouring to work out in advance the conversation he would have with her. But it would always turn out differently. When the red colour-splash of Marianne's coat appeared on the central avenue and when, as they drew closer, Renato saw her small head slowly take shape against the ground of the grey fur-trimming, it would at first not seem hard at all to begin his narration of Hauff's *Othello*. But once he had begun to submit the story to her, it would very soon be borne in upon him: the admiration he intended thereby to arouse, the admiration he had to transfer from Othello to his own person too – that admiration was not forthcoming. He would not succeed in extracting from Marianne anything except an indifferent: 'Yes, yes, I'm listening.'

But he would still not abandon his recital, would strive to get the utmost out of it – all that was most compelling – while his own voice would seem to sound more and more alien and mechanical to him; the brilliant formulations he worked out, decimated to wretchedly lame creatures, would not find their way to Marianne. But she, meanwhile, would stare in front of her, without altering her expression even for one instant. Only a strand of hair would from time to time be blown into her face by a gust of wind, all the more emphatically bringing into view the immobility of her mouth, her slender curving nose, as in the relief on a terracotta.

To be sure, Renato would occasionally take comfort. He would think: 'She's younger than I am, she can't understand all that.' But when she once said: 'I was at the Concert Rose yesterday, they played fantastically beautifully again', or when his Mama recounted at table how she had heard that the little Gérard girl was a quite unusually precocious creature, then Marianne and her mystery would immediately be wafted off into an inaccessible domain.

The Town Park was traversed by three avenues, the upper, the lower and the broad central one. The upper avenue – which ran alongside the station – they would visit only to make a change, and would always soon abandon. This upper avenue was frequented by people who used the Town Park only as a thoroughfare, and it was as if the aroma of the railway compartment, the aroma of soot and orange peel, had been transported into the open air along with the packages they carried, the women's straw bags and the soldiers' black wooden trunks. Here the man with the wooden leg used to sit on his bench. His world of shadows, with its horrific images of hospital and lodgings, had so thoroughly cast its spell over him that time and again he would be seen to come only here, only to the musty upper walk, rather than to the lighter regions of the lower walk and the central avenue.

The lower walk was always deserted. The children

greatly enjoyed going there and, at the start of their promenade, used to turn off in order to lead their nannies there unnoticed. The path was a winding one and the disposition of its flanking bushes – in winter a dense, entangled mass of branches – would time and again present a surprising aspect. If Renato had managed to make Marianne laugh – this could occur as a result of the most unbelievably simple remark, such as: 'Look at that man's beard over there in the Gasse!' – then he could hope the whole outing might pass off like that.

But they used also to visit the lower walk just before returning home. They would be on the point of leaving the Town Park when, at the last moment, the governesses would appear to change their minds and would say: 'We'll just go once more along the lower walk.' By this time one or other of the windows on the adjacent Mariengasse would already be lit up and the odd vehicle would be passing by, so that with the thud of hoofs and the clatter of the carriage as it traversed the roughly paved surface, the silence from which the noise emerged and into which it faded away again would seem to grow all the more conspicuous. Though Renato had been unable to reach any understanding with Marianne, as he walked along beside her he would already be thinking of the next occasion. Next time – he used to think – he would try to talk to her about *Der Freischütz*, repeat to her what Felix had been saying about the play at school that day. He would play Felix's role and she would be obliged to feel the same excitement that people always used to experience when listening to Felix.

But they did not, in any case, venture all that often into the lower walk either. The nannies favoured the central avenue. Broad and laid out straight as an arrow, it offered an extensive view and the other children with their governesses could be recognized even from a great way off. So sometimes all would come together in a crowd, a great flock of children and a great flock of nannies. But they would usually remain standing only for a short while with the others. Miss Florence and Miss Harrison did not come there to the central avenue to have their conversation all too frequently disturbed! It is not certain, mind you, whether matters may not have stood quite otherwise: whether they may not have come there precisely in the hope of being able to walk with the others. (The respect with which Miss Florence used to speak of all governesses makes this hypothesis not entirely improbable.) Perhaps it was the others who sought to avoid any sustained intercourse with the English women. But perhaps even both parties were interested in winning the friendship of the other, and the only impediment was their mutual awkwardness.

They used to walk with Helene Pauer and her governess, though, whenever they met them. If Marianne saw Helene coming she would be delighted and Renato would know the walk was definitively ruined. He would have to watch the girls strolling off to one side, closely entwined, speaking to one another in low tones and sometimes even laughing. He would then, of course, endeavour to look as though it were all of no concern to him, but it was very questionable whether he succeeded. For Felix Bruchhagen had already once said to him: 'I was watching you yesterday, old man, it was really charming to see how the girls left you in the lurch and the expression on your face.' On the days when they walked with Helene, therefore, he had also to fear being caught unawares by Felix.

From that distance, he would be unable to follow what the girls were telling one another, but he would hear what the governesses were saying and hear Fräulein Stöwe's lamentations about the state of affairs in the Pauer household. 'It's all just a sham', she used to say, '"Outside – ooh! Inside – pooh!", as they say in these parts.

It wouldn't be possible in our country, anyway, for a strong, healthy man like Herr Pauer to attend to his profits and his affairs at home, while out there so many flourishing young human lives are being sacrificed. But you just can't imagine how mean and stingy they are into the bargain. Madame came to me recently: "Oh, Fräulein Stöwe", she said, "you might come and see the new war film with us." But when we arrived there, it suddenly turned out they'd taken only a small box and I was given such a bad seat that for three days afterwards my head was ready to split from the flickering. But from the outside, everything grand and tiptop. Well, a person in our position sees exactly how things really are. One only has to see the common way in which Sir and Madame quarrel with one another. It goes on all day long, and even at table they don't mince their words. For a child like that, of course, it's pure poison.'

Miss Florence would nod with the utmost gravity, yet also with satisfaction, at Fräulein Stöwe's accounts. She dreamed of a world that would be ordered in accordance with better laws; of a world in which governesses, overwhelmed with honours, would run the lives of families, perhaps even of nations. So she used to receive Fräulein Stöwe's descriptions with the dignity and sense of responsibility of a general accepting a report on the enemy's strength; but at the same time also with the superior smile of the historian being informed about new factual material, new research findings, that accord very well with his conception of history, supporting his thesis and his political convictions.

A meeting with Helene and Fräulein Stöwe, though, was a none too common occurrence. Living in another part of town, they usually frequented a different park. Miss Florence and Miss Harrison, on the other hand, remained faithful to the Town Park, remained faithful habituées of its main avenue. Only in the summer months would they not walk there. Outlying gardens would be the answer then, the crush was really too great in the Town Park. In wintertime, however, visitors to the main avenue would be distributed at such distances that it was impossible not to believe in the existence of a higher law, which had stripped the trees of their leaves and laid bare large expanses of grey sky only in order to make space on all sides, thus enhancing the delights of the cold season through transformation of the earth into a clearly visible terrain.

If November were in, it would doubtless have wrapped all the facades on the city streets in a blanket of mist and, by early afternoon, submerged the church interiors in a twilight through which the people now entering the precinct would see the sanctuary lamp glimmering infinitely far away in the distance. But here in the park November would have raised the other side of its Janus head over the scene. Once the leaves had been cleared away for good, the chestnut man with his little engine would have taken up his station on the main avenue and the children too, dressed in leggings and warm coats, would be ready to set out on the journey into winter.

But in order to enliven the melancholy cheerfulness of this image of departure with one last touch, the painter had not refrained from adding a few splashes of carmine red amid the pale-grey tones: the noses of the old gentlemen whose small phalanx used to proceed slowly along the main avenue. Admittedly these were not the noses which, in the paintings of Jordaens or Ostade, figure as the showpiece in the faces of greybeards; which, wreathed in the aroma rising from a wineglass, reflect in their subdued radiance the unconcern of the years that, as an epilogue, are freed from the flow of time and hence resemble the years of childhood, not yet caught up in that flow. The noses of the old gentlemen were quite simply reddened by the air – by that air in which the first cold (like siphon bubbles artificially forced into drinking water) was rising and advancing with all its asperity against the tenderness of living tissue. And the nostrils of these noses, already trembling at the first whiff, would vainly seek to recapture the atmosphere from which they had been driven and which, carefully preserved with the help of rugs on the window-sills, furnished their proper abode betwixt the lion heads of their armchairs – with its mixture of warmth from the stove, the aroma of plush and that wood aroma emanating from the sideboard which, for forty years, has stood in all its oaken splendour anticipating imaginary festivities. To be sure, these old men too had returned to the land of childhood; yet only their renewed need for protection had shown them this path, a path that despite everything was still fairly arduous. For if there was anything to be said, they would stand still, turn their heads towards one another and thus hold a daily rehearsal for the funeral procession which would move off just as slowly from the house of mourning and time and again make a little halt at some street crossing, or at the club premises where the deceased had functioned as a committee member.

Renato used always to be detained by the Valenta brothers. It would usually be the younger of the two, the 75-year-old Doctor, who would address him. 'How is your dear Mama?' 'Well, thank you', Renato would reply. He would say it without considering how his Mama really was. But there would be no variation in Dr Valenta's response either. 'That's all right, then, that's all right', he would say, then he would always stand there for a little while longer. He obviously believed it would not be polite to turn away at once, and for this reason would seek some friendly word to say to Renato. However hard he strove, though, he would never find one, so there would be nothing left for him to do but freeze his features into the smile that had accompanied his last words. And, like some great boulder hanging in solitude above sea level, this smile would appear to project into the embarrassment of the conversational void, but without thereby mitigating the wildness of Dr Valenta's exterior, the terror of his huge form or the menace of his beard which, not yet grown grey, fluttered in wispy strands about his face.

How different this beard was from the other brother's beard! Herr Valenta senior was only one year older than the Doctor, so it was impossible not to think that nature had made one of those leaps here, such as may often be observed – for example, when a liquid is heated and, rather than being transformed by degrees into a gaseous state, is volatilized at once when its boiling point is reached. The older brother's beard had crystallized into silvery-grey ridges of ice and – as the frame for a handsome, ruddy countenance and one component of a well-groomed exterior – was an element of the brighter world. People said of Herr Valenta senior that he was the victim of religious delusions and, as he stood beside his brother (he never spoke so much as a single word to Renato), he would all the while keep his gaze fastened on the heavens, so that one could not help thinking he saw there the Madonna enthroned, surrounded by angels making music. Renato, incidentally, would not know what to say either, so they would all remain standing there mutely. But in the end Herr Valenta senior would awaken from his ecstasy, would very slowly – and as if still overwhelmed by the signs of received grace – turn to his brother and would say in the gentlest of voices: 'All right then, let's go.' Only then would the two gentlemen move away.

If Renato told his Mama when he got home that Valenta had asked after her, she would usually say: 'An extraordinarily intelligent person.' And she would often add that in his youth he had been a dancer and a great admirer of her Aunt Melanie. The image she thus conjured up showed the Doctor in front of Aunt Melanie as she sat in her armchair, forcing his gigantic body into the faint suggestion of a bow while his wrinkled, bearded face was pulled into an embarrassed smile. The advance of time is a fact which we do not wish to apprehend; and if we think we see no young faces in the snapshots of bygone decades, it is not just the fashion of that time which is to blame, it is just as much our own protective instinct by which our vision allows itself to be determined. Hence, the image of those conversations at dances, of that old flirtation, was not so very different from the picture that necessarily imposed itself when there was talk of how Dr Valenta, even today, still put in an appearance at Aunt Melanie's every evening. Only the element of excitement, of an illicit game, had vanished from the picture. The Doctor no longer had to restrain himself. He did not even let himself be deterred from bringing a long pretzel stick with him, in the breast-pocket of his fur coat (since, as he said, one could never be sure that the biscuits one would get at Aunt Melanie's would not be quite stale). Since he now had the custom of not taking his overcoat off even in the room, it would more and more often happen to him as he spoke that the end of the pretzel stick would become entangled in the strands of his beard. Behind his armchair the volumes of the encyclopaedia had been arranged on a shelf in meticulous order. Dr Valenta was very learned and could provide information on every question that came up. But if it did ever turn out that some fact mentioned in conversation coincided with a gap in his knowledge, he would have no inhibitions about rising slowly to his feet, reaching for a volume of the encyclo-paedia and reading out the relevant passage in a loud voice.

On Tuesdays, Miss Florence used to interrupt the walk with the words: 'Today's Tuesday.' Miss Harrison would then nod and say: 'Piano lesson, I was just thinking that.' When they arrived home they would sometimes find Fräulein Konrad already in the room, sitting at the piano and leafing through the music sheets with one hand as she deftly struck a few chords with the other. Miss Florence would always be very flustered then, since she greatly esteemed Fräulein Konrad. She used to say there was no one in the world who could play the piano better. She had got hold of this notion even though Fräulein Konrad had never voiced it – but had always found only the most discreet ways of allowing the fact to be divined. But Miss Florence understood entirely. If Fräulein Konrad said that last night she had been at the piano recital by pianist X – the pianist whom 'Messrs the critics' found so 'world-shattering' – and if she then added: 'It was a disaster, heaven help the pupil who played like that in one of my lessons', then Miss Florence would shake her head in wonder and say: 'There has never been anybody with your ear for music.' Or if she had said: 'All right, now for once I'll play something for you' and then rendered in the highest treble pitch those passages which she maintained sounded like a waterfall; and if, on completion of the piece, she remained sitting quietly for a little while, kept her eyelids – which seemed made from leather – half-closed and raised her snub nose in the air; then Miss Florence would say every time: 'I can find no words!' And she would repeat over and over again: 'No, I simply cannot find any words', until Fräulein Konrad closed her eyes completely. But she would at once reopen them and turn to Renato with a smile: 'You see, Renato.' Then Miss Florence would nod her head several times. Renato would not have been listening very closely to Fräulein Konrad's playing. But as he could see Miss Florence, and now Fräulein Konrad too, starting to nod and waiting almost with exultation for him to shrink visibly as he played, in the face of such expertise, he would feel that he really must contract his body as best he could – though not so much in consideration of Fräulein Konrad's playing as because both ladies expected it of him.

In any case, Renato knew from Helene Pauer that Fräulein Konrad praised his playing very highly and said he was her best pupil. When speaking with his parents too, she seemed to be delighted with his playing. So his parents were very pleased and, on evenings when some stranger was visiting, they would tell Renato to go over to the piano and play Chopin's 'Mazurka' or Mendelssohn's 'Spring Song'. 'Marvellous', the visitor would then say, 'astonishing for his age'. But Miss Florence would always comment afterwards: 'Well, they've had an opportunity to show you off again, thank the Lord!' And she would be fond of recalling the afternoon at Aunt Melanie's when he had been invited to play. Dr Valenta – so she had learned from the housekeeper – had subsequently opined that he did not play well at all. 'It's just that he has been brought up so artistically', Dr Valenta had said.

But however much Fräulein Konrad might enthuse about Renato in front of Helene or in front of his parents, she did not praise him to Miss Florence. To Miss Florence she would say that the lessons were pure purgatory. 'It would be difficult to find another creature as inattentive as this boy', she would say again and again. And if Renato made a mistake as he was playing, and if the mistake were repeated, then she would emit the kind of groan evidently uttered by Prometheus as portrayed in that pen-and-ink drawing in *Tales from Classical Antiquity*, which – with its depiction of the fear-distorted face and the tangled beard apparently alive with vermin, and with its finely hatched vultures – immeasurably intensified the horrors of the book with its yellowed, shiny paper and old black binding. Fräulein Konrad groaned and maintained that a lesson like this gave her a migraine from which she would be bound to suffer all day long.

During the lesson, Renato was fond of saying he was thirsty and needed to fetch himself a glass of water. When he entered the kitchen, he would see Cook sitting in a corner on a low stool and reading her own newspaper, with the aid of silver-rimmed spectacles whose extended ovals rested on the extreme tip of her nose. Even if Herr Knobloch were standing in the kitchen, mulling over with her what Mama used to term 'high politics', she would not relax her grip on the page, but would look up at Herr Knobloch over the newspaper and over her spectacles.

'I've always said it, only artillery can do the job', he asserted. 'We can build gun barrels thirty centimetres thick, in Germany they've got them forty-two centimetres thick. But there has to be cavalry too. Just imagine what a squadron like that can do, all galloping along together.'

'They need the horses for food now', Cook said.

'True, true, you're right there', Herr Knobloch answered with a chuckle. 'They're already slaughtering rabbits now and the other day one butcher was selling a dog.'

'Bread's getting dearer and dearer too', Cook asserted.

Herr Knobloch nodded: 'And nobody knows how it's going to be now with the bread coupons either.'

Cook flared up: 'Oh, for goodness sake, the ones with the money will always have plenty to eat, they get hold of it all right. But for the people, the ordinary people, it's just misery all along the line. Having to queue just for a bit of sugar, that's if they can get it or buy it at all.'

'True, true', Herr Knobloch said. 'But look at all the shooting that's going on down there in Italy again, on that Doberdo Plateau.'

Cook seemed grumpy: 'It isn't called Doberdo, it's called Dobaredo.'

'All right,then, Dobaredo. It was in the paper recently, that Archduke Silvator himself went up onto this plateau. I saw an archduke too last year, riding through the city here. He kept saluting all the time.'

'I can't help thinking about our poor soldiers', Cook said. Her nose twitched and she wiped it on her apron. 'All they're having to go through. They stand in the trenches with the water coming up to their knees. My niece's husband got an illness from it, couldn't stop screaming all day and all night.'

'The soldiers what can't stop shaking', Herr Knobloch said, 'you know, the ones what've had such a fright in the war, the ones what get treated with electricity now, they scream like that too!'

Cook regarded Herr Knobloch angrily. 'You always believe everything. Plenty of them are frauds, they just need it knocked out of them. It's all stimulated. But if someone gets a splinter of that there sharpnell in his leg and his leg gets amplotated, that's when it really hurts. That's when they've got something to scream about. But lots go under too. They get gangrene. Then they're buried outside and get only a wooden cross with their name on it.'

Fräulein Konrad was angry when Renato returned. 'The idea of having to take so long, just to drink a glass of water', she said. In the meantime she had put ready a book of music by Czerny. Renato played the étude with the demi-semi-quavers and saw his fingers moving quite of their own accord. But that did not surprise him, since the passages of the Czerny étude were not palpable in the least. They were unreal, just like the conversation that Cook had been having with Herr Knobloch or like the war which had been the subject of their discussion.

But suddenly Renato came to a halt. For Fräulein Konrad had snapped at him: 'How often do I have to tell you that on this C you have to put your thumb underneath!' – and in the same instant it had occurred to him that his thumb too was unreal and that the thumbs of the soldiers partook of the same unreality, the thumbs of the soldiers who screamed and of those who were buried after their bodies had turned quite brown in the field hospital. But the sight of their screams was now all the more terrifying, in that one could see them hanging like great, elongated fish bladders in the air beside the carbolic fumes and one had no idea where they belonged.

'It's dreadful', Fräulein Konrad said, 'he keeps on getting stuck.'

She was irritable and rapped on the upper ledge of the piano with her pencil.

II

Renato used to tell himself that the way Miss Florence tested him in Latin grammar had no sense. At school, you see, Dr Brischta would always ask about quite different things. It never occurred to Renato, though, to speculate as to whether there was any more sense to be found in the translation Dr Brischta wanted or the formulae he required to be known. But perhaps Dr Brischta himself had no thought of any sense there. One day, you see, he would find a translation containing three mistakes excellent, whereas on another day he would be very shocked at just a single, little mistake. So it was easy to believe that he had no definite meaning of the Latin phrases in mind.

Soukup admittedly used to give another explanation. He said that Dr Brischta's marriage was unhappy, and that everything depended on how his wife had treated him on that particular day. As we all know, the channels through which information of this kind has threaded its path usually lie wholly in the dark. But it should not be forgotten that the less we are able to say about this path, the stronger the truth of a fact grows (the subjective, believed truth and sometimes also – by means of an equally obscure return path – what can be termed in such cases, if need be, the objective truth).

They knew Dr Brischta's wife and often used to see her towards midday, pacing up and down in blonde splendour in front of the high school, with an impatience that appeared understandable on a visit to the school – an errand which a personality such as hers could not help considering a trivial and unworthy affair. They used accordingly to think of her if, in some book title in a shop window or on some cinema poster, they read of 'the demonic nature of woman'. They would think of her blue dress and her large hat, and they would think too of her glances – which seemed, when she emitted them, to touch things in their orbit like terrible, magic wands of silver. When Frau Brischta came along on the school excursion, they admittedly noticed that she was much smaller than had appeared from a distance, noticed the lobster-red skin in the cleavage of her linen blouse and saw a wart with a hair growing from it on one of her rather plump cheeks. She spoke like any other woman, moreover, about apricot cakes and about fine weather (she used to say 'abricot gakes' and 'fide wedder'). But despite all this, they did not underestimate her demonic nature. It almost seemed, indeed, as though they now for the first time saw her demonic nature leap forth among broken saucepans, past hair bleaches and hardened cheese – as though it now for the first time revealed its true power.

Dr Brischta would be thinking about his wife if he sat mute on the rostrum at the start of the lesson. He would keep his mouth open beneath his small dark moustache and would tap one cheek with his hand at regular intervals, so that each time his pince-nez would quiver. That demonic nature had settled like a layer of mist upon his spirit, causing the Latin words to dance in his head as they saw fit and also regulating the order of good and bad marks in his pocket-book.

Dr Brischta, always busy with his own thoughts, also had his own way of speaking. (He would rap out every

word and then always close his mouth very hurriedly.)
Sometimes they would see him standing at the end of the
corridor. He would stand with knees flexed, the hemisphere
of his black hat sitting at a tilt on the back of his head.
With one arm raised aloft he would move his index finger
up and down and, as he rapped out the words 'Gangway
clear' to the rhythm of this movement, he would stare into
an indefinite distance.

But that may perhaps have been a joke, just as what he
used to do when his class was over was obviously a joke.
Since the Latin lesson, you see, was always the final hour
that concluded the afternoon, it would fall to him to take
the class register back to the office. Well, he would always
take a pupil with him to carry the register. But the
latter – Renato was most often chosen for the task – the
latter would have to keep at a fixed distance behind him
on the way to the office, so that the two of them, teacher
and pupil, used to stride through the corridors and the
stairway with the sacrament of the register like a priest
and his acolyte.

If Miss Florence had things to do in the vicinity of the
school, she used to pick Renato up. They would then
usually stop for a while in Frau Zuleger's little stationery
shop. The space was almost entirely filled by the form of
Frau Zuleger, who – mighty and endowed with knowledge
of higher decrees – used to dispense 'teaching materials':
who knew the rulers that Dr Weinzierl wanted and the
notebooks that were required for Dr Brischta; who would
always allocate pupils the right thing, without brooking
any contradiction. But Miss Florence used to savour the
pleasure of breaching official norms. She enjoyed good
relations with Frau Zuleger on a private basis, and Frau
Zuleger used to show her the military postcards her son
sent from Russia. 'It's really terrible', she would say, 'the
winter in Russia', and she would let Miss Florence see the
cardboard boxes of comforts which she used to send her

son, the woollen socks and the salami sausage. Sometimes
only a red card would arrive from the front, with a pre-
printed text which read: 'I am in good health and doing
fine'. 'They're not allowed to write themselves', Frau
Zuleger would say, 'I don't know why, I think it's so the
enemy won't pick anything up.'

Frau Zuleger had many other things to complain of too,
things that she did not like to mention in front of Renato
or whose relevance Renato did not understand. But Miss
Florence likewise intimated that her life was impeded by
adverse factors. 'As you know', she would say to Frau
Zuleger – and if the two of them then looked at one
another, shook their heads a little and now and then
glanced down at Renato, he would think to himself that
his parents must surely be the cause of Miss Florence's
complaints, and would preferably do something to make
himself invisible there in Frau Zuleger's shop.

Sometimes a piano would be heard from the living-
room. It used to sound as though the hammers were
striking sheets of glass. Fräulein Zuleger, the daughter,
was the player. She, too, had taken lessons from Fräulein
Konrad and she now offered tuition herself. But if
Fräulein Konrad was a good teacher, Fräulein Zuleger
was undoubtedly a bad one. Fräulein Konrad could in any
case hardly remember her. 'Oh, her', she used to say and
cast her eyes heavenward, 'yes, well she didn't really study
with me, but with one of my pupils.' Sometimes Fräulein
Zuleger used to put in an appearance behind the counter.
She had dark eyes in a pallid face. Miss Florence would
say that Renato was a pupil of Fräulein Konrad's.
Fräulein Zuleger would nod and, as she surveyed Renato,
would undoubtedly be thinking something appropriate
and not very flattering to him. But Renato himself would
be struck dumb in the presence of Fräulein Zuleger, who
radiated about her all the majesty of her insipid face, her
dismal room and her badly paid lessons.

For Dr Weinzierl's mathematics classes, in particular, there were many purchases to be made at Frau Zuleger's store. Dr Weinzierl required pupils to bring a geometry set to school; small, medium and large rulers; a small and a large set square. 'It's incredible', one of the mothers once said to Miss Florence, 'he must think we're made of money.' But Dr Weinzierl was implacable and imbued with the dignity of mathematics. He was so convinced of its majesty that, when presenting some new method of calculation, he would be quite unconcerned about whether the class was following or not. And when he then made one after another of the pupils – those 'grubby fellows', as he was wont to call them – sit down with an 'unsatisfactory' grade, it would come to pass that each time he recorded the mark a smile would light up his magician's head with its pointed beard.

Dr Weinzierl was also a great patriot. He used to run the pupils' funds for War Sponsorship, for Blind Welfare and for the Red Cross. He also used to accept subscriptions to the war loan. There were some pupils who used to maintain that he related the marks he gave to the level of patriotic service. It was incidentally Dr Weinzierl too who had introduced the collection of metal. Since the army, so he claimed, needed all kinds of metal – copper, nickel, bronze (in his deep bass, he could pronounce the word 'bronze' with French distinction) – it should all be brought along. Frau Martin allowed two copper pipes to be removed from the kitchen and Renato carried them to the physics room. Everything was stacked up there and Dr Weinzierl was finally photographed in the midst of his magic world. Saucepans, lamp-shades and sugar mortars, together with the regiment of small objects – inkwells and door latches – all this lay on the ground or was arranged on the benches in the physics room; he himself stood upright in the centre of the picture and surveyed the dimensions of what had been achieved; while in the background the physics apparatus, rammed close together, failed to disturb the solemn scene with its shadowy, humdrum presence. The view that it was possible to obtain Dr Weinzierl's goodwill through patriotic contributions incidentally seemed disproved as a result of this collection. For Fiala had brought along a large pot made of pure nickel, and Dr Weinzierl nevertheless notified him of an 'unsatisfactory' mark in his half-yearly report. So they had not found the secret of Dr Weinzierl's classifications after all.

But with Dr Piller things were different. For in this case it was quite clear who was going to get good marks. Dr Piller had his 'little protégés' and if one of them came to a halt in his Greek translation, there would be a silence during which nobody knew what would happen. Dr Piller would twist the ends of his moustache up, then fold his arms and present his hook-nosed, cuirassier's face in profile. He would display his handsome, knightly form, which seemed the product of an epoch long gone by. But when he proceeded so deliberately with the rudiments of Greek that they knew it all without listening; when his movements were so slow that they could tell themselves they had never seen such weariness; then it was quite clear that in that knightly figure, for all its stateliness, only a last remnant of the old juices still survived. It was a remnant just as, despite all outward monumentality, one perceives it only as a remnant when one enters some castle of the late Middle Ages: the owners' line has died out, been reduced to poverty or finally abandoned the castle as an abode; the furniture has been cleared out; the sentinel has forever relinquished the watch-tower; and in the courtyard overgrown with grass one can hear crickets chirp and see a clump of daisies standing in the sun. Such a remnant of knightly splendour, however, had nevertheless survived precisely in the master's person. And even if all bellicosity had taken refuge in the sentences of the

Greek textbook (which spoke of the sentry who stands before the tent), they would nonetheless sometimes see a faint semblance in Dr Piller's face, as when in subdued tones he used to translate some Greek sentence or other into German: when, for instance, he would say: 'Virtue brings honour'. What virtue was it, of which he spoke? And what honour? His knightly virtue? His knightly honour? The black eyes would from time to time suddenly light up in his great, immobile face. But the blaze would soon be extinguished again – and from the playground they would hear two planks banging together or the clink of bottles being unloaded at the mineral-water store.

If the school day began with Dr Piller's class, the comfort of morning repose would be prolonged for an hour. (A comfort which, let it be said, we discover in morning repose precisely when a rather difficult day lies ahead of us: one of those pleasures which grow stronger in proportion to the shakiness of the ground upon which they rest. But who knows, perhaps such pleasures should not be seen as anything special. Perhaps, in reality, there is no other pleasure and no other joy. For the subterranean action of our anxieties evidently cannot be suspended. Aside from despair, therefore, it is perhaps not unreasonable to assume nothing but a weaker and a stronger state of alertness: a weaker one in which our loves and our anxieties exist in a certain apathy, and a stronger one in which these possibilities appear to exert themselves. And that is how it is with intensified love, perhaps intensified anxiety too – anxiety about an imminent existential disaster; anxiety about the possibility of a million-year-long void that we are destined to enter with our imminent death – it is perhaps this anxiety too that our word 'happiness' encompasses.)

Sometimes Renato would indeed tell himself that he was happy. He would tell himself this if he woke up in the morning and saw that it was still dark in his room. In front of the windows an occasional tram would already be rounding the bend and its sounds – the ringing of the bell and the squealing of the wheels on the tracks – would extend for a little while against the background of the dark, empty square. Once Renato got up at this hour and he then had the good fortune to feel corporeal as had never previously befallen him. He positioned himself at the window and was able to see out through the shutters. On the opposite side, amid the black terraces, a shop selling provisions was brilliantly illuminated. At that distance, the dimensions of the scene were greatly reduced: the cabbage heads on display, the apples and pears, the woman handling the scales, all this was shrunk to tiny proportions, but at the same time intensified in its plasticity – which, enclosed in those little bodies, was obviously all the more powerfully effective. Renato saw the coloured fruits in their lovely, pitiful toy existence; he saw the woman moving slowly and steadily about the shop – another woman came in despite the early hour, purchased something and placed the object slowly in her large, black bag – and this scene, in its as it were pastoral contentment, was so finely embedded in the street, whose nocturnal peace and darkness seemed all the more precious in this morning hour, that Renato did not know what he should do. He leapt back into bed, so that the springs rang and the brass frame jangled.

But the darkness of the room and the chant of the tramway outside on the square – all this was not really there if, on waking in the morning, Renato suddenly noticed how his limbs had scattered in the most disparate directions and if, as he then collected together the separate parts of his body, he was terrified by the question of whether what he was assembling was also a human among other humans. What he then glimpsed would vanish in a trice, though. And if he then thought about what the terrifying thing was that he had seen, he would know only – know very faintly ('with the faintest of memories', it might have been put), just as the terror beneath his ribs too was now faint – would know only, I say, that in that instant he had seemed to himself infinitely large. He had been so large that all other humans – who were accustomed just like himself to call themselves 'I' – were accommodated within that largeness, and had even found so much room that all of them merely covered the floor of that space like a thin layer of sand (and he himself like a small being among them); while above them (hence above him and at the same time also within himself, the large being) arched a chamber stretching to infinity.

If Miss Florence at breakfast then sat and reached for the jam – she said it was not proper jam at all, though, and spoke of an unimaginable English substance that consisted of whole fruits – if she held her knife in thin, unnatural fingers to spread a little of the stuff slowly upon the bread (she would again be staring in front of her, during this little English ceremony that she had managed to preserve), then Renato would see she had no inkling that, between him and her and behind their backs, there was a truth; and that it was possible to think about this truth also (without being able to find it again just then, though, or to keep hold of it at all).

In winter, when they arrived at school the gas-light would be burning in the classroom. They would have plenty of time and often Renato would not yet have any thought of getting down to learning his Greek vocabulary. But when Felix Bruchhagen entered the classroom – he would often remain standing in the doorway for a moment or two and his profile would be visible against the background of the darkness outside on the corridor, which only at isolated points seemed diluted by the wavering light of the tongue of flame – then Renato would sometimes even leave be his Greek vocabulary for good.

Miss Florence did not like Felix. 'A rude, cheeky boy' was her customary expression. And to Frau Martin she used to say: 'That schoolfellow is a bad influence on Renato.' Then his Mama would nod meaningfully. To be sure, she did not prevent him from visiting Felix and even inviting him to the house. But if his Papa on returning home should happen to encounter Felix accidentally on the stairs, he would come into the room with a smile that he obviously considered crafty and say: 'Aha, that was young Bruchhagen.' And Renato would reply: 'Yes, that's right, Papa, it was Bruchhagen, he has read a tremendous amount already' – but Herr Martin would appear unconvinced even by this revelation and reach for the evening paper without answering a word. The poor things were basically to be pitied, remaining immune as they did to such an apparition – Felix, in their eyes, being nothing more than one of the 'friends' who used to visit Renato, simply a schoolfellow like Fiala, Pollak or Zimmermann.

But when Miss Florence said: 'That Bruchhagen, he'll soon be making sure you know everything a boy doesn't need to know', she was much mistaken. She did not realize that things are usually not just simpler, but at the same time always also more complicated, than we ever think.

For in school Felix used always to say: 'We mustn't corrupt young Martin.' Then Fat Pick would laugh and the others, Woska, Krebs and Soukup, would laugh too. But even the rest of them used to repeat it and say: 'Young Martin mustn't be corrupted', and one would find Thin Pick himself fending off some question from Renato merely with a wordless gesture. This was intended to be the gesture of a person who smilingly intimates: 'I really mustn't betray that secret.' But in spite of the movement Thin Pick used to execute with his hands – he would seem to be trying to push an object aside with the back of his hand – and the smile he used to force onto his horsy countenance, he never succeeded in reproducing the gesture. On other days, though, Renato would be able to talk to Thin Pick about *Der Freischütz* or *Die Meistersinger*, just as Felix used to talk about such things; and if the other boy bent down his head as he listened and made a movement with his hand that was meant to appear casual, Renato could even tell himself that Thin Pick now admired him.

Fat Pick, on the other hand, had little interest in *Die Meistersinger*. The oldest in the class, before high school he had attended a middle school for two years and, in addition, had already had to repeat one year of high school; a large if indefinite tally of years had, as with a tree trunk, deposited the layers of their age rings round his body. So he would sit behind Renato on the farthest bench, filled with the substance of the lost years which seemed all the more dreadful for being hidden, and would transmit nothing to the surface of this world but a light, high, husky laugh (which on its way always dyed Fat Pick's ruddy face a little redder).

During lessons Renato and Fat Pick used to talk and they talked so much that Dr Brischta said he would suggest to Dr Piller, the form master, that he move one of them to another place. Once Dr Brischta said to Renato: 'Your friend Pick', and by doing so made him as sad for a moment as we are all obliged to feel when we suddenly and – however often it happens – with fresh surprise see ourselves confronted by human error; by the underestimation or overestimation of a person; by one of those countless misconceptions with which men live and which they carry with them to the grave. Thus Dr Brischta thought of Renato, that it was possible for him to share the life of a mythical creature like Fat Pick in his secret kingdom; and thought at the same time, indeed, that he did not see the horror of the abyss towards which Fat Pick was drifting.

Well, if one thought about this abyss – however in-

definite it might seem – one could of course pity even Fat
Pick; and Renato sometimes used to believe he could do
his own bit to save him. He used to believe then that he could
perhaps 'educate' him, just as Miss Florence was trying to
'educate' Renato himself when she punished him on days
when she found in the morning that he had blue circles
under his eyes. The fact that he almost never received the
punishment, though, on the actual days when he had done
what Miss Florence called 'misbehaving' – on those days
she usually noticed nothing – this had hardly anything to
do with the matter. Miss Florence had her own purpose,
and Renato would have liked to make the same purpose
known to Fat Pick. He saw the furrows beneath his eyes
and said (just as Miss Florence was accustomed to say):
'You should give up that bad habit.'

Fat Pick grinned: 'What do you mean then, what bad
habit?'

Renato was scared to give the thing a name. So he said:
'I mean what you probably do in bed.'

But Fat Pick burst out laughing: 'What I do in bed.
That's really gorgeous. In bed! This Martin's really
marvellous. In bed!' The word 'bed' seemed to impress
him mightily. And while his laughter was already abating,
he continued to gasp it out, though at longer intervals and
more and more faintly, in the end only as a barely audible
gurgle – just as an orchestra, slowly calming down after a
big explosion, will come out a few more times above the
now-subsiding billows with the theme of that explosion, as
so to speak an echo; but lets it venture forth more and
more faintly, with more and more delicate groups of
instruments and more and more bashfully, before the
whole thing finally fades away.

But Fat Pick did not grow calm, however. He asked:
'Right, why should I give up that habit then?'

'Because you're ruining your health by it', said Renato.

Whereupon Fat Pick turned aside with a careless gesture. 'It's already ruined', he said.

Well, however alarming this was, it was still clear that they had not understood one another. Each had probably been speaking about something different. But whatever the stupendous inferno might look like, into which Fat Pick had relapsed in endless raptures, he had nevertheless ruined his health. It could now be seen, moreover, that he had sacrificed himself coolly upon the altar of the unknown felicity, without ever breathing a word about it; and the fat cheeks and thick lips of his bloated face – the entire surface layer of which used to be conspicuously suffused by an even red colour – every separate patch of that flesh had all at once revealed itself as a truly precious substance, in the magic of his ruined health.

If Felix noticed that Fat Pick or Woska were signalling to him, he would follow them at once and leave Renato standing; and if he then paced up and down with one of them in front of the first row of desks, and laughingly huddled against him (laughing about those things of which he would always say to Renato: 'You don't understand anything about that, old fellow') – then Renato would see that, on his face too, a little flush had mounted right to the hairline. When asked who was his best friend, Renato would certainly always say: 'Bruchhagen'. But he knew he was thereby conjuring up a picture that was too simple.

At any rate, it would also sometimes happen that on entering the classroom Felix would pay no attention to the others. He was just reading a big novel. '*War and Peace* by Tolstoy', he said. 'It's marvellous. But a lot of it's very hard going', he added without looking at Renato at all. He was staring ahead of him, as it were at an invisible interlocutor who like him understood the book.

But then he turned again to Renato: 'Yesterday I read a

splendid chapter', he said. 'Prince Bolkonski, he's an incredible person, you see, he dies in the war against Napoleon and as for the first time he thinks he's dying, he sees above him only the blue sky growing bigger and bigger.' And as he recounted this – he was standing leaning against the classroom wall, in the gas-light that cast its friendly shadow – one could believe that he himself was that Prince Bolkonski, so young and handsome, who had to die in war. Thus did he lie upon the alien, dark-green soil, in front of those white horses, silken banners, blue-and-gold uniforms which a many-coloured paintbox had recorded with the martial brilliance and melancholy of Napoleonic water-colours, isolated at fairly wide intervals against a broad horizon; and with his fine, pursed lips, the strand of hair that had fallen across his face and his gaze that vanished into the furthest reaches of the sky, he was so exactly like Felix – who could sit motionless and silent on the bench and simply let it wash over him when Dr Brischta was holding forth – that the hero first revealed his neglected virtues, his suffering and his youth through the quivering of just those lips, before filling the landscape with the poignancy of his death.

But Renato could not even contemplate reading *War and Peace* himself. 'Oh, of course', said Mama, 'young Bruchhagen reads that kind of book, a fine idea at your age! But just tell you that you should read *The Bride of Messina*, and naturally you show no interest.' Then Renato would think about the cinnabar-red Schiller volume, that contained nothing but the skeletons of small, alarming characters that looked as though they were jostling and clattering against one another – as did the words too, though they only appeared to clatter but were in fact supposed to be spoken in chorus (as if it were possible for people to speak in chorus at all). But the green Tolstoy volumes were shut away in the glass-fronted shelves. A delicate, golden design covered their spines and made their well-proportioned, curved forms glitter faintly.

Sometimes, in the afternoon, Renato would enter the room in which the library was situated. Miss Florence would be out of the house. When he turned the electric switch, the click of the contact against the wood panelling would produce a sharp, hollow sound. The light which then illuminated the library area dispersed gradually to the rest of the room, in whose darkness – through the aroma of wood and unused materials, astonishing each time one entered this room after several days – the pieces of furniture made themselves perceptible: those strange, shapeless beasts who lived their own life here in such seclusion, almost always undisturbed, and formed their own, probably sceptical ideas about humans – an unknown sphere of life in the midst of the apartment, comparable only to those unseen world orders of which philosophers speak, which perhaps intersect our own existential space and our very bodies in great number, and in which immense mass migrations and diluvial catastrophes occur as we drink a black coffee after our meal or lie on the sofa leafing through an illustrated paper.

Untouched and cocooned in their own life, the books stood behind the glass panes of the library, and since they were left in peace here for years, they had found enough time to develop this life of their own to the full in all its beauty. They had not been exhausted by restless readers tearing their agitated opinions from their bowels, but stood there proud in their youthful, beautifully fashioned binding, as on the first day, in that room where they hardly ever came into contact with humans: an aristocratic elite, in full possession of their arrogance, their irony and their optimism.

And if one looked more closely, one could perceive how the books that Felix was permitted to read were recognizable by their bindings. The green Tolstoy volumes, green like the woods against which the cannons' thunder reverberated and over which the sharp wind came blowing, stood beside a compact mass of dark-red books which bore the inscription: 'Zola'. 'Zola', said Felix, 'shows the awful truth, it's called naturalism. It shows us everything as it really is.' Renato saw the titles on the black title panels of these books – *The Beast in Man*, *The Belly of Paris* – and he saw how these panels afforded a vista, a peep through into the night of disgust and those bloody excesses that shone in the sinister gleam of reality.

But Renato would also have liked Felix to read Hauff's Tales. 'Really', the latter asked, furrowing his brow. 'Should I really read that?' He was so well up in everything that he already knew in advance what would please him or not. 'Yes', said Renato, 'those stories are really excellent.' But he was embarrassed himself as he said it. It sounded as if he merely meant: 'Yes, excellent, you know, just like what those stupid grown-ups call excellent.' And he thought about the Tales and saw them, kindly and helpless, imploring him to speak with Felix on their behalf, and knew that he had failed.

But one day – Renato had in the meantime spoken several more times to Felix about the Tales, for the idea of seeing their fine things, the opera coats, prima donnas and ministers, drawn into Felix's mind with softly beating drums and of then seeing Felix say: 'Yes, you were right, those stories are really wonderful', this idea rose before him again and again – well, one day Felix said: 'Yesterday I read that Hauff of yours, you know.' But he had nothing more to add.

Felix could also be very nice to Renato, though. Once he was ill and stayed away from school for a long while. 'You ought to visit him on his sickbed', Mama said; and with these words she effected that shift of perspectives we so often experience when someone has said something unexpected – whether because they are forgetful; whether because, in a sudden fit, their life and what they think of that life seems not to count for much; or whether because, in a periphery round that life, unknown and contrasting possibilities lie (possibilities which, even if we know nothing of them, nevertheless perhaps for the first time make this life seem endearing). Well, at any rate, Mama spoke about a sickbed visit and spoke of it as though it were a matter of going to see Aunt Melanie or Thin Pick. But since she treated this 'business' as a 'matter of form', its content was for that very reason made manifest – the visit to Felix in all its uncertain beauty – rather as the name of a great writer is made most intensely manifest to us when we see it figure as an inconsequential name among others in the telephone directory.

Admittedly it was not at all certain what Felix would say to so unexpected a visit. But Renato did not have to wait for long in the room to which he had been conducted. Felix soon came towards him. He came in yellow pyjamas, a garb in which Renato was not permitted to walk about the apartment even on days when he was healthy. Otherwise Miss Florence used to say: 'If you catch cold, obviously that's your own fault. But who has to take care of you afterwards? I do, of course.' And if he ever actually did 'take a chill', as she used to term it, then she would not be satisfied simply by his spending the day in bed, but at her bidding unsuspected bolsters and quilts in ever greater numbers would reach the light of day from some unknown locality, they would be thrown over him and while, in the glow that increased in an incomprehensible way, the chill would in an incomprehensible way be 'driven out' of his body (just as, in the glow of purgatory, sins are driven out of the soul), during that time Miss Florence and Mama would stand one on each side of his bed and watch imperturbably over the splendid spectacle of annihilation like gatekeepers to Hell. Of course, Miss Florence and Mama were perfectly right to insist upon the execution of these rites, and the machinery standing at the end of the universe approved their procedure and corroborated it, by bringing the illness to a close. And had Miss Florence and Mama seen Felix in that 'get-up', then the machinery would have endorsed their horror, it would have nodded approvingly when it heard the two of them say, 'If you let them grow up wild, see what it leads to' and, behind a thicket of coarse white beard, its gloating smile would have revealed a row of large teeth. But at the other end of the world there stood another set of machinery, which winked and was delighted that Felix showed such imagination even when ill, watched benevolently how everything came to pass here so naturally and without any fuss, how casually as it were his two trouser bottoms flapped around his bare ankles.

'It's fantastically nice of you to come and visit me', said Felix. He had adjusted an armchair for Renato and was himself sitting on the edge of a chair facing him. Renato saw that the visit pleased him. He even seemed only just able to hold on to his chair. But then he leant back again and laughed in amusement at the remarks Renato was making.

Renato himself was surprised and thought Felix was deliberately overlooking how helplessly he sat in the armchair, with his winter coat and burning face. He was still astonished even when he left. For he had spoken only about trivial matters, about Thin Pick and Dr Brischta, about the hat which the latter had put on so askew that it had fallen off his head. But he very soon stopped thinking about it and could not help noticing how his feet had begun quite of their own accord to move faster and faster over the pavement, between the brown house rows and the rows of black trees, on the road at whose end the light-grey sky was visible like a removable stage-set, like a thin curtain behind which the next scene already stood prepared in hues of purple and gold.

He told himself that in the afternoon he must try to

make it all comprehensible to Marianne. 'Marianne', he should perhaps say, 'I've got a friend! A friend, Marianne, that's what I've got!' And he could hear how this cadence alone contained it all, how the sound alone of such words comprehended in itself all the surprise of that friendship. Only thus would he first attempt to show Marianne what it was all about; of course, his eyes too would doubtless shine in the same way that Felix's eyes shone when he spoke of anything beautiful; and Marianne would take cognizance of the matter in silent astonishment, and even on the way home would still be shattered by the idea that such a friend and such a friendship existed.

But Marianne was not in a good humour when she came to the Town Park that afternoon. The only thing that seemed to interest her was a big fish, which kept leaping above the surface of the water in the middle of the pond. A boy stood on the bank throwing stones at it. Each time the fish sped upwards, its body curved into a semicircle, Marianne laughed and in the pauses she kept her gaze fixed on the pond. Her laughter grew louder – she laughed rather hoarsely, her mouth unmoving and half-open, and only her upper body was shaken by this laughter which sounded like that of a boy – eventually it grew so loud that the lad on the bank turned round. But he merely glanced at her once, then immediately reached for his pebbles again, to fire them off at the water just as before, at short regular intervals.

In any case, Marianne soon had to go home as well. Miss Harrison said she still had some jobs to do and Miss Florence too decided to bring the outing to an end. She said the dampness 'cut' right through one's clothes that day, an observation that Renato never quite understood. When they left the Town Park and arrived on the big square, a gust of wind drove into their faces from the far end. The wind instantly abated, though, leaving behind only a slight warmth in their cheeks, like some bitter medicine which, once in a while, seeks to vindicate itself through a pleasant aftertaste. The square was empty, apart from a man pushing a handcart in front of him on one side. One could see how the mass of the buildings was motionless, even though the earth was revolving at head-long speed and, according to Dr Weinzierl's assertions, was also flying at headlong speed through the universe. But the buildings did not confirm this. They stood unmolested, in a time that was not passing at all and that had suddenly spilled its emptiness into the afternoon.

Though Marianne seemed quite indifferent to the news about his beautiful friendship, Renato was still happy when Felix at some time during the next days said to him: 'You always go out for your walk with the little Gérard girl. She certainly seems to be a charming rogue. I must take a closer look in the Town Park.' Renato was glad to effect the introduction, and was sure of winning respect thereby not just from Felix but also from Marianne.

But when they met, though, Felix behaved rather differently from what Renato had expected. At the moment when he extended his hand to Marianne, he turned red, stuttered occasionally in his speech and was also all too ready to agree with everything Marianne said. It was incidentally astonishing that he could speak about nothing except school, about Fiala and about Dr Brischta, about the hat which had fallen off his head (an event that he had not even witnessed himself, but that he knew about only from Renato's account). But all this did not seem to bother Marianne, she was ready to laugh at the least remark Felix uttered and never before had Renato heard her talk so much. (By the way, speech seemed not to come entirely easily to her either, she too did not always find the right word.)

But Renato was nevertheless to remember this little scene of the first encounter between Felix and Marianne for a long while, and even many years later. It had been preserved in the form of one of those snapshots which our mind produces perhaps quite at random, but which when strung together yield the album we leaf through from time to time and see as our life. They had stopped at the end of the main avenue, at the spot where on one side the grass slopes away to the little pond. Marianne had leaned against the low wire fence, half-sitting and half-standing, supporting herself with her hands on the upper edge of the mesh. It was as though her embarrassment had caused a thin mask over her face to melt, so that the faint pink hue of her cheeks seemed to be exposed for the first time. Her eyes too were released from the compulsion to stare into the distance, so she was able to let her gaze rest on Felix. But she kept her mouth slightly open, as though a low guttural sound were seeking to escape from her throat, in order to carry directly to the open air something of the mystery that her body held confined.

When, after this day, Felix sometimes used to say: 'I like the little Gérard girl terribly', or if he said: 'Yesterday the little Gérard girl looked charming again' – as he said it, he screwed up his face very slightly – when, in other words, Felix praised Marianne, Renato could not help saying to himself: 'He got to know her through me', and was happy at the idea. But his happiness was over when Felix said: 'I had to explain the new guessing game to her first, of course', or when he declared: 'Your galoshes were really comical yesterday, Marianne found them very amusing too.'

So Felix came in this way to the Town Park. He did not come regularly, and in school Renato always used to ask him whether he was going to put in an appearance that afternoon or not. But it once happened that, following this question, Felix looked at him for a few moments. 'You needn't be afraid', he said eventually, 'I've got no time today.' Renato did not know how to reply. But he did not ask his question any more, and thus mostly remained in ignorance thereafter as to whether Felix would come or not.

If he came, the walk could also pass off very nicely, of course. They could talk about the theatre and Felix would try to explain to Marianne why the opera *The Valkyrie* was to be preferred to the opera *Siegfried*, or why *The Barber of Seville* was more beautiful than *The Marriage of Figaro*. It would then always happen that Renato would get a painful feeling in his eyelids, as though his eyes were about to fill with tears. What, after all, was better than this consciousness that everything in the world combined so beautifully?

But it could never be determined in advance how Felix was going to behave. For he found it necessary every now and then to entertain Marianne with comic stories. He would then report how oddly Renato had behaved in the mathematics lesson; how he had stuttered until Dr Weinzierl could not refrain from imitating him in front of the whole class. Or he would recount how Woska had hit upon the idea of tying the arms of Renato's overcoat together, so that the sight he had presented when he put it on had been quite indescribable. Then the two of them would look at one another and laugh. In the end they would evidently not know how to manifest their happiness. So they used to run ahead and pant for fun with exaggerated force, so that even from behind Renato could see the little clouds of their exhalations, before they dissipated in the air.

Among the scenes that Renato's memory retained from those years, a particular place was occupied by the scene depicting the children's party to which Marianne had invited her friends, both boys and girls. In Frau Gérard's dining-room, the fireplace, the wood panelling and the sideboard lie in darkness and only the oval table is brightly lit. The children sit, quite far apart from one another, on tall, dark chairs. They talk softly and when one of the boys lets himself sink back – so that his white sailor blouse stands out against the backrest in the same contrast to be found in the work of the great Spanish portrait painters, when a bright garment appears against a dark background – then, as with the utmost self-satisfaction he allows a piece of chocolate icing to melt in his mouth, one will rediscover in the arrogant face of the infante the frivolity and the sadness of precocious youth and declining empire. That afternoon Marianne wore a dress of black velvet. The yellow tint of her throat was brought out with total clarity. With her head tilted slightly to one side and with a fixed smile, as though her thoughts were elsewhere, she merely answered in a low voice such questions as the children put to her.

But suddenly everything had gone absolutely still, for the door had opened and Frau Gérard came floating in as soundlessly as a magical golden carriage. It is not certain whether she was really clothed with excessive lavishness that afternoon, or whether it is merely to be ascribed to remembrance (remembrance whose powers are already tossing reality into confusion within the hour) if subsequently, in Renato's mind's eye, the thought of Frau Gérard's first appearance displays her that afternoon in fantastic garb, as though she had been festooned with countless tiny little bells or with Christmas-tree decorations; also, moreover, as an apparition without physical substance, so that had anyone ventured to poke through the tinsel, their hand would evidently have plunged into a void – would have found no body at all. With a deliberation that revealed her awareness of the significance of this action, she now drew herself together – setting all the profusion of her filigree burden in motion – before lowering her head with its blonde hair arrangement and pressing a kiss on Marianne's forehead.

When she had straightened up again, she said: 'I hope

Fritz will play something for us today.' Renato could not help taking fright at the expression 'play for'. But after the tea party was over and they had left the dining-room, it was nonetheless another boy for whom the piano was opened.

He played a waltz by Chopin. Renato wondered whether his playing would have pleased Fräulein Konrad. Fritz did not play as she liked. But when the piece was over Frau Gérard, deeply moved, went up to him, stroked his head with her hand and said: 'You've learnt a fantastic amount again', so Renato could not help thinking that he must have played well after all.

The children too applauded, just as at a concert. 'He really is a splendid fellow', Felix said to Marianne, 'he's a genuine virtuoso.' 'Yes, he plays marvellously', Marianne replied. She said it in a low voice, with a nod of her head and a little sigh, just as many grown-ups do when they give no different expression to the highest admiration or most intense delight than they do to the deepest sorrow or most extreme resignation.

Renato looked at the pianist: he stood leaning against the wall, kept his arms clasped behind his back and, as Frau Gérard spoke to him with great animation, alternately raised first his right then his left leg. He had also drawn in his cheeks so that his mouth looked like a snout, his face narrowing from the height of his large glasses downwards.

But Felix seemed still in the grip of Fritz's playing. As he strode up and down in the middle of the room, his eyes fixed on the floor, he was the very picture of a person overwhelmed and possessed. Perhaps the music had really reduced him to this condition, perhaps he wished only to prove his agitation to himself, but perhaps he would also have liked to be noticed by Fritz and by Frau Gérard. Renato made one attempt to detain him. He could not help being afraid, though, that he would be able to utter only words that were banal in comparison with what Felix was now feeling. And as he heard himself say: 'He played wonderfully', he knew at once that he was not saying the right thing. Nor did Felix make any reply. And even when Renato went on to ask him: 'Couldn't we tell him that?', he merely shrugged his shoulders as though to say: 'If you want to be importunate, you can certainly try it.' Then he began his wanderings again.

Of course, Felix could have drawn attention to the fact that Renato too knew how to play. Mendelssohn's 'Spring Song' might perhaps even have sounded very good. Marianne too could have spoken to her mother about Renato's piano-playing. But neither of them said anything. And Marianne listened without a word as a boy addressed Renato and said: 'It's amazing when someone can play the piano like that, isn't it?'

So the afternoon took its course. One week ago, Renato had been invited by Marianne; one week ago, this afternoon had risen before his eyes – an hour one could see in advance becoming immersed in time, like the hour of Christ's birth, of which historians maintain that after it history first began to run forwards and backwards. But now that Renato found himself in the middle of this hour and nothing extraordinary was happening – it was an afternoon such as the children very often spent – he seemed to fare like the researcher who wishes to plumb the inner depths of Nature, but again and again, as his knowledge progresses, uncovers only fresh surface layers. He did now see here, to be sure, the realm in which Marianne and Frau Gérard spent their day. Yet as he walked up the stairs, as he traversed the red carpet and entered the apartment, he could not help seeing how the secret had continually shrunk back a step. Indeed, in the very instant when the drawing-room door had been opened before him the mystery had fled – and the armchairs, the sofa and the cabinets had straight away allowed it to vanish into their interior. And disclosing only their smooth exterior, the pieces of furniture stood there like an assembly of great scholars obliged to attend some boring ceremony, or like society people at a burial. Thus did they seem to be winking at one another here: 'Oh well, just for today we've got a children's party, we'll talk again tomorrow.'

Renato, to be sure, even managed to go on thinking that everything here was just a prelude to the moment when, with her magic key, Frau Gérard would throw open to him the fairy kingdom. He thought about the impending moment of general departure, and thought to himself that she would then stop him and say: 'I've heard a great deal about you from Marianne. This afternoon, you know, was really nothing. You must come back next week and what's more alone, then we'll have a talk.'

But when the time came, she seemed to be overcome precisely by a slight absence of mind and evidently found it impossible to concentrate on the moment. For she stretched out her hand to him quite mechanically and said nothing. Only when, in the line of children, Fritz came to be standing before her did she shake herself out of her reverie. 'I hope, dear Fritz', she said, 'that you'll be coming back to play for me really soon.'

At home Renato had to recount everything about the afternoon. His Mama asked after the boy who had played the piano. 'What', she asked, 'Fritz Burda?' And she grimaced just as though she had swallowed something hot. 'My God, my God', she said, 'I know exactly who he is, it's really sad, those people live in such misery! Frau Spiess lives in the same building and she's always telling me. Those Burdas have a hole of a cellar there, a woman with four children, Fritz is the oldest and there's a one-year-old into the bargain. The woman plays the violin in a cinema. And in the meantime the boy has to look after his brothers and sisters. He even does the shopping. The woman is meant to be very respectable, and apparently

the boy is particularly talented. But what misery that
must be, quite dreadful.' And then Frau Martin said a few
words to Papa in French, which Renato was not supposed
to understand.

Renato was alarmed and pictured Fritz standing in
front of him with gigantic spectacles and his mouth
twisted into a snout, and could also see the brothers and
sisters standing in a row beside him, arranged by height
('like organ-pipes' people used to say in such cases), but
they all had identical faces and each – even the one-year-
old – wore large spectacles.

A few days later Renato was caught by the sleeve in the
street. It was Fritz, but he seemed instantly to regret his
friendliness and turned aside. Renato asked him whether
he had already been to visit Frau Gérard. 'No, not yet',
said Fritz and smiled, as a person smiles when he is
recounting how he has played truant from school for a
day.

So Renato could not help thinking everything was
arranged senselessly. For he would have given his own
life – of which Herr Knobloch always used to say: 'The
boy has really chosen his parents very well' – he would
have given up this life most gladly in order to exchange it
for Fritz's life, which other people found so sad. At any
rate, only for a foolish person was the room nothing but a
slum; in reality, it was filled with a fine gold dust, the
visible sign that Frau Gérard dwelt over this spot as a
tutelary spirit. And had he now handed one of his little
sisters her bottle, as he did so he would be thinking of
Marianne, who had said to him how happy she always
was when he came. And while peeling the potatoes he
would suddenly have been able to tell himself: 'I'm a friend
of Frau Gérard's.' But if he ever had time, he would run very
fast to the Gérards' place. The footman in his brown
jacket would open the door to him, greet him and call him
by name as a good friend of the house. Then he would be

shown into the room, they would play music and chat to one another at great length. But just before the evening meal, at the last moment, Frau Gérard would ask him whether he wouldn't like to stay, another guest was coming too. And once the stranger appeared, she would take him aside saying: 'Come into the next room with me, I like to leave him alone with Marianne, the two of them get on so exceptionally well.'

In view of the Gérard home, the idea of the afternoon which Frau Martin wanted to arrange for Renato was a sheer embarrassment. Without the shadow of a doubt – so Renato thought to himself – everything would be tackled ineptly and in Marianne's eyes the afternoon would merely be a fiasco. As there had been a burst water pipe, the casing had been removed in one place in the hall; the bare, dark-grey wall was visible – it was said that the masonry had to dry out.

When Frau Martin proclaimed her intention of inviting the children, Renato's first word accordingly was: 'But Mama, the hall...' He thought that Marianne would receive a poor impression immediately on arrival. But it was not possible to contend with stupidity. Frau Martin simply laughed: 'I'm not actually inviting the Emperor.' Miss Florence, on the other hand, at once seized the opportunity to put her oar in: 'That's just one more example of what his head's full of, trying to put on airs and play the fine gentleman. A boy like that should be ashamed he's got nothing better to think about.'

On the following day, when Frau Martin spoke about it in real earnest, saying she now wanted to get down to inviting the children, Renato asked: 'Wouldn't you rather wait, for that?' But all the reply he received this time was a look so protracted that, in view of his mother's injured devotion, in view of all the anxiety she felt about him and the disappointment he caused her, his own life – which, after all, was also a life with hopes, anxieties and disappointment – this life seemed instantly to drift away. Older people believe in the curious privilege of being able to set their own sufferings, be these ever so insignificant, over the sufferings of their youngers. Perhaps they claim it only because power lies in their hands; but perhaps also because they believe in the existence of a divine balance that weighs sufferings against each other and upon which their own scale-pan always predominates, loaded down by the fact of their lost youth (youth which so often they have lost only thanks to that same privilege of the previous generations). Renato turned away and ran his fingers through his hair, as he always did when things had become so complicated that there was no chance of controlling them.

The wall in the entrance hall was repaired in good time, after all. But when Renato arrived home on the day of the party, an alarming sight met his eyes. Two long tables were just being moved into the nursery. For the meal was to be taken there, not – as had been a matter of course at Marianne's – in a grown-up living-room. Miss Florence was delighted to demonstrate her acumen in relation to Renato, by once again playing the 'psychologist' as she was wont to call herself: 'It seems to me something's bothering you again...', she said. But Renato could see it would be pointless to make any reply. He did not say anything either when his Mama arrived home laden with presents which she had bought for some ridiculous reason. They would most certainly all find it odd and off-putting, to be invited and then given a present. What were they supposed to do with the presents, anyway? How could Felix use a pocket-torch or Marianne the writing paper with the War Relief Bureau's insignia? The whole thing was doomed.

As they all gradually appeared at around four o'clock, Renato found himself confronted by the problem of how it came about that this process worked. For the fact that four o'clock was the same hour for all of them and that the given address had to mean exactly the same thing to all of them, so that they all really did coincide at the same time in the same place – all of this presupposed a machinery of life operating so amazingly that one was tempted to believe that their confluence, indeed life as a whole, did not exist. However, if one could assume that life did nonetheless exist, then the precision of its mechanisms was all the more wonderful in that it was no well-defined goal that united the others here, no goal that would have been the object of an instinct common to them all or a desire common to them all: nothing brought them here save the execution of a disagreeable task – an as it were abstract duty. That morning, in the Town Park or on the telephone, one of them had undoubtedly said to another: 'We have to go to Renato Martin's this afternoon, unfortunately.' Thus although no allure was involved, no place that would have had the power in itself to attract and unite them, and although at the moment of leaving home they could say only: 'We're having to accept an invitation', this thought nevertheless did not lead one of them to one street and another at a later time to another street, but they all came at the same time, to the same street, to the same house and up to the same floor.

This miracle was soon thrust into the background though, and to some extent diminished, by a new miracle that came to pass at the same time: by the fact that the place itself was transformed. For Renato could not help saying to himself that it was perhaps not so strange after all that they had found the way there, when he saw how his room began to metamorphose, ceased to be his room and had simply become the assembly ground for those who met up there. There was Marianne talking to Felix, here stood Helene chatting to another girl. All this took place just as though they had been anywhere else and not particularly in Renato's room. Marianne perceived a chair and sat down on it. The chair had ceased to be Renato's chair, had become a chair upon which Marianne was sitting. Sometimes, quite suddenly, we think we learn that the reality we have constructed from the raw material of our sensory impressions is merely a chance one; and as we build a new reality before our eyes out of the old materials – just as when we make a new pattern appear before our eyes in a kaleidoscope – we experience the pleasure that art and love afford us. But the pleasure is merely transitory. It sometimes happens that the new pattern is replaced by a third, but for the most part the picture reverts to the first, original pattern (whether because habit reimposes the first picture upon us, or because we have learnt that it is nonetheless a degree more real than any other). Thus too did Renato's room start to return, to grow into the conversational gaps that now developed and to fill them with its ungainliness. 'It's terrible', he thought, 'they're more bored than I'd expected.' Without any doubt, Marianne was finding the occasion exceptionally ridiculous.

But, to cap it all, Frau Martin eventually came in and sought to do her own bit to entertain the children. She brought a gramophone with her, set it in operation and obviously thought the others might be glad of it. They sat against the walls – the position of the chairs, indeed the entire room in general, had lapsed definitively into disarray – and obviously had no idea how to while away the time. Then gradually they left and went home. By the end only two quite small boys were left behind, rolling on the floor to the sound of the gramophone and pummelling each other meanwhile with their fists, until a nanny intervened.

It was quite natural that, next day in the Town Park, Marianne did not utter a word about the party; that while they walked she stared in front of her as rigidly as ever, and only occasionally opened her lips to transmit a brief reply.

Meanwhile, though, they were getting very close to the Christmas holidays. At the same time, very belatedly, the year's first snow arrived. They had already ceased to think of the possibility at all, but at the last moment the sky – which until then had swathed the bare, winter earth in a damp shroud – at the last moment the sky seemed to have second thoughts, seemed to burst open, allowing a whole stock of brightness to dance down with the load of white flakes and thus getting the country into condition just in time for the festival. The snow had submerged the earth and created a suspended living space that in its artificiality – only now and again enlivened by the small, black form of a person making his way across the white surface or incidentally embellished by a slender column of smoke that rose into the clear air as peacefully as the line on a Japanese woodcut – a living space that thus provided the right scenario for the melancholy puppet theatre of festive joy. People said to one another: 'I wish you a happy Christmas!' They were honest enough to think: 'Christmas, there's really no such thing, so I'm not really wishing him anything.' Precisely for that reason, however, it is possible that underneath it all they harboured the most splendid wishes for one another.

The week after Christmas Eve, the last week of the year, was like an epilogue set in an unreal sphere. In the afternoon, one went to the ice-rink. In the club-house – in the room whose floor was overlaid with a dirty layer of caked snow and whose cold atmosphere, behind its tightly closed doors and windows, exuded the preserved flavour of a winter afternoon even through the charcoal aroma and smoke from the vainly struggling cylindrical stove – there in the club-house skates had been strapped on, then, as one stepped out on the silvery surface, one felt oneself met anew by the stream of air which, like the air over an unknown sea, seemed to bear with it the vastness and desolation of strange continents. At the other end of the rink, the master skaters were addicted to their unfeeling arts, each for himself alone. Their forms stood out like solitary sailing vessels against the dim horizon, against that horizon behind which the new year was already arising, blue and cold and without mercy.

Marianne appeared in a dark-blue sports outfit with dark-blue trousers. If she herself had expressed anything about this apparel, or if Miss Harrison had asked Miss Florence how she liked the new outfit, then there would have been nothing astonishing about this change of costume. But since it had come to pass without anyone finding it necessary to express a word, since Marianne had glided up in the novel apparel as though it were the most natural occurrence, it transpired that her beauty disposed of possibilities even beyond Renato's expectation. Marianne was no longer a child, she was a young maiden.

So she too was full of the mystery that nestled at the edge of the ice-rink and whence the new year seemed to emanate. But not just the new year. For the War welled up, gigantic and black and cratered. In silence it had watched 40,000 Russians perish all at once before the fortress of Przemysl, their round faces and brown caps sinking into the mire and each time the mystery reaching up with its thin fingers to grab them. But that was only the beginning. For the mystery spread and spread, from 40,000 to 80,000 and then to a million. One could see how easy it was for the mystery – in war, but also with those who died at home – and that it did not have to think twice. But it was all the harder to understand that which was required of a single individual: namely, that he should think everything over – whether he should go skating, whether he should study for school, whether he should strive to become a grown-up with a tall, dark shape and a large, pallid face.

Renato went back into the club-house. Miss Florence found him there. 'Why ever are you crying then?', she asked.

He had not known Miss Florence was there, so he said: 'Oh, Miss Florence, there's a new year coming!'

Miss Florence recoiled: 'What's that stupid nonsense?' Then the skating instructor entered the room. 'Tell me', said Miss Florence, 'he's crying because a new year is coming, have you ever heard of such a thing?'

The skating instructor was a man of worldly experience. 'That's just like those spoilt children', he said, 'they never know why they're supposed to be crying.'

III

But the War continued, sliding right over New Year's Day. A year before already, it had detached itself from a figure. That had been the scorching hot 14, which seemed planted on the sun-molten, bloody soil like a banner and a gallows. Now the milder 15 had itself come to a close. It had turned winter warfare in dugouts and trenches into a daily monotony. The figures had dropped behind the bulkhead of New Year's Day as though behind a high parapet. They had left the War behind and definitively taken with them all the beauty that blossomed in the crannies of their digits like some unexplored, delicate flora. Now the empty 16 stood there, holding its mouth open and staring towards the War. To this there was now no longer any sign of an end: one could see its grey waters rising higher and higher and see how, on their surface, all the year figures to come were being borne away more and more swiftly.

The pupils were taken to the Iron Warrior. He stood in

a bare courtyard and a wooden roof was erected over him. His head was already covered with nails. This part of him, incidentally, was not immediately recognizable as a head. It could have been thought that the warrior had no head at all and that his neck was merely broadened towards the top. But Fiala said he was wearing a visor.

Dr Weinzierl stepped out in front of the pupils and delivered an address. He said that the Iron Warrior was a noble symbol. Anyone who entered and made a financial sacrifice in order to drive in a nail was contributing to the reconstruction of the fatherland, which would be consolidated by the self-sacrifice of patriots, just as through this spirit of sacrifice a simple wooden figure metamorphosed into an iron warrior. Then he himself drove in the first nail – he held it elegantly between two fingers of his left hand – pronouncing as he did the watchword: '*Viribus unitis!*' Dr Brischta followed him, his head jerking, and rapped out each individual word as he said: 'Black-and-yellow for ever!' Then it was Dr Piller's turn. He contemplated the warrior dreamily and his motto – 'German and loyal' – sounded as though spoken from deep slumber.

If one now came in the afternoon to the Town Park, it seemed as though the avenues had widened; as though the air had become entirely white; as though this patch of ground had prepared itself for a new and endless journey. And when one returned home, one could not help noticing from day to day how, between four o'clock and evening, the brightness rammed in a wedge that grew broader and broader; and how the sluggish light, which now would not budge from the room, sought – as an isolated harbinger of spring – to concentrate all the desolation of the coming season upon this narrow space, at this one hour.

Marianne would come to the Town Park and, if Felix was not there, she would ask why he had not come. 'I don't know', Renato would hasten to say. He would say it in that deliberately mysterious manner in which one speaks when, for the other party's sake, one is trying to emphasize a person's importance. But at the same time he knew he was quite ridiculous, speaking in that way.

At bottom, though, he thought that Felix could never be closer friends with Marianne than he was himself. He knew, indeed, that he himself was Marianne's best friend. He knew it, even though on their walks it was hard to get Marianne to speak, and even though he saw how glad she often was when she could go home. But his Mama would always say: 'Renato is friends with the little Gérard girl', Miss Florence and Miss Harrison likewise treated this friendship as something self-evident and thereby, time and again, disclosed the veritable truth: the truth that was guaranteed by the higher powers and before which that surface truth – which derived its thin, dubious substance only from Marianne's outward behaviour – used instantly to evaporate. The real truth, moreover, also held imbedded within it the law that no other person, not even Felix, could ever figure as Marianne's friend.

A prosperous man who invests his fortune may see ruin coming for ages. Once he is actually ruined, he still wakes every morning with the certainty of having riches at his disposal; and he retains this illusion until some brutal fact brings him to his senses. So too was Renato surprised, when another reality broke through. It occurred before the mathematics lesson. Felix was sitting on a desk, with his back turned towards the teacher's rostrum and his feet propped up on the school bench. He had tilted his head back a little and, without any warning, suddenly pronounced the formula which caused the earth to stand still for an instant: 'I was at the Gérards' place yesterday', he said, screwing up one side of his face very slightly as he did so.

One reads about the pain a piece of news causes; one reads about it and thinks to oneself that the word 'pain' has only a figurative meaning there. But one forgets that even this kind of pain is a physically ascertainable fact, like a headache or a sore throat. Just as Nature with wise foresight makes a woman forget the pangs of labour, so does she – in the interest of preserving the species, of course – make such pains too fall time and again into oblivion and we are astonished each time we feel it anew: the weight that has settled between our upper ribs and our heart spontaneously diminishes and then intensifies once more, eventually filling our entire upper body with its inert mass and compelling us to breathe in deeply when it expands to new, quite unexpected dimensions (this can occur at any moment: merely, say, if a beautiful face, a particular combination of muscles, teeth and hair, has come into our view again or if a particular mouth has smiled). Felix smiled and was obviously thinking about the day gone by.

But during the mathematics lesson the bulky weight remained stuck in Renato's body. Dr Weinzierl spoke of equations with three unknowns, and it was as though his voice came from one of those gramophones playing their records independently of the surroundings they find themselves in; letting their records continue to the end anyway, while in the same room some drama is taking place. Dr Weinzierl spoke of the method of solving such equations and had no inkling of what had occurred in reality. He may even perhaps, as on other days, have sent Woska and Soukup back to their bench immediately after the first question, may have expected this to constitute an event – even though Felix had been at the Gérards' place the day before, Frau Gérard's blue gaze had passed over him (at the moment when, from her corner of the sofa, she held out her hand for him to kiss) and at the last perhaps even both of them, Marianne and her mother, had accompanied him out to the hall, where there had been no end to the laughter and farewells.

Renato learned nothing, though, about that afternoon. When he asked Felix, the latter made no reply, acted as though he had not heard the question and let it be understood that he was too noble-minded to recount something that could not fail to give pain to the other party. And only as if through inadvertence did he let drop in the following week that he had been to the Gérards' place a second time.

When Renato now walked beside Marianne and when he observed her face; her nostrils, which she occasionally twitched; and her cheeks, which seemed taut but nevertheless on contact would probably have been quite soft – this flesh which she carried home after their walk, to the apartment in which she, like her mother, had dispatched the invisible essence that her body held enclosed in the most disparate directions and allowed herself to settle in the most hidden corners – when, in other words, Renato saw Marianne like this, he could not help thinking at the same time about Felix, who together with her in that apartment could rummage in the secrets of her life.

Once, at about midday, Renato saw Marianne and her mother in the street. They were coming towards him very fast, in conversation with a tall gentleman who was laughing politely. Frau Gérard seemed in an unusually good mood and during their rapid exchange also found time to call something to the large, pale-grey dog she was holding on a leash at her side. Her dark-blue dress, her fur and her dazzling, pale-coloured gloves were full of freshness. But Marianne was walking beside the dog. She was obliged to take big strides. She was laughing as well and, in order to see the strange gentleman, she was craning forwards, while her throat was slightly flushed from her laughter. Renato did not know whether he should now raise his cap, but while he was pondering the others had already gone by. However, he thought for a long while thereafter about this apparition, which had flown swiftly past clad in gold armour and which bore within itself, deep beneath all the integuments and layers of its great and arrogant beauty, in great profusion and to the indisputable surprise of any stranger, a new and very special mystery: namely, Marianne's life. He also thought of this encounter when, a few days later, Felix told him how he had accompanied Marianne and her mother on a shopping expedition in town.

Renato still had the walks in the Town Park, of course. But he was soon to discover that he could no longer expect much even from these. For Miss Harrison had applied for permission to return to England and was speaking quite seriously about the prospects of obtaining the authorization, indeed was already even discussing her itinerary. Miss Florence said what a pity it was that there would now be an end to their joint walks. But since she was thinking only of herself here, it seemed to be precisely she who was definitively elbowing aside Renato's happiness and all his hopes.

Miss Florence had incidentally surprised him during this month. One evening she had taken his music stand, placed it on the closed piano and then set upon it the first volume of his piano exercises. Finally, quite softly and with long pauses, she had begun to strike individual keys. She had taken a piano lesson with Fräulein Zuleger, the daughter from the stationery shop.

She had revealed her secret, however, only after Renato had worked it out for himself, and she was determined in any case to shield so fragile and noble a thing as her playing and the lessons with Fräulein Zuleger from the general incomprehension – but above all from his parents. She practised in the evening, when she knew that nobody else would come into the room. And her notes – she often did not strike them correctly, but always only after she had with the aid of her spectacles looked first at the music book and then at her hand – well, these notes, which in themselves would probably already have been very faint, in view of the secrecy had contracted still further. But Renato saw how over these notes – notes which in the case of other pianists had to be regarded only as 'first steps', and which thereafter always ran impatiently into the open air of recital pieces and sonatinas – how over these notes, I say, an entirely new sense of piano-playing had arisen, which came at once to a standstill above the spectacles that Miss Florence wore, then settled tenuous, delicate and insubstantial in the furrows of her brow.

On one of these evenings, however, Cook came into the room unexpectedly. She saw Miss Florence at the piano and was astonished. Miss Florence was alarmed at first, but then she told Cook the whole story. She also spoke of Fräulein Zuleger: 'She coughs all the time during the lessons', she said, 'she's got something really wrong with her lungs.' Cook had set her hands on her hips. Now she shook her head in amazement and seemed quite stunned by the idea of so much suffering and piano-playing.

Renato had a dream at this time. He dreamed that he was watching a lesson given by Fräulein Zuleger. He saw the room behind the shop, saw Fräulein Zuleger, the pupil of Fräulein Konrad (properly speaking: the pupil of one of her pupils), and saw a girl sitting at the piano beside her. There was something strange about the scene, though. Everything was much dimmer and much smaller than Renato remembered it. And he was very surprised, until he realized all at once that the teacher in the room was not Fräulein Zuleger at all, but one of her pupils, actually even a pupil of one of her pupils. And everything here had such infinitesimal dimensions – the girl who was giving the tuition; above all, the girl who was taking the lesson and the tenuous notes she struck, which still existed right at the frontier of audibility; the piano; and the stationery shop – all of this was so small and consumptive that, in view of this minuteness, Renato woke up.

Miss Harrison's departure was settled, so the joint walks too would be coming to an end before long. But during these weeks Renato was often able to forget this. If he was walking alone at Marianne's side, or if Felix was there, he felt as though things would continue like that for ever; and he was able to believe he would really succeed some time in pronouncing the right word, would manage to recount something so interesting that Marianne would stand rooted to the spot and say: 'But I must tell Mama about that. She'll be delighted. She'll certainly want you to come and see us tomorrow on your own.' But then Miss Florence suddenly happened to mention to Miss Harrison how she had heard that people travelling to the Entente countries were all stopped for a week at the Swiss frontier. She said that and, by so doing, provoked an irruption of the world order which the grown-ups had monopolized for themselves, in which they made the trains leave and gave the signal for the black, misshapen ships to move off and stagger across the Channel – they made the whistle peal forth short and shrill, saying as they did so: 'We've no time to think about what these silly children here may want.'

But if Renato was not thinking about Miss Harrison's departure, he was nevertheless not entirely in the wrong – in conformity, you see, with a law of life which ensures that things seldom suddenly go so well for us, and seldom suddenly so ill, as we expect (while catastrophes befall us from a quarter about which we were not thinking at all). For like one of those little fairy shapes which have no sooner vanished who knows where than they appear again, emerging from nothing in a quite different part of the room to stand suddenly on a casket or in a nook – so Renato would see Marianne reappear as if coming, so to speak, from an undreamed-of direction. It was said that, after Miss Harrison's departure, she would be coming for natural-history and, art lessons to the high school, which for the past two years (in the two classes that came 'below' Renato's class) had been admitting girls too. Furthermore, she was already supposed to play a part in the 'Entertainment' – the public evening performance by the pupils with whose organization Dr Weinzierl was busy.

This evening, announced by Dr Weinzierl in an animated speech and already prepared with very considerable expenditure of time, now floated like a vast, immovable barrel, jam-packed with details from the gigantic hall – the brightly clad pupils reciting; the stage-set upon which the curtain was raised; the spectators searching for their places with bewildered looks, then before the start leaning forward in their seats, turning to one side or to the rear, thereby setting in motion all the machinery of their voice which, rising and falling and trilling in the high register, filled the space with a stirring orchestral piece – it was like a great receptacle packed full in this way that the evening floated in the air. Strange habit, which induces us to imagine over and over again what is impending! If we have once reflected upon this, then we have grasped one of the most depressing facts of our existence. But we have not gained much by our reflection. Neither does knowledge avail us, nor the most extensive experience – telling us that it has never come to pass that a pencil lies on the table just as imagination has depicted it; telling us that no embrace or alien body feels, that no noise sounds, as we have pictured it beforehand – all that does not prevent us, in the future too and throughout a whole lifetime, from producing the doomed images: expending our whole life, our spirit and our sensitivity on those works of art which are destined for no other end than for the infinite arsenal of the void.

Dr Weinzierl had asked what everybody could perform at an artistic evening. 'Everybody should tell me where their aptitude lies', he had said and at the same time, all at once, evidently had a sense that he was presiding over a chosen band of little artists; and the half-turn he had given his chair, the sensitive smile with which he gazed in front of him, the delicately intimated flourish with which his left hand accompanied his speech – all of this indicated that as a discoverer and patron of talents, albeit in his little circle, he now felt himself to be a friend of the arts.

He took mute cognizance of Renato's communication that he played the piano and assigned him to hold up a palm frond in the patriotic scene 'The Apotheosis'. But a lady of Fräulein Konrad's acquaintance told him that he really ought to let Renato play. Whether this had happened at Fräulein Konrad's suggestion was not clear.

But at all events – without Renato really noticing how it happened – a system of levers operating high above his head very speedily ensured that his playing became a settled affair. Even his parents agreed. His Papa simply still found it necessary for Dr Weinzierl to hear Renato; this must happen 'for form's sake', he declared. He said Dr Weinzierl should come by on the following Sunday – and thus perpetrated one of those blunders Renato's parents so often perpetrated when, not realizing that other worlds of which they were ignorant existed alongside their own, they would wander quite unconcernedly into those other worlds, innocently causing a shock there and confusing the order of things. Thus Papa did not shrink even from exerting himself personally to 'invite' or actually 'summon' mathematics; from expecting it to climb the stairs with its ray-crowned head as naturally as any other visitor, to deposit its stick in the hall and then 'go on in' and take part 'in there' in the conversations which, as unending and hopeless as a train's rhythmic rattle, would often penetrate as far as Renato's room with the wheel-screeches of laughter and the long-drawn-out signals of civility. It was an arrogant innocence to expect this, an innocence that could not but offend Dr Weinzierl very deeply, but which at the same time, without his being aware of it himself, also made him seem pitiable, since he almost certainly did not know what to do with his stick in the hall and would indubitably lay it with its dirty end on one of those chairs which Mama was always saying should be treated with consideration. But unbeknownst to himself Papa too was to be pitied somewhat at this moment, since he was prepared to meet mathematics with all imaginable friendliness; whereas the latter, in its alien splendour, would not heed the kindly preparedness that had settled upon Papa's cheeks and would let all his courteous speeches bounce off it, not responding to them with even a single expression of civility.

But when mathematics came, it smiled and the steel scaffolding of geometrical figures that held its face together seemed to melt in this smile. And as though thawed in a beatific moisture, so the contours of that face dissolved in a new and gentle flush while Dr Weinzierl, who after a series of bows had accepted Mama's invitation to sit down, with numerous satisfied nods of the head found Renato's piano-playing excellent. Miss Florence, too, had been greeted by Dr Weinzierl in the friendliest manner, as had Fräulein Konrad, who for her part appeared much quieter than one might have expected, but at the same time had laid aside the incorporeal armour which always seemed to hold her erect. At all events, at the moment when Dr Weinzierl offered her his hand, her face had been overlaid by a purple bloom.

But when one saw the Doctor himself sitting in his armchair, holding his fingers politely splayed against one another as he conversed with Mama; and when one heard how he always uttered his majestic sentences only after a faint growl, a rumbling of his deep voice, which he obviously emitted only because he did not know what to say – one could not help finding it strange and even alarming. One could not but be astonished, moreover, not just at mathematics which had dropped from its cloudy heights, but also at Mama: for she did not, as might have been expected, find Dr Weinzierl's discourse 'silly, conceited nonsense', but listened to him very attentively (more attentively, in fact, than she had any good reason to) and eventually even without reflecting told a story of her own – complained to Dr Weinzierl about how Papa could never wait for the end of a meal, but would always have the newspaper handed to him beforehand. His parents and Dr Weinzierl too had thus left their posts, the order of things had meantime collapsed and in the resulting confusion, far below, they were attempting to cling on to one another, to the embarrassment of both parties – his parents and mathematics alike. The inevitable consequence was that their insecurity led them to say things which they would not have permitted themselves on another occasion: to clutch at every topic that seemed available to them, drawing it down to their disordered world and placing it with its porous reverse side beneath the light.

'I believe the little Gérard girl is taking part', said his Mama. And with a smile she added: 'That's really something, for Renato. But it seems to me that he has got a dangerous rival now. Young Felix Bruchhagen is courting her too.' She laughed, with no thought of mentioning 'courting' in connection with Marianne as though she were one of those numerous girls who were to be read about, and who were talked about – one of those girls who, with scarlet faces and contorted limbs, let themselves be subjected to the frightful and humiliating action of 'courting'. Mama did not shrink from lying in wait, as if crouched in a corner, for Renato himself and Felix; and even upon Marianne – whose slender form was planted out there in the Town Park, its precious substance motionless before the drifting clouds – even upon Marianne she did not shrink from quite simply pouncing and, despite her resistance and the exertion that tinged her countenance in pathetic impotence with a delicate flush, dragging her down into the slimy mass of her laughter.

Dr Weinzierl laughed too, incidentally, although he probably had not quite understood what it was all about. 'Of course', he said, 'young Bruchhagen.' And his laughter faded into an approving smirk, as he evidently allowed himself – in consideration of this private visit, this extraordinary and so to speak holiday occasion – to 'loosen the reins' and for once viewed a 'rascal' like young Bruchhagen from the standpoint of amusement and the fine art of living, with a benevolence which seemed also quite casually and absurdly to embrace Marianne.

After Dr Weinzierl had left, Renato's parents said he was a delightful person – and Renato at that moment found them more pitiful than ever before.

Miss Florence too was charmed by Dr Weinzierl. She had, by the way, in the meantime already given up her piano lessons with Fräulein Zuleger. She had done so after a sad piece of news had arrived at the stationery shop. The young Zuleger had fallen on the Russian front. Why, indeed, Miss Florence decided just at this moment to cause the family the loss of a lesson as well, was admittedly not easy to see. But she said: 'It's really impossible to think of piano-playing now.'

Instead of which, she would now often sit for several hours with Frau Zuleger in her room. She used doubtless to sit on the large sofa with her upper body bent forward; she would clench her lower lip in her teeth and look up at Frau Zuleger; and the latter, over and over again and with tears running down her cheeks, would give a rapid little nod of the head.

'You must offer her your condolences', Miss Florence

told Renato. And to the question of what he ought to say, she replied: 'Stupid boy, not to know that.' But eventually she declared: 'You can at least say: "I'm terribly sorry that Herr Zuleger has fallen in the War".' But she did not perceive how sad it was to speak of 'Herr' Zuleger; in other words, that Renato – who had not known the dead man – should now after his death for the first time address him as 'Herr Zuleger'. He should use the title 'Herr' – the title which the barber gave to his client and wherein lay enclosed the route by which the stranger, after leaving the barber's shop, would hurry through the streets and also all the unknown beauty of his future life – whereas, for the young Zuleger, the word 'Herr' could contain nothing but what it denoted (the body lying on the brown earth), so that this word manifested itself here for the first time in all its desolation.

But after Renato had arrived at Frau Zuleger's shop and seen her standing behind the counter, selling a pupil a booklet and then slowly fetching another from its old position, as he had noticed nothing unusual in the little stationery shop apart from the black dress she was wearing, he went outside again very hastily. For, without understanding why, he had felt precisely in view of this limited alteration that he was on the point of weeping (which would have been very disagreeable for Frau Zuleger, who was not weeping herself).

When the month of February had marched in – its lightly built name filled like an airy portico with a pellucid brightness, but at the same time in the symmetrical (neither rising nor falling) sound of its syllables forcing the year to a brief standstill* – it could occur that at the noonday hour, when school was over, the surface of the streets and the facades of the houses would be seen

*The word used is not the usual *Februar*, but the Austrian form *Feber*. [Trans.]

trembling in the sunlight and a warmer air would suddenly be felt, which introduced a spring day quite unexpectedly into the midst of the cold season and which also brought with it from far away a scrap of undefined beauty. But the clouds would very soon close in and, under their sunless illumination, the month of February's level road would lie there once more, the short road along which no progress was made and at whose side from time to time in the afternoon – not as deceptively as in the noonday light, but in its actual reality – the empty, beggar shape of spring would be seen to rise up ever more menacingly.

Miss Harrison said that her departure was drawing closer, but in reality nothing indicated this. Even the concert, about whose approach there was constant talk, still lay as far ahead as when it had first been perceived. Thus Renato was unable to conceive of establishing any connection whatsoever between the pieces he was preparing with Fräulein Konrad – Paderewski's Minuet and Schubert's Impromptu – and that evening, whose square, densely packed gondola with its vast dimensions could be seen swinging on the furthest horizon. Behind our backs, however, time progresses and is able to bring things down even from quite unknown orders and thus to condense situations.

So the walks with Marianne still took place during those weeks. And if Felix came along, it sometimes happened that he would suddenly look mutely at her and then she would smile, would draw the corners of her mouth apart and also widen them, so that beneath her body – beneath that shell which had always until now been seen walking erect, tranquil and tightly closed through the avenues of the Town Park, but which she had now all at once opened up – precisely beneath this body a new corporeal being made its appearance, consisting of a moist, smooth material, an as it were cheap, everyday material. But inserted in

Marianne's life and overshadowed by Marianne's name, it appeared fit to fill this life with a new and painful beauty. One now saw this life raised to a new level; saw that Marianne unhesitatingly bestowed upon it the content of her name, without a care for its costliness, using it as the cheap content of all other names was used – those other names from which the name of Marianne certainly differed only slightly. From the small foundation of this difference, however, all the sweetness of her life now rose up in quite unprecedented strength and concentration.

It happened at just that time, incidentally, that she would sometimes suddenly behave in a friendly fashion towards Renato. She once even allowed him to recount one of the Hauff Tales to her, and what is more listened with interest. But as her mouth was closed and she was taking firm, pounding strides, it could be thought that a splitting of her small personality had taken place, so that there remained here only the Marianne who did her homework and whose grey coat contained the body of a girl who laughed or played guessing games with the others, while the remaining part of her person – incorporated as a new being, borne by the wings of her smile – had definitively vanished into some other region.

Thus did time quite imperceptibly effect a shift of scenes and, just as imperceptibly, cause the boy Renato to slide deeper and deeper into its most dubious realms. For one day the telephone rang. And when Renato arrived at the instrument, he saw at a great distance – infinitely reduced and sitting in a tiny capsule – none other than Marianne. He could also hear her voice coming all that way through to him. She said that Miss Harrison was busy with her travel preparations and he should tell Felix, who did not have a telephone at home, that she expected him tomorrow at two in the afternoon, in order to go with him to their rehearsal for the play.

Renato had not known at all that the two of them were

acting together in the play. And it thus came about that this fact which had suddenly become visible – they had told Renato nothing about it, although he had walked along beside them time after time – that this fact revealed itself as an accidentally fallen fragment of a life that had already long united Felix and Marianne and that already bore within it its own firmly ordained legality, so that they no longer found it at all necessary to inform him about a particular point, be it ever so innocuous. They never thought of speaking about a matter such as their joint acting, because precisely this matter – which in isolation, and viewed so to speak from an abstract standpoint, could be a colourless, banal state of affairs – was in reality harnessed with a thousand threads to that life which they inhabited and which had already long lain there in its unattainable, blue distance. But the telephone rang once more and rang on repeated occasions. And it occurred to Renato that Felix was summoned even on days when no rehearsal was scheduled at all.

IV

Miss Harrison had departed. Her departure had occurred during the week preceding the Entertainment. But not by a single word did she suggest that she regretted being unable to attend the evening or hear Renato play. On the other hand, she did leave behind for him a photograph of herself. Renato said to himself: 'If one receives a photograph from somebody on parting, it doubtless means in effect that one must have been fond of that person.' And he looked at the photograph, saw Miss Harrison's protruding upper lip, which he did not find agreeable at all, and also the hat which sat askew on her head. 'I probably am fond of her', he declared and immediately reflected how strangely it was arranged that one was fond of people who seemed quite indifferent to one. He also thought about how Felix would see the photograph and laugh at it. But Miss Florence would have been angry if Renato had not hung the picture up. So it was fixed upon the wall.

Marianne's arrival in the school also occurred in those days. This event took place, after all, without any great preparation and quite noiselessly. For suddenly, in one of the breaks, she was simply standing in the doorway to the class, standing there like one of those little figures which a magic lantern can transplant into the middle of the room. Renato would have like to show the class how well he knew Marianne. But when he saw her make a sign only to Felix, with a slight movement of her head, he was obliged to remain where he was.

On the way home, however, he thought about the Entertainment and thought about how he would see Marianne there in four days' time. He could not help saying to himself, though, that this Entertainment – which he had always seen at the same distance before him, and which thus could not help appearing like something so to speak standing outside time (it moved further and further away in step with time) – this Entertainment in reality would not take place at all, and in reality it would not be possible to count on meeting Marianne there.

But the fact that time and the Entertainment were fleeing one another was evident on the next morning too. At one stroke, though, the situation had been reversed. For the Entertainment was suddenly standing outside the door in its fluid immensity. And a few moments later when it had entered, time had already left the room, had fled – just as reality flees before a dream, or one dream before another. And one could now see the room and all the days stretching up to the concert evening dangling in empty space, as though in a crystal housing. But even the street outside was enclosed by the walls of this glass palace. For when Renato stepped out into the street at a time when the others were at school, going in an unfamiliar manner to Fräulein Konrad's apartment – she had said this 'extraordinary' lesson must be held in her home, since only with the greatest difficulty had she managed to 'squeeze it in' between two others – when Renato went outside, I say, he saw the passers-by and the trams, which normally travelled through time with such assurance, all at once moving in a space without hours. For the Entertainment had suppressed the hours.

Fräulein Konrad lived with her father. Renato climbed the stairs, entered a dark hall and then a bright room. The piano stood near the window. A dark table with a bare marble top and pieces of dark furniture stood against the wall. 'We know we're poor', said the furnishings, 'and we're proud of it.' They said this so categorically, puffed themselves up so, that one did not dare to look at them.

Fräulein Konrad was unwontedly amiable. She praised Renato, suddenly said that he was playing excellently (she said it even though he did not himself notice any difference with respect to other times). When he had played a piece through to the end, she would nod her head. She had nothing more to find fault with and could hardly manage to say anything. And when Renato looked up, in the silence that now reigned in the room, he suddenly found it very sad to look at her.

Renato had never seen old Herr Konrad. But he could be heard right through the wall, pacing up and down and coughing. So Renato could not help fearing that he might all at once step wordlessly through the door – small and hunched and dressed in black, with a red nose and gummy eyes – like some small sea monster and in egotistical unconcern fill the room with the terror of his ninety years. But then it came upon him all at once that the Entertainment had settled in and was causing all objects to totter. And he felt how, over his fear lest Herr

Konrad might enter the room, a new fear was thrusting its way: much greater in its dimensions and covering the lesser one like a flat sheet. This was the fear of not escaping again from the crystal palace of the Entertainment; of not rediscovering time or anything else at all; and of not even seeing Marianne again.

But within this timeless space there was nevertheless a certain something, a kind of power, which set another something in motion: something akin to hours and to days – so to speak, a novel kind of time. It was not time itself, to be sure (since one was situated on the terrain of timelessness); but it was a copy of time, which rendered itself perceptible and caused a copy of the afternoon preceding the Entertainment to present itself in Renato's room. If anyone had asked Renato on this occasion what afternoon it was, what the date was, he would have said: 'Today's the afternoon of 25 February 1916' (the date of the Entertainment). He would have said this, however, only because other people expected that answer. In truth, he would have known that there was no date. So he would have given a false answer. And although a 25 February had nevertheless now planted itself before him, his answer would not have been the right one. For this 25 February, fashioned from a light material, which stood on the shaky ground of timelessness in the mist that pervaded the air of his room with its tiny pearls in the white, transitional light of the afternoon – this 25 February had nothing to do with the firmly established day in which other people believed.

Fräulein Konrad had said that Renato should not take his music with him to the concert, and that he should not look at the pieces again, since that simply made a person nervous. Miss Florence was busy with the kitchen book. She was adding up, though not as other people did; for, as she calculated, she at the same time muttered series of English numbers with great rapidity and also moved her fingers as though she were playing a scale in the air. It was a clumsy way of calculating, there was no doubt of that. But it was an English way and it would not have been possible to eradicate the habit: this habit which was evidently also that of her father and her brothers and sisters, and which suddenly revealed once again that she – as one was always prone to forget – had brought a little fragment of the great, green England quite intact within her across the Channel and had kept it intact, only to disclose it suddenly all at once in its clumsy beauty in the midst of Renato's room. It was a fragment of that England which appeared also too chivalrous even to ask whether the figures with which Miss Florence was busy (the figures from the butcher and the baker who had their shops in the street below) – whether these figures were worth mentioning in the English language; which thus, in its magnificent indolence, treated these figures as though they were figures from the great, wide world; which perhaps even, in admirable innocence, had no idea at all that such unworthy figures existed as these ones here: figures, by the way, which precisely in their worthlessness caused the dark-blue, steely beauty of the English figures to appear only all the more plainly by contrast.

'You could really keep yourself busy with a book, instead of standing around here', said Miss Florence. 'But Miss Florence', Renato declared, 'I've got my concert today!' 'Now, you, just don't you be too conceited about it', she said, 'practically anyone can do that, after all, with lessons from Fräulein Konrad and even extra lessons into the bargain. When a person has all that!'

Mama had instructed her to supervise Renato's dressing. A dark-blue necktie with white spots was to be knotted round his stiff collar. She tried again and again, but it did not work. Suddenly she flared up: 'Oh, keep still for once, you're absolutely hopeless today!'

Renato thought about the impending concert, and thought how people used to say it was always very exciting to play in public. 'Miss Florence', he said therefore, 'I shan't let you get me excited.'

But that was the signal for Miss Florence. 'What?', she cried. 'Excited? Excited? I've never heard such a thing. The artful little wretch. Lets me dress him, lets me wait on him, then reproaches me. See what I have to put up with. What a lout!'

Mama came in and took Renato to her room. There he found a thread which he fastened to Mama's wardrobe, to one of the hinges. He plucked at it, first holding it loosely then more tightly. The thread thus emitted low notes and higher ones, just as according to Dr Weinzierl's explanation the strings of an instrument always produce different notes according to the tension. But it suddenly occurred to him that he had to have another look at a passage from the Paderewski Minuet. He had utterly and completely forgotten the passage. But then Papa entered, in his overcoat and with a snow-white scarf round his neck. 'It's high time', he said, 'we're already late.' It was no longer possible to pick up the Minuet. And as they drove in the carriage – his parents and Renato and Miss Florence, who offendedly kept her head turned towards the carriage window – during this drive Renato was thinking that all was lost, since he had not found time to have one more look at the Minuet.

The thing was a success, though. And as he sat on the podium – not on a concert podium, but on a stage with its curtain raised in front of the auditorium – he could hear the performed music reaching his ears from afar and playing quite on its own without his help. He thought of Dr Weinzierl, who had stood there with his great, white shirt-front and whose face had thawed into the same red moistness when he greeted the grown-ups as on the day when Renato's parents had received him. Indeed, it even seemed to have become a degree softer, and was on the point of dissolving completely, as he now made his bows – including to Fräulein Konrad, who once again was unable to prevent a slight flush mounting from her neck to her face and right up to her temples. Dr Piller, who was pacing up and down behind the stage, had his hands clasped behind his back. Exactly as though he were holding a corridor inspection, he moved a piece of scenery aside and endeavoured to keep order here, just as in school he used to make certain there was no sandwich paper lying on the floor. Dr Brischta crossed his path, went up to Renato, but at the last moment stopped a little way away from him, his head jerking. 'Oh well, I suppose you're playing today', he said – and would have liked to say more, if anything had occurred to him. The teachers shifted about, were arranged according to height and jostled one another. And Renato said to himself: 'How strange, now I'm sitting and playing in a concert and can think at the same time.' And above the floor upon which his playing moved he saw an upper storey in which those thoughts moved. And he saw, too, how above that storey a second storey rose up, inhabited by his reflection upon those thoughts; and since he could think about this as well – that is to say, about his thinking concerning those thoughts – the third storey was already there in an instant; and thus it rose, higher and higher, until suddenly a gentle fear came stealing into his breast. He saw that he was sitting in the concert and was supposed to play (the pieces he had practised with Fräulein Konrad), and saw too that he was not at all sure whether those precise pieces were crystallizing in the air through the movement of his fingers. But at that moment the Schubert Impromptu was already almost finished.

The audience applauded so heartily that Renato was surprised. The playing had evidently pleased them. Probably not the playing itself, though. It had been correct, as Fräulein Konrad wanted it, but for that very reason it could not please them. And even had it been able to please them in spite of its correctness, they would not have recognized it as being correct. On the contrary, a little creature had evidently swooped swiftly down on fragile wings from some uncertain height, had settled on the forestage before Renato, between him and the audience, and had unobtrusively arranged everything in its own way, without Renato deserving it and without any reason.

When they then applauded after the next piece, Renato could recognize a face among the round, swaying heads. Over to the left, at the end of one row of seats, sat Fritz, clapping his hands and laughing so that his spectacle lenses quivered. Then he even stationed himself as the first on Renato's path. 'Excellent', he said and gripped Renato's hand very firmly. This was much more than Renato had expected. With Fritz too, however, it must have happened that an ill-defined something had edged in between Renato's playing and his ear; something that had not been in the playing, that Renato had not contributed at all, but that had supervened fortuitously to distract Fritz from the pieces performed. Had it been possible to suppose that Fritz had heard accurately (with an accuracy which, however, was not at all to be expected of Fritz), then it would not have seemed impossible that he should have approved the playing in itself. But it was not the playing in itself that had pleased him. The alien something had arrived and sounded in his ear. It always turns out like this: without a little measure of bad conscience, great happiness is not conceivable; indeed, it almost seems that the presence of this slight warning of conscience first allows us to recognize the achievement of happiness and success.

Later the curtain went up on the theatrical scene. Prince Eugene entered an inn and spoke sentences whose meaning Renato did not understand. Marianne was wearing a costume with a black bodice and gigantic white sleeves. 'That's the little Gérard girl?', asked Mama, 'well, but she's not really pretty at all.' She raised her opera glasses. 'Look', she said to Papa, 'she's even got a hooked nose, a real hooked nose. She walks badly too. I must confess, I'm disappointed. I'd remembered her being much prettier, she's certainly not to be compared with her mother.'

In the next interval a gentleman came over to greet Renato's parents. 'Congratulations', he said to Renato, then turned to Mama. 'That little girl was la Gérard's daughter', he said. 'The mother's an interesting woman.' He clamped his monocle rather more firmly into place and looked across at the box in which Frau Gérard had taken a seat, thus introducing into the theatre hall – where the parents of the other pupils jostled one another, grey-bearded, bespectacled and nodding their heads fatuously – introducing into the midst of the hall all the regalia of her invisible little state.

'Well, just you watch out', said Mama to the stranger, 'If you can't take your eyes off her, I fear for your virtue.'

But the other smiled. 'One really can't help liking her. She has the most interesting life, by the way. Not long ago, when the writer Gerhart Hauptmann was here in town he had a meal at her house, and I believe Richard Strauss has dined with her too. She keeps up a correspondence with all manner of such "celebrities".' He laughed, laying particular emphasis on the word 'celebrities', as though they were dubious apparitions with whom serious people naturally did not come into contact.

Renato was as little surprised by this communication, though, as we all are if the object of our desires is revealed to us in new and yet brighter colours. We then believe our inclinations to be in a manner of speaking confirmed, when we perceive how, without our participation, the world of which we dream coagulates to a hostile bulk and a yet more painful beauty. So Renato was not even very astonished to learn that great composers had entered the Gérard house, over the red stair carpet; that they used to sit in the gilt armchairs with their oval armrests, while Frau Gérard served them black coffee; that Marianne had perhaps just arisen from a midday meal with Gerhart Hauptmann when she used to come to the Town Park at three, to stare before her in silence amid the bare beds and the dark, branching trees.

He himself, however, was to enter the Gérard house once more in the next days, though not in the way he had expected. 'I absolutely must meet up with Marianne this afternoon', Felix had said in school, thereby at once nipping in the bud any argument regarding the urgency, the seriousness of this meeting. 'But, you see, just today it's very difficult for Marianne to get out of the house, so she has said we've got an extra performance for the Entertainment. But so as her mother doesn't get the idea she's with me, we thought you could pick her up. That would be terribly nice of you.'

As Renato stood before the brown door of the house, he thought: 'Now I'm pulling this bell.' Any spectator would have seen that this moment had arrived. It would have escaped the spectator, though, that Renato was by no means entering this house as a normal visitor (as he had all the time been wanting), but with an illegal, so to speak intimate, purpose (hence as if he had simply skipped a stage): as a deceiver of Frau Gérard and this whole house; and therefore, at the end of the day, as a deceiver of Gerhart Hauptmann and of Richard Strauss. They were perhaps just now sitting at the table upstairs, with half-emptied glasses of red wine standing before them. And if Renato were to be shown into the room, they would grin and say: 'Aha, so this is a little friend of the family, he's taking the pretty wench off to a school function.' Nodding approvingly, they would contemplate him idly, while in reality their attention was directed towards the works they were creating – to the music that crackled in the word 'Elektra' like the white sparks in an induction coil; and to the plays which Felix read – the works that marched past like great, luminous clouds on the horizon, far away from this little scene here. But should someone come in and point out to them: 'It's not so simple as that, there isn't any school function at all', then they would grow bewildered, touch the table-top with two fingers and say: 'Well, I never! That's not bad. Children of that age, too! You wouldn't have thought it of the little lass and this scamp.' They would, perhaps, even bunch their heads together and laugh, and their works would move a bit closer. But should another person come eventually and announce how matters really stood, then Strauss and Hauptmann would suddenly no longer understand. They would shake their heads and say: 'Those are foolish pranks, one can't make head or tail of them', and at once they would turn away bored.

Renato pulled the bell. A girl with a red skirt came to the door, obviously one of the housekeeping staff. The household was not ready for a visit at present. The sound of a floor being scrubbed with a hard brush came from the upper floor. The woman did not understand what Renato wanted. 'Josef', she shouted, 'Josef, there's somebody here!' The footman, dressed in an apron and with his shirt-sleeves rolled up, came bounding down the stairs. He listened to Renato, nodded wordlessly, did an about-turn and bounded back up the stairs. The red girl called after him: 'You've left the steps down here again. If they topple over and smash something again, then there'll be trouble.'

Renato glanced round the hallway, he saw the white walls and the stone which, in the lethargy of this unofficial hour, revealed that it was entirely unaware what manner of house it was holding together; which saw no difference at all between him, Renato, and Frau Gérard; which offered itself up unthinkingly to view and access, because it regarded itself simply as ordinary stone, no different from the material of the neighbouring houses. The domestics, too, obviously had no inkling (the footman had been in a great hurry to perform Renato's errand); they judged this house in terms of the wages they were paid and the food they were given; and in their next 'position', to the question where they had previously been in service they would quite simply say: 'With Frau Gérard' (they would pronounce it 'Sherart') – and say it, moreover, with the same naturalness with which a prince's son, if he should arrive in the first class as a newly enrolled schoolboy, would speak his name, never suspecting that the sound of this name would at once cause the reflections of a shining castle, a wooded landscape, ancient wars and masterpieces of painting to flicker about his temples.

The footman arrived, but then ran back to the stairs again. 'All right, come on then Mariandl', he called and clapped his hands. 'Come quick, the young gentleman's waiting here.' 'Yes, yes, I'm just coming', Marianne could be heard calling. She had hurried so much at the footman's behest that when she arrived she was still buttoning up her gloves.

Felix was waiting at the corner. Then the three of them went a short way together. They walked down the monotonous street along which Renato often walked in the opposite direction with Miss Florence, and which bore the ugly name 'Bredauergasse'. Felix and Marianne were laughing. They were not thinking about the fact that they were walking along the Bredauergasse, whose worthy grey houses in their arrogance seemed all at once pitiful, because Felix and Marianne were not paying them any attention.

Marianne looked sideways at Renato: 'Oh, let's take him with us', she said to Felix. But Felix said nothing. All that could then be heard was the sound of their footsteps on the pavement, until the moment when Renato parted from the other two.

It was a few days later, moreover, that the event took place which should doubtless have figured as the main element in our account, but which already at the time spread so much uncertainty around that today it is really not possible to present the full facts. One thing at any rate is certain: the unknown, ruddy-cheeked teacher – it was known of him only that he was called Schulte, and that for a while he was in temporary charge of geography for the fourth year and in the upper school – this teacher came into the classroom in a fury, compelled Felix and Marianne to follow him, asked Felix his name and then made the entry in the class register. What he entered there is approximately known too: 'Bruchhagen is committing improprieties with a young female external pupil', it must doubtless have said. But they did not all have time to read it, since Dr Brischta arrived in the classroom immediately after the bell to give his Latin lesson, as the last lesson of the afternoon. No one was quite sure, by the way, how to envisage those improprieties. Woska maintained that the unknown teacher had extracted the pair of them from the cloakrooms. That was not accepted without further ado. But Woska stuck to his assertion even subsequently, saying over and over again that he had seen the whole thing with his very own eyes.

It was incidentally Woska too who whispered to Renato – at the moment when the latter was accompanying Dr Brischta from the lecture room (in order to carry the class register behind him in the usual manner) – it was Woska who whispered to him that he should tear out the page with the entry. 'The blockhead made his entry on the wrong page anyway', he said. 'There isn't anything on that page yet, nobody will notice anything.' This, of course, could not have been complied with had Dr Brischta not been accosted on the stairs by that lady who used so often to make inquiries after her two sons, and who held him up for so long – until the staircase was emptied and until

Renato felt his hand clutching at the sheet in the class register. He was filled with consternation when he felt the sheet yield. But he had not noticed that behind him, slowly and soundlessly, Dr Piller had mounted the stairs; and only when the latter was standing at his level – at the moment when he was closing the book with his left hand and stuffing the crumpled sheet into his coat pocket with his right – only at that moment did Renato realize that the master was looking at him contemptuously, the eyes in his face, deep behind his pupils, like smouldering coals. 'Ah, so it's young Martin, is it', he said very slowly. Then he stared once more at Renato for a long while in silence. And stressing each word in turn, he added: 'I shall have to have a talk with you, in great detail, there's no doubt about that. Not today, but tomorrow, you'll please report to me of your own accord.' Then he left Renato standing there and all the possibilities – decree handed down by an extraordinary staff meeting; expulsion from the high school; exclusion from each and every school in the kingdom – slowly mounted the stairs with him, covered by his great, black back.

You will unquestionably be able to picture what happened that afternoon: to wit, that Renato told the whole story to Miss Florence. You will be able to picture it – if you think of the exceptional circumstances, the excitement, the menacing danger; and if you relate all that to the bundle of hopes and fears which, in the course of this account, we have learnt to condense as the character of our hero (however dubious such condensation cannot but appear, even in the case of such a dubious youth as Renato). So you have already pictured it and – who knows – perhaps someone has already been found to forgive him for it too. Even if Felix and Marianne were unable to forgive him.

In any case, the communication to Miss Florence – she had not been satisfied with any explanation, wanted to know everything, and eventually found out even about Woska's hypothesis – this communication, I say, had a consequence which Renato did not foresee. Miss Florence, that is to say, decided to go instantly to Frau Gérard. 'That's appalling', she said, 'that can't be tolerated' – and without waiting for Mama, who was spending the afternoon and evening out of the house, she set off.

Well, however unexpected this consequence was, what Dr Piller said the next day – or, strictly speaking, what he omitted to say – was just as unexpected too. For, after once again staring for a very long time at Renato, he declared: 'Yes, I asked you to come and see me, because I haven't spoken to you since the Entertainment. I just wanted to ask you, who teaches you the piano.' And when Renato had proffered Fräulein Konrad's name, he said: 'She certainly seems to be a capable instructress', stood up and intimated that the interview was over.

Now, what Miss Florence talked about with Frau Gérard and how it all passed off – whether a lightning bolt sped from Frau Gérard's head, so that Miss Florence could only subside scarlet with shame for her importunity; or whether Frau Gérard had eagerly laid aside the golden mantilla of her artistic friendships, leaned forward and said: 'Please go on, I'm enormously interested' – all this was impossible to ascertain. Miss Florence recounted nothing of her visit. But the fact that Marianne no longer came to school and that Felix was no longer prepared to talk to Renato, saying to the others: 'One doesn't talk to such a ridiculous baby' – without the visit this would doubtless not have occurred. It must, at all events, be said that Felix remained implacable. Even when Fat Pick tried to remind him: 'It was for you that he tore the page out of the class register', even then he would not hear a word about Renato. 'He's still a ridiculous baby', he declared – at which Fat Pick (without understanding what it was all about) said, with an easy laugh: 'Very true, no doubt about that, of course.'

But so far as Marianne was concerned, it did not end with her now no longer coming to the Town Park, or to the school either: she had even vanished from the town. Her mother had taken her to Vienna. 'She's gone to the Sacré Coeur boarding school', said Mama; and with this French name – syllables whose faint bell chime would accompany the sisters as they walked through their garden to vespers – with this beautiful name Sacré Coeur, she caused the thin golden hoop which had now unexpectedly coiled round Marianne's figure to gleam.

Mama, by the way, had not taken too much notice of this incident with the class register. For it had so happened that, precisely during the days in question, she had been kept very busy by a family event. Namely, Aunt Melanie had died. She had died and, through her death, had been belatedly awoken to a life whose bare possibility had never until then been contemplated. For on her account the trains were suddenly set in motion, from various directions, and brought her relatives together at the same place. People spoke about her, they held urgent telephone conversations, and Mama – in a black skirt and black blouse – touched a handkerchief briefly to her eyes during the midday meal. However did it come about that Mama all at once found herself obliged to cry over Aunt Melanie? Of course, it may be that death, arriving from his invisible nether world, brought with him at the same time other nether-worldly aerial forms – rather like the life which people claim to have led before we were born, and which seems governed by the same fabulous laws as the life of those antediluvian beasts which, in reality, probably never existed and whose immense bone fragments, tied together with wires, cause the symbols of futility and boredom to arise so magnificently before us in the stillest halls of the natural history museum. It may be that death had come to surround Mama with a life that had never been connected with her real existence by the least common ground – wherein she sat in a garden with Aunt Melanie and the two of them, despite the discomfort caused by their stiff blouse collars, bent their thin, yellow faces close together in rapt mystery. Well, perhaps such a life existed and – with the acknowledgement: 'She was my aunt, after all' – had quite suddenly gained power over Mama. But perhaps it was also the case that death, like some mechanical alarm device, with a little jolt had set a far-ramified system of levers in motion: a system of levers which had already long been standing ready and wound up and which – with the ordering of mourning clothes and funeral invitations, with the receipt of condolences and with emotion over the loss – now performed its complicated task.

For Renato, it would certainly have been welcome if one of these two mechanisms had functioned. Then, in the knowledge that the deceased woman was in good hands, he would probably have thought no more about her death. As in the theatre, the scenery of the spectacle would here have blocked his view. But when Mama actually explained that afternoon: 'I was just intending to go up to the Semmering for a few days, this aunt has really died at an awkward time', and as the uncles told their war jokes and even laughed a bit about poor dead Aunt Melanie, Renato in fact seemed to glimpse – through the damaged places in the scenery and the gaps left where it was badly positioned – the vista of a backstage laid bare: a backstage which extended into the gloom and whose presence took his breath away, as he observed Aunt Melanie in her black casket journeying alone into this darkness.

The fact that Aunt Melanie even now struck the others as comical was due – sad as that may be – to a circumstance of her death. She had suffered a stroke, and actually on an evening when for the first time in twenty years Dr Valenta had not come to visit her. One after another of the relatives asserted that agitation over a possible infidelity had killed her. But the more serious members of the family realized that it was nonsense to maintain such a thing – so eventually they all recognized that the conjunction of the two events should be regarded as a mere accident, albeit a comic one.

Dr Valenta himself must have taken the loss very hard. He fell ill, and when he came later to the Town Park it could be seen how severely he had been affected. Raising his hat had always been hard for him. But now he could lift his arm only with such difficulty, moved his hand so slowly and falteringly to his hat, and so often missed his mark, that Renato decided henceforth to spare him the effort. When he now met him, he would look to one side and act as though he had not seen him coming at all. A few years later, though, he learned that Dr Valenta was terribly angry about this and used to call him the most appalling brat he had ever met in his whole life. But by this time it would already have been difficult to begin greeting the Doctor again, so it came to pass that the latter died without the matter ever having been elucidated.

In relation to his funeral, which Renato attended 'as the family's representative' – and perhaps also in order by this gesture demonstratively to return the Doctor's salutation – in relation to his funeral, I say, one further detail must be reported. Renato, already no longer at high school, was surprised to notice Dr Piller among the funeral guests. Then, as they were leaving the cemetery, the latter came up to him. 'I'm glad to run into you here, Herr Martin', he said, 'and particularly at the burial of such an estimable man. You will perhaps be wondering what has brought me here. In point of fact, I should perhaps tell you that I benefited more than anyone from his generosity. He supported me throughout the entire period of my studies, and did not deny me his assistance even subsequently. He was a noble man. He was also very well disposed towards you, by the way, and spoke up for you on every occasion. But especially in the earliest years.' Renato was about to take his leave, but when he sought to withdraw his hand, he felt the schoolmaster clasping it in his own. He seemed to be pondering very intently. Eventually he released Renato's hand. 'We can speak as two grown men now', he said. 'I think I must tell you about it. You see – it was when you were a third-year pupil, I think – you see, you got into a serious scrape with a page from a class register, you must certainly recall it yourself. I happened to be watching at the time. I already knew about the entry in any case. My colleague had already told me about it, since I was the form master. So I knew that you had not done it out of self-interest. But you were nevertheless the one who could expect the most serious punishment, perhaps even expulsion from high school. Just imagine what that would have meant, for you and for your parents. But before deciding to do anything, I thought I had better consult with him, so I went to see him that afternoon – our common protector, I mean. He told me at once that I should ignore the whole thing. But at first that seemed to me a monstrous suggestion. I must confess, it was my first dispute with him. He told me you were a good boy, and also spoke of the fact that your mother was ailing. He took the most astonishingly far-sighted overview of the situation; he asserted that nothing would be noticed, since the colleague who had made the entry was only temporarily employed at our school and was due to leave the institution before the staff meeting. All that could not persuade me, and even when I left I had not changed my mind. But that evening he suddenly came to my apartment. Climbing stairs was by then already terribly difficult for him. He said he had come to plead for you once more, and drew my attention to the fact that he had thus omitted, for the first time in twenty years, to make a visit to a friend's house. I can still recall exactly how he put it. "There they've put in a lift for me", he said, "and here I am, visiting you on the third floor though you don't have a lift in the building." Then I decided to let the matter drop. But the other two, your friend Bruchhagen and that little girl – I can't recall what she was called – they benefited too, of course.'

. . . With this conversation, however, we have already anticipated by a long space of time. For one would then have to ask what Renato had been doing, in the time following the Entertainment and the incident with the class register. Well, so far as the Entertainment is concerned, it should be mentioned then that Dr Weinzierl was awarded a medal. Everybody congratulated him, but after that nothing more was heard of the evening or Renato's playing either. Only once were they reverted to. To wit, Mama had heard a curious rumour. 'Apparently something comical has been brewing', she said, 'between Dr Weinzierl and Fräulein Konrad, who actually got to know one another in our house. People even say she has persuaded herself that he wants to marry her. But he has never dreamed of such a thing, of course.'

When Fräulein Konrad came for their lesson now, Renato would often steal a sidelong glance at her. He would notice how her dark-red fabric dress would occasionally rise and fall when she took a deep breath. Then he would think: 'Aha, she would like Dr Weinzierl to marry her.' And he did not find it hard to picture the latter getting ready to embrace her, his movements abrupt and his pointed beard awry.

Renato, incidentally, for the most part spent his afternoons alone. It was not to be expected that Felix would come. On the other hand, Thin Pick did come to visit him now and then. When he came, he would before entering send his visiting card into the room in a sealed envelope. Mama and Miss Florence used to laugh at this and Renato would laugh with them. Then he would play to Thin Pick from *Der Freischütz* and explain to him what happened in the opera, more or less as Felix used to explain it. Thin Pick would appear entranced. But when at seven o'clock he would already have to leave, Renato would not detain him.

No one else would be with them now, when Renato walked with Miss Florence through the Town Park. Miss Florence had discovered a new little path, which led past a few birch trees on one side of the central avenue. 'Look', she said, 'the crocuses are already coming up.' 'She thinks one has to be happy about it', Renato said to himself. 'That's what she thinks, just as it's written in the German reading book. People don't know what's beautiful. Perhaps', he said, 'somebody once said that spring was a beautiful thing, and since then they go on repeating it and they write it in books.' And he looked up at Miss Florence, who in all probability was thinking about spring.

Three Early Tales

The Taxi-driver

I made a big mistake. Arriving home from a journey – the train had come in at about nine in the evening – I asked the taxi-driver to carry my suitcase upstairs to my apartment. The man agreed, turned off his meter and hoisted the piece of luggage onto his shoulder. Upstairs, he deposited it in the hallway, I paid and then the odd thing happened. While I was taking off my topcoat, instead of leaving the apartment he went on into the room. I found him there, standing in front of the bookcase.

'You have some interesting things', he said, 'art history and literature too.' In pronouncing the word 'literature' he drawled and kneaded the sounds in the most curious way, so that they were not in the least like our customary ones. Those sounds are quite impossible to reproduce. So I am simply forced to write down the word 'literature' here, though it actually sounded quite different. Then he went over to the adjoining shelves and said: 'Here's history-of-music.' This term too he pronounced in his characteristic exaggerated way, it sounded really strange and yet I understood the meaning. The thing was quite uncanny. Now the man could surely have gone. But he did the opposite. He took a volume, sat down at my desk, switched on the lamp and began to read. I was able to observe him and could not help noticing another oddity.

Standing in front of the bookcase, he had been a fat man wearing an ordinary broad-checked overcoat, with a reddish pate and of medium age. Now he was young and slim, and wore a livery that fitted him like a glove; a livery that had once perhaps been very elegant, but was now in many places already shiny. His hair was immaculate and combed straight back. Drawing closer, I saw it was greased with a pomade that gave off a sharp, rancid odour.

The taxi-driver sat on in my apartment for a long time that evening. Since because of him I could not go to sleep anyway, I asked him various things: I asked him about his work, about his wife and his children. Often he gave me short, but very polite answers. Sometimes, though, he would seem not to have heard my questions, so deeply immersed was he in his reading.

Two days later he came again, and now he comes regularly. He comes, takes his book and sits down at the desk. Sometimes, if I come home dead tired after a strenuous day, it even happens that I discover him already in my room. Usually he sits there without a sound, but the repose I so badly need is nevertheless done for. I have no idea how he has got in, since nobody apart from myself lives in my apartment. If I am at home, then he rings very briefly – by now I always recognize it, this brief ring – I open up and in he comes.

Mostly he devotes his attention to the books. But sometimes he brings a geometry set with him, spreads paper on my desk and begins to draw. The first time, I asked him what it could be. 'Trigonometrical logarithms', he asserted, saying it in his own, rather alarming gobbledegook. Once in a while he goes to the piano and plays a little melody with his right hand. He plays without touching the piano, letting his hand just hover over the keys – which then, however, set themselves in motion. It is doubtless supposed to be a merry tune, but it always sounds very melancholy. Sounds are emitted that fall between the squeak of an old instrument and the whine of a fiddle. He often plays a wrong note, then corrects himself or starts over again. It sounds strange, almost heart-rending. I should like to stroke him then, but as I go up to him I notice that his hair is very thin and stands on his head in black, tousled clumps, among which numerous tiny little worms are nestling.

He comes, even if I am holding a business meeting right there at home, sits down unconcernedly in the other corner and listens. If he perceives some failing on the part of my interlocutor, he begins to laugh at it or winks at me, which is then always extremely embarrassing for me.

It is plain that the taxi-driver is ruining much of my work and almost all my precious leisure hours. A friend asked me why I did not notify the police. But that was a very naive question. You can just imagine it! So I ring up the police and say: 'Please, Inspector, the taxi-driver's in my apartment.' If I were a police inspector, I should laugh at such a call. And anyway I cannot be at all sure whether the police would only laugh. Probably they would in fact become suspicious and persecute me. So I prefer to leave that be.

The man is becoming more and more tiresome, though. It now very often happens that I suddenly wake up around midnight. Half a minute later, I hear that brief ring. I open the door and there is the taxi-driver. He goes to the desk and begins to read or draw, or he goes to the piano to play his tune. 'Hush', I say then, 'it's midnight. One's not allowed to play music here at this hour.' Then, of course, he stops. But instead of playing, he now whistles his song, whistles it very faint and low through a gap in his teeth, and this sounds so pathetic I cannot help flinging myself on the floor and sobbing.

Whatever am I to do? The thing should just never have occurred. It would have been less trouble to bring up my own suitcase.

The Murderer

They were at table eating and in came the murderer. He had a black uptwirled moustache, he was brandishing the axe over his head and in the right-hand corner of his mouth a gold tooth glittered.

The murderer remained standing in the doorway for quite some time. In brandishing his axe, he had struck one of the doorposts. He had started back and now held the murder blade motionless over his head. His stance as he stood there was awkward. But the look in his eye was still murderous.

Nobody dared move. Eventually it was Monsieur who broke the silence. 'Sit down then', he said. He said it in an almost annoyed tone, but his voice quavered like the note of a small trumpet blown feebly and badly.

Madame and Eugénie looked at one another. Papa had been the first to see that there was suddenly a fourth place at table for the murderer. He had noticed it, even though he was ordinarily very slow to notice things.

The murderer sat down and unfolded his napkin. Then he beckoned to the footman. He beckoned with a broad, sweeping gesture, rather vulgarly; he had propped the murder blade against his chair.

The footman had been discharged by Princess Coubilesco, on grounds that were unclear. But Madame

thought him very good-looking and, since he had at any
rate been in service for three years with the Princess . . .
Now he was sparing no pains to serve the murderer.

The murderer took big mouthfuls, from time to time he
wiped beneath his moustache with the napkin, occasionally
he would hawk. His hawking came from deep down and
resounded like faint thunder.

It was a fine warm day, so the big sash window had
been pulled down. The sea glittered with its deepest blue
and on the farthest horizon two little white sails twinkled.

The silence continued. Eventually Monsieur plucked up
courage. 'It is', he began, however he got no further. But
the murderer had clearly guessed in a trice what Monsieur
wanted to say. 'Yes', he said, 'you're right, it is a fine day.'
Then he nodded contentedly. Madame made haste to take
up the conversation. 'Yes, today', she said, 'today it's
really fine and clear, we can see Corsica today. Yesterday
we still couldn't see Corsica.' Monsieur cut her short.
'Our coast', he asserted, 'genuinely merits the name Côte
d'Azur.'

The murderer grinned, his mouth stretching uncommonly wide, then he looked round him, looked around
him once more and suddenly stopped smiling. Then all
was silent again.

But this time it was the murderer himself who broke the
silence: 'Ah, the Côte d'Azur', he said, 'how does
Mallarmé put it? "The backgrounds of eternal blue . . . " '

Eugénie looked up. One could not assume that this was
anywhere in Mallarmé. But a murderer who quoted
Mallarmé, even a false Mallarmé, was strange enough.

Eugénie now noticed that the murderer was sitting there
in a darkish violet fur. The temperature was almost
summerlike, but the murderer seemed nevertheless to feel
perfectly comfortable in the fur. Eugénie also saw that
under his fur he was wearing rusty brown breeches and
red socks, obviously very cheap. But while she was

looking, it happened that the trousers altered their colour
and changed via a dull lilac into an indeterminate dark
shade. At the same time she could not help noticing that
the trousers were frayed, that whole pieces were even
missing from them. But along the loose threads dimly
glowing worms were wriggling. And since these were
multiplying at an ever-increasing rate, soon the material of
the trouser leg was replaced by a sheet of worms. Eugénie
closed her eyes. When she opened them again, she saw
that the murderer was simply wearing shabby black
trousers, quite ordinary black murderer's trousers.

'Won't you have any salad?' Monsieur asked the
murderer. The murderer gave no answer. Eventually he
said: 'Stavisky came to blows over a capon.' Monsieur
did not understand what this meant, but he nodded
several times very vehemently. His eyes did not leave the
murderer's lips. He saw how the murderer was looking at
Miss Eugénie and hastened to say: 'Of course, a bit of
rape, a bit of sadistic killing, I can understand that quite
well. It's even necessary – that's the way of the world. I
have always told my daughter that one must prepare
oneself for life.' He nodded at this and made a chewing
motion, though he had put nothing in his mouth.

Eugénie thought about how her Papa was Adminis-
trateur délégué of the Crédit Lyonnais and Chairman of
the Usines Céramiques; about how it was said he would
become a deputy; and about how the family had received
an invitation to Princess Coubilesco's for next Thursday.
Because of all this, she found it very sad that Papa was
currying favour with the murderer so obsequiously.

But Monsieur pulled his chair still closer to the
murderer's chair. And as he smilingly craned forward, he
asked: 'Couldn't you actually have a go at my mother-in-
law?' Madame affected a minor revolt. 'Now Émile', she
said, 'you and your constant joking! You must know', she
said apologetically to the murderer, 'my husband is

always making these mother-in-law jokes.' Monsieur had turned red, he felt that he had gone too far. But the murderer after a brief pause began to laugh. He laughed uncommonly loud, in short, absolutely regular gusts; it sounded as if not just one voice, but two or three voices were laughing, one average and two deep male voices. The gusts of this laughter were so loud that they made the air in the room vibrate. A silver fruit épergne standing on top of the buffet vibrated too, causing the head of a tiny putto to knock against a little baldaquin. This then kept emitting a faint, delicate sound, a very precise accompaniment to the single gusts of laughter. Despite the enormous strength of this laughter, the silvery sound could be heard each time very clearly. The murderer laughed long. But all of a sudden – without it having grown weaker – his laughter ceased. Then he once more sat silent.

Eugénie looked at his moustache and his livid skin, which was full of tiny little craters. She thought to herself that he must be a very big murderer. Even the shabbiness of his outward appearance brought her to this hypothesis. For she said to herself that surely only little murderers were elegantly dressed and looked like the gentlemen who stayed at Le Claridge. But, of course, that was only a conjecture. For perhaps everything was much simpler in reality. Perhaps precisely the big murderers were elegant and had the appearance of Ivar Kreuger. But in that case, this one here would be only an average murderer or one of the little ones – a possibility for which admittedly there were no clues either. Then, finally, it was equally conceivable that precisely this one here was the biggest of all murderers, the president so to speak of all the murder regimes in the world. It was impossible to tell. Chance sometimes plays very strange tricks in life.

The murderer had incidentally become very companionable. He pulled out his wallet and took from it a couple of photos. 'You must take a look at my lad's pictures', he said to Madame. 'The little rascal's five now, look, here he is, sitting in a boat, and here he's standing on his little skis.' Madame was full of enthusiasm. But Monsieur had a question. 'Incidentally', he said, 'what do you think about Canadian Pacific? Should I hold or sell?' But this was overdoing things. The murderer's face turned to stone. Monsieur and Madame were intensely frightened. They could also see that nothing could now get the murderer talking; he was staring in front of him, motionless and unfathomable.

But Eugénie was saying to herself: Perhaps he's only pretending, simply because he doesn't understand anything about the stock exchange. But the murderer seemed instantly to know what she was thinking, he looked at her and she felt a cold shiver down her spine such as she had never experienced.

Now nobody could speak. The footman cleared away the dessert and brought in the fruit. They were all looking at the murderer. He did not move. Just once he twirled the right point of his moustache. A little wisp of smoke rose from it. But that lasted only an instant. Nevertheless they knew that something was going to happen. Time was now passing very fast. Simultaneously the minutes were becoming filled by their expectations – each arriving minute somewhat more than the one that had just passed. They saw the minutes rising ever higher, everything within them was being compressed further and further, they had long been full to the outermost brim, it was a wonder they did not burst. But suddenly – quite unexpectedly – there came an entirely empty minute. Precisely during this minute the murderer stood up. With outstretched arm, he swung the axe high in the air. He swung it now very dexterously and fast, without any effort, so to speak with professional ease, then he cut off their heads. First Monsieur's, then Madame's and finally – here he hesitated for an instant – finally also Miss Eugénie's.

Then he climbed into his car – it was an old Rolls Royce – and drove to Cannes, to his next scene of crime.

The footman had noticed nothing of the murderous deed. He had just been busy placing the coffee cups on a tray. But when he handed Madame the black coffee and saw how she lay headless on her chair, he dropped the serving tray.

What the Dead Man Said

'Excuse me', said the man who was advancing towards the counter, 'I'm a dead man, you see.' He said it in a low voice, as if he were ashamed. The woman behind the desk appeared to accord no significance to his communication. Without raising her head, she went on arranging the pins and buttons which were spread out in front of her. It was only when she looked up that she realized that the man genuinely was deceased. It was not that his eyes had glazed over or that his cheeks were particularly pale. But his face with its occasional stubble; his black hair, which was very soft and which, despite its shortness in places, hung thick and tangled over his brow; and also his emaciated hands – in fact all parts of this small body allowed no possible doubt, not for the least fraction of a second, that they belonged to a dead man.

For a while there was silence in the shop. But soon the dead man began to chatter: 'So you'd like to know', he said – the woman had asked no question whatsoever – 'so you'd like to know how things are among us dead people?' 'Oh', he asserted, 'you have no idea!' He smiled and gestured with his hand, as if to convey: 'You think it's nasty, but in reality it's much nastier.' 'The worst thing', he said, 'is the wrong telephone connections. It hardly ever happens that a correct connection is achieved. Yet everything has to be done by telephone. Anyone who's still unused to it finds the experience intensely bewildering. For instance, at first I was manager of a fruit wholesale business. I called up an apple firm to order a load, and the next day a wagon full of second-hands arrived. Of course, it was too late to cancel the purchase. But even if one knows the ropes, it doesn't help all that much. And then the wires make contact and become entangled during conversations; you begin to have a conversation with one person and, before you notice, you're obliged to continue it with a different one. So the result is businesses don't make progress, ill people get no treatment, and there's permanent turmoil and indignation. Moreover, not a single marriage can survive. The divorce courts are permanently overburdened, I can tell you a thing or two about that, for I was a divorce lawyer myself for a time. But the individuals are mostly not to blame at all, it's just the wrong telephone connections.'

'But with the radio', the dead man continued, 'it's just as bad. And yet we have to listen to the radio a great deal there', he said, nodding his head concernedly. 'If you switch on a station, you know, what usually happens is that you run into two quite different stations, which are transmitting all muddled together. If there were at least some regularity, then of course one wouldn't need to complain so much! But you can never tell which station you've obtained, especially since the number of stations is increased daily. What's more, when new transmitters are introduced – and their numbers have already gone up almost inconceivably – when that happens, there's no announcement, and even if as a special exception some old transmitter is closed down, you get no notification. As you can imagine, of course, it's virtually impossible like that to listen to anything on the radio. And yet we're obliged to do so.'

The dead man fell silent for a moment. He looked down

at the counter upon which a couple of cigarettes now suddenly lay. The dead man picked up one of the cigarettes and lit it. He held it clumsily between index finger and thumb, like someone unaccustomed to doing so, and exhaled the smoke through puckered lips. But soon he continued speaking. 'There are far worse things, of course, where we are', he said. 'The crush and the noise, that's not it. Though every time, when you've grown accustomed to one level of noise, a new noise of previously unimaginable proportions starts up. It has been increasing like that for centuries. But what's far worse is the pace at which everything proceeds. You're carried along by that pace. You join in, it all appears very easy, and yet it's impossible to reconcile oneself to it. You see, I died only three days ago. But the things I've seen already in that time! I've pursued at least twenty careers and I've come to grief much more often even than that. I was a film promoter, I was a lamp-lighter, I was a clerk with a sugar cartel, a worker in a rubber factory, president of a bank, room attendant in a museum – I've quite lost track already of everything I've been!'

But all of a sudden the dead man stopped and looked anxiously around him. 'Or do you think', he asked, 'I've been there longer than three days? I was still here on the day Pilsudski died, at any rate.' He fell silent for a while. 'But when was Bismarck dismissed?', he next asked unexpectedly. 'I know that fact made a big impression on us there.' He knitted his brows and seemed to be thinking very hard. But suddenly his forehead cleared. 'Recently', he said with a smile, 'somebody brought us the news that the Emperor Franz Joseph had died. But we laughed at that, of course. For after all, the whole world knows the Emperor Franz Joseph still has at least twenty-five years to live!'

The woman was staring at the dead man in astonishment. Throughout the entire time she had spoken not a word. Nonetheless, the dead man behaved as though she were questioning him. 'Yes', he said, 'why I've come back here, I really don't know. But I must tell you one thing: however bad it may be there – for me it's now far worse here. You know, of course, about ill people who are prescribed a saltless diet. Food is then so tasteless that it's repugnant to them. Everything here seems equally tasteless to me, but a million times more so. So terribly saltless! And when I wake up in the morning, this dreadful saltlessness descends upon me right away. Things here are so remote and hollow, I really don't know what to do in this agony. Believe me, it's the greatest misery that can befall a person. If, for instance, I see a woman here, then I'm seized by a desire that's more irresistible than any I experienced in the old days. But the thought of satisfying this desire is the most repulsive thought that exists.' As the dead man said this, his mouth twitched and a cold shudder could be seen to run up his spine. In the meantime, though, he had turned to go and it was not even quite clear whether these last words had been spoken inside the shop or already outside.

He could be seen walking down the empty street now, his shape growing smaller and smaller. His capacious yellow cloak was lifted a little by the wind, the bottoms of his legs could be seen lumbering rhythmically and slowly over the paved surface. He was already a long way off, but his voice nevertheless sounded in the shop as if he still stood in front of the counter. 'I must endure here', he said, 'I've no idea for how long. It may even turn out that I shan't find the way back. But I don't dare think about that. Only when I have it all about me once more – the noise and the crush, the confused radio signals and the wrong telephone connections – only then will there be any peace for me.'

Wedding in Brooklyn

Seven Stories

Disarray in the Spectre Kingdom

The palatial buildings lie in peace now. In sunlight their surfaces are outlined sharply, towards evening they huddle a little closer together and later still a small lamp burns behind a window and the faint sound of a bell occasionally peals out through the night. Count Abelard still walks around, of course, but it appears to be just an old habit, the embassy staff do not give it a thought. He walks in the room where the golf clubs and the ping-pong table are kept, and nothing has happened yet. He no longer appears regularly, after all – perhaps somewhat more frequently of late, but that is certainly just an accident. On average he comes more and more rarely, soon no more will be heard of him.

But in the district where the long terraces run, it started several years ago. And now it is spreading further and further afield. You walk past the rows of brown, grey and dark-green houses, you go over the little crossroads where the chemist-shop windows are already lit up and all at once you stand still in alarm and you know: here and there, on one old upper storey or another, something is astir. Here, the little girl sits at her pianino and practises. But suddenly it steps through the plush curtains into the room and there stands the spectre. It is her grandfather, small and fat, in his dark lustre jacket and with his white goatee. He steps slowly across to the piano and looks over her shoulder at the music book. The child leaps up, screams loudly and runs into the far corner. Meanwhile, of course, all has long since vanished.

But the spectres have not changed merely their haunts. It can be seen that their hour too is different now. It is the hour after sunset, the hour when the lamps are already mingling with the daylight on the streets and the mixture of lights resembles a mixture of salt and sugar. At this hour it comes to pass that a motionless form may be seen, in the half-lit stairwell between the door to the janitor's flat and the dustbins. And as the family sits drinking coffee, their deceased aunt abruptly settles in all her massiveness on the middle of the table and her hands have swollen to near-gigantic proportions. At the same time, they know too that the man with the crutches is now moving up and down the stairs outside. Often he enters the hall and stands in the corner by the coat-stand – and sometimes, for a few seconds, he will even step through the wall into the room itself.

But it cannot be said that the spectres now keep to just that one hour. At night too, if a person is lying in bed it can happen that he will notice something. So he will take a look – and there on the chest-of-drawers two obscene, round heads will be grinning.

Now, alas, there is great disarray in our spectre kingdom. Formerly, as we know, times were different. One could ask the porter and would even receive a very precise reply: 'This place is haunted, and that one, and always only at a very specific hour.' Now the porter smiles and says all is quiet in the building. In the place to which the spectre folk have vanished, however, there nothing at all is known. They always come unexpectedly, sometimes in pairs, sometimes in the strange shape of an unborn, half-grown child with no legs and just two fingers on its shoulders in place of arms. They also no longer have their own particular houses. Anybody who has lived in one house must make his appearance in another, to the alarm of its inmates and to his own alarm.

So everybody suffers from the confusion, even the spectres themselves. Will it last much longer? Will this misery not soon be brought to an end? No one knows. Here and there a voice makes itself heard speaking of the approach of better times. But anyone who has brought himself to gaze for a while upon the visage of one of the spectres – and a person can accomplish this only very rarely, at most once or twice in his life – anyone who could thus bear to look one of those poor creatures in the face, that person has abandoned all hope for ever.

The Nanny

She looked like the dachshund Waldi. Admittedly the outlines of her face were far more angular, especially her nose which had a little lump on it and terminated in a long, thin point. Nowhere else was such a nose to be seen. Even Bibbi and Tommy always looked at this nose.

Bibbi was six years old and Tommy was nine. His parents liked taking Tommy out with them: when the airman Bleriot came to town, for instance, and put his enormous machine on display in a hotel, in a big white room, while explaining everything himself unintelligibly but thrillingly and once giving the propellor a twirl with his own hand.

On such occasions she had to stay at home with Bibbi or take the customary walk, go to the river, over one of the bridges, then over another bridge on the way back. 'You're the neglected child', she would say to Bibbi and in the evening, when she had placed him on the table to wash him, she would address him imploringly: 'You poor child! How will it all end! Neglected, cast aside! Always and everywhere, only the big boy! He's spoiled and pampered, while they don't want to know a thing about you.' And then she would recount how dreadful things would usually befall such children, she spoke of one boy who had turned into a zombie and said: 'That was exactly the same case, always neglected, always rejected.'

If some stranger came into the room, an uncle or an aunt, then she would remain sitting in her corner, just nod her head and at once hunch her little body over her work again. Bibbi and Tommy felt that these were awkward moments. But then they would see her gleaming black eyes and big, loose mouth, which used sometimes to twitch while the visitor was there, and they would think she was quite right if she despised these people, who always used to say only such stupid things.

'The old witch', their uncles and aunts used to say and they would laugh. And the children's parents would laugh too.

Tommy had been given a camera, a Kodak No. 2. Once he came into the room and saw Bibbi winding the spool. He had exposed and ruined a whole roll of film. But she smirked and admitted she had been encouraging him. Then Tommy wanted to smash everything in the room, including Bibbi, into small pieces.

She incidentally had one great passion. She loved the theatre. 'I always go only to the left side-gallery', she used to say, 'those are my favourite seats.' She used to tell them about festival productions, about splendid evenings, about Caruso and Battistini. Only *Pelléas and Mélisande* had displeased her. But *Hamlet* with Kainz, that was her most beautiful evening.

She told Tommy that Hamlet had been a Danish prince and, as she was showing him how Kainz played the role, Tommy all the while believed he could discern in her ugly features something resembling a princely tenderness and did not know why it made him so sad.

If while being washed Bibbi took it into his head to let out a sudden shriek, then she used to say that one day he would certainly have a magnificent voice, become a great singer. And since he had black hair, she said he would be a bass, another Arimondi.

Tommy had a strange dream at that time. He dreamed that Battistini had come to the city and had lost a diamond. He Tommy had noticed it, had seen from behind how the big, black-clad singer accidentally flicked the diamond from his coat pocket. And then he had seen the diamond sparkling on the pavement in another street. He had picked it up there and taken it to Battistini in his hotel. But as Battistini was advancing towards him, in order to clasp him in his outstretched arms, just then Tommy woke up.

In the theatre he was shown the side-gallery, a row of chairs behind a balustrade and set apart from the other seats. She had to sit there, of course.

Once in the winter – their parents had just gone away on a long journey, to Switzerland or some such place – Tommy came home from school an hour late. She had in the meantime cabled to his parents: 'Tommy lost'. His parents were very angry about it, and she had to quit the house.

She took two rooms, one for herself and one for 'lodgers'. Bibbi and Tommy came to visit her. 'Sh!', she said and pointed to a glass door, 'that's where my lodgers are. They study at the university.' Bibbi and Tommy looked at the room in which they were standing. It was big and low-ceilinged and dark, and only a black trunk stood against the wall beside the bed. They had never liked a room as much as this. And at the sight of the glass door, they thought of the terrible lodgers of whom she was so afraid.

Next time they came, she said: 'The lodgers have walked out and now no others want to come any more.' Bibbi and Tommy were very frightened. They saw how her loose mouth, and now her nose too, twitched. 'How can that be', though Tommy, 'she only took on the room, after all, so that the lodgers could live with her.' And he looked at her, saw how she was ready to summon up all the sweetness of her ugly face for the lodgers and saw how the lodgers nevertheless came to the door only to say: 'No, we don't want you, we don't want to live here.'

Bibbi too noticed how sad she was. 'They don't want to come', she said. 'And yet I give them everything. Breakfast and whatever they want.'

At home they said: 'It's unfortunate, but you can understand why nobody wants to live with her.'

A couple of weeks later it was reported that she had gassed herself. Tommy had never experienced anything so dreadful. It was the lodgers, the terrible lodgers. They didn't want to come, although she had gladly given them everything. Coffee and buttered rolls and even two eggs for breakfast, if they had wanted it.

Bibbi and Tommy went to the funeral.

Afterwards her black trunk was opened up. Apart from clothes and old shoes, they found a great quantity of photographs there. Photographs of la Duse, of Caruso, Scotti and Battistini, of Kainz, of la Destinn and la Farrar. They also found theatre programmes and a lot of little yellow tickets bearing the imprint: Side-gallery, Left.

The Moonlit Night

Soldiers lay in the trenches, in Russia, in Rumania and in Italy. Soldiers, as everyone knew, were giving their blood; they were the shield, the vital strength of the monarchy, which was now in its third year of war. A young ruler had ascended the throne, in the picture palaces people saw his coronation in Hungary, the illustrated papers showed him visiting front positions and chatting with the men. Soldiers were seen in the streets of the city, many with curious hopping movements; others had been blinded, for gas warfare was making headway. And since a private relief association had been established in Vienna on behalf of incurable war invalids, Frau Counsellor Klier had a happy idea. A branch should be set up in the capital of our great and important province; and the initial funds needed should be raised by means of a concert, through ticket sales and benevolent subscriptions.

The Counsellor approved the plan. He was delighted to see his wife's activities so universally esteemed: activities which now, at this great hour, had developed so prolifically and so diversely – on the War Assistance Board, in the Fatherland Association and for two afternoons at the hospital. He was a true servant of his state. He had his own spacious room now on the first floor of the administration building. 'My state within the state', he would say with a smile when a visitor noticed the Persian rugs, the inlaid cabinets or the family photographs. In the spring the Counsellor would observe how the trees outside on the little square put forth buds and green leaves: the hoot of an automobile or rattle of a cart seldom pierced the quiet of this neighbourhood. The Counsellor particularly approved of the plan to invite the Governor's consort to patronize the evening: a visit was made, the opportunity was taken to impress the war invalids' plight upon Her Excellency and the Counsellor's lady came home well satisfied and in a buoyant mood.

So far as the programme for the evening was concerned, she had already worked hers out. For Frau von Zeisel, a young niece, had recently joined her husband in our city from Graz and brought with her not just her own youthful charms but also a certain reputation as a singer. Flattering press reviews from her home town and an occasional performance in Vienna increased the young lady's renown; there had even been talk of negotiations with various opera houses. The Counsellor and his wife were childless. They liked young people, the Counsellor's lady saw the evening as a fortunate opportunity to bring her singer at once before an audience of the city's elite, while delighting the public for its part with her amiable niece. And as she was still secretly hoping that on an occasion such as this her beloved sister would not shrink from the journey, she was able to look forward not just to a charitable enterprise and a concert, but to a joyful family reunion.

The ladies' committee, which soon assembled, received the ideas of Frau Counsellor Klier with approval: they knew her efficiency and tact could be relied upon; they praised the noble aim of the project; moreover, they had already heard gratifying things about the young singer. The meeting was taking place at Frau Körner's house, tea was served with little pastries, then they discussed the remainder of the concert programme; they were anxious

to include a certain colour, a certain measure of variety.
The ladies made one suggestion after another – Frau
Worlitschka a local string quartet, Frau Siegel an artiste
from Reichenberg who gave recitals – they deliberated and
at last they found a solution. Young Zimmermann, a
violinist – though not a professional, an amateur of the
best kind – who had been called to the colours a few weeks
before, was to Frau Neidhart's certain knowledge stationed
very close at hand; and since Frau Colonel Seidel
confirmed that in view of the patriotic objectives it would
be possible to arrange a short leave, the decision was easy.
As for the piano number without which the evening could
not really be imagined, they found a solution here too. A
male or female pupil from the masterclass at the State
Conservatory was the obvious thing – and certainly only a
modest burden on the budget. So they were able to part
from one another well contented: the date of the
concert – in the first week of April – was as convenient as
could be, the Princess's patronage already in itself a
success and, so far as the programme was concerned, they
could certainly place very high hopes in the appearance of
Frau von Zeisel, who so advantageously combined the
singer's art with ties of blood. The choice of violinist,
too, was a wise choice: they thought of the uniform in
which he would appear on the stage, and in which he
would embody the military spirit so charmingly and so
opportunely.

In the next weeks the Counsellor's consort, now
president of the association, had nothing but good to say
of the ladies: of Frau Körner, who looked after the job of
treasurer so conscientiously; of Frau von Greinz, who saw
to the matter of the hall and its decoration; and of Frau
Siegel, who had taken on press publicity and the layout of
the programme – in short, the domain of print. And as the
evening approached, all the seats were taken, the hall – it
was the big hall in the German Institute – was bedecked

with green foliage and two green trees even stood in containers in front of the main doors.

Nikolas Körner attended the concert with his mother. At her side he mounted the low, commodious stairs with the carpet running up the centre; he looked at her, saw her dark, silken cloak, her smooth, lightly powdered skin and her sparkling ear pendants.

'Is that her younger son, the one who's still at high school?', asked Frau von Neidhart. 'Yes', said Frau Siegel, 'she complains about him, she says he's a dreamer.'

Now, as they mounted the carpeted stairs, Frau Körner was saying: 'Be friendly if we run into Frau Counsellor Klier.'

But the Counsellor's lady was very busy. She was giving instructions to the ushers, as well as to the young maidens who stood at the doors all dressed in white. They were handing out programmes, even their long gloves were white. Two of the girls came up to Frau Körner, they were smiling. Frau Körner seemed to recognize them. 'Mimi Greinz', she said, 'isn't it? And Marion, her sister.' The girls made a curtsey. Nikolas looked at them, he saw that Marion was tall and fair, he saw her deep-set eyes and felt his head swim slightly. 'This is my son', said Frau Körner. The girls glanced at one another.

Later, as they sat in their places, Frau Körner said: 'They're nice girls, why didn't you talk to them?' 'What was I supposed to say to them?', asked Nikolas. His mother laughed: 'You're certainly no cavalier.' He saw that Marion was selling a programme; she curtsied, then laughed with her companions.

Meanwhile the hall was filling up. Two large plate mirrors had been installed in the wings, the stage too was bedecked in green. 'So this is the charity concert', thought Frau Springer as she came in, 'I'm glad I shall be seen here.' She thought about her dark-red evening gown and her rope of pearls, and she saw ladies and gentlemen with whom she was unacquainted conversing with one another. People conversed in little groups, they leaned over to the rows behind and many of the ladies kept their fans in continuous motion. Frau Springer noticed an old gentleman with a ruddy face and carefully groomed beard subjecting her to a lengthy scrutiny; this was Dr Weigel, she did not know that his gallbladder was just playing up and he was hoping he would not have to go home, since his wife had been longing to attend the concert. Then Herr von Hölty and his wife arrived. He was smiling in all directions, his fair moustache trimmed in the English style was sprinkled with a little grey, he had just received a new state commission. The factories were working two shifts now: however the war might be decided, he had built up his industries considerably.

Nikolas had to stand up, since Herr von Hölty and his wife were sitting in the same row. The lady sat down beside his mother and asked: 'Is that your younger son? What news do you have of the other one?' 'Still on the Isonzo front', said Frau Körner, 'and for a couple of weeks, only pre-printed cards. You've heard about those cards, I suppose? "I am in good health and doing fine".'

Frau von Hölty bowed her head deeply and closed her eyes. Was she doing that in order to think with greater concentration about events out there at the front – about the dead and about the overcrowded field hospitals?

Almost all the seats were occupied now, it was half past eight and suddenly all conversation died away. The white-clad maidens stood still, they held their unsold programmes gracefully at their breasts, the centre doors were flung wide open and the Prince and Princess stepped into the hall. The Counsellor and his wife led them to their seats, then the Counsellor stepped out in front of the audience.

First he cleared his throat, then he said: 'Your most illustrious Excellencies! Ladies and Gentlemen! At this great hour, when all our thoughts are directed day and night to the dear fatherland, when young and old are standing shoulder to shoulder to oppose victoriously the insidious foes assailing us on every side, our thoughts travel also to those heroic defenders of the fatherland who have incurred permanent physical injury.' The Counsellor then spoke about the amputees and about those who had lost their sight, occasionally he would glance at a text and grasp his Van Dyck beard in one hand. He spoke of great advances, by virtue of which the new technique of pro-thesis was causing new possibilities and new hopes of life to spring forth. 'And yet', he continued, 'and yet we still have our hands full, we have to give and give, the agony still cries out to Heaven.' And he paused and looked upwards, as if he could see that heaven through the ceiling of the hall. His listeners, including Their Excellencies, maintained an unmoving silence, as did the white maidens, who were now sitting on an upholstered bench along one of the mirrors. The Counsellor concluded on a note of confidence. For the willingness to make sacrifices on the home front, he said, was a worthy counterpart to the great deeds of the armies. 'And while we all stand at our posts', he said, 'we look confidently towards a great and victorious future, and we all make the mighty cry resound: Long live Austria! Long live the sublime Imperial dynasty!' The audience, it must be said, did not make the cry ring out in reality, but they all applauded heartily and the Princess, rather stout, did so by lifting her arms in the air and clapping her hands together with quick little movements.

No sooner had the Counsellor taken his seat in the front row and expressed his thanks on all sides in the friendliest fashion, than Herr Zimmermann, the violinist, was already standing on the stage. The buttons of his uniform gleamed in the light of the chandeliers, he tuned his instrument softly then set it in place, his mouth twitched –

the military collar was causing him problems – then he looked up at the accompanist, who was orchestral director of the theatre, though in the theatre, of course, he conducted little or not at all. Herr Zimmermann was playing Mendelssohn's Concerto, and the Counsellor's consort told herself that his tone was particularly sweet. The young girls looked up at the stage, they noticed that the violinist's face had turned very red and that he was making great efforts with his bowing. Frau Dr Weigel listened with great interest and, if one of the high notes struck her as not quite right, she thought sympathetically about military service, about drill practice in the dawn light; while her husband, the schoolmaster, could now tell himself that the pains in the area of his gallbladder had vanished and the whole thing had obviously been a false alarm. Marion was sitting not far from Nikolas. He could see how her form was discernible through the tight-fitting dress, he saw the line of her neck, saw how she breathed and how her blonde hair was a little lighter where it framed her face.

But was anybody listening to the accompanist, who, as Herr Zimmermann fiddled and moved his upper body to and fro, sat at the piano and played without a break? It was certainly not necessary, since one could depend upon it: the accompanist played well. Frau Springer, in a red evening gown, leaned back and displayed her profile in an advantageous manner, and Herr von Hölty suddenly had an idea: the supply of yarn for trouserings could much more favourably be turned to account for military capes. Frau Worlitschka, in one of the middle rows, saw the critic of the morning paper pick up his programme and write down a few words. 'I hope he isn't writing anything bad', she thought, 'that wouldn't be very pleasant for our committee.' Journalists, her husband was wont to say, are vile, they often do it on purpose. And as she watched the critic, his pince-nez and his little blonde beard, she thought about the bad pay of newspapermen, about the articles they write in order to vent their discontented humours, and about the world in general which is so full of malice.

After the violin recital had come to an end and there had been a short interval, when Frau von Zeisel the singer stepped out on to the stage a perceptible whisper ran through the audience. It had to be admitted, she was a charming sight. Her shape was rather plump, but above her cream-coloured lace dress sat a little head with finely curved mouth and delicate nose. Her eyes sparkled. Herr von Hölty, in the third row, could not restrain a smile, old Baron Landis opened his eyes wide, and even Colonel Seidel nodded.

Frau von Zeisel began and her voice trembled a little. 'Self-consciousness', thought the critic, 'it can happen.' The ladies from the committee were all looking up at the stage. 'A lovely voice', thought Frau von Neidhart; *'charmant'*, said Frau Siegel to herself. And as the second song came to an end, the critic thought: 'No striking material, but well trained, very good diction and thoroughly musical.' He wrote something on his programme and Frau Worlitschka noticed this.

Frau von Zeisel sang a group of lieder. 'Schubert', thought Colonel Seidel, 'that's what I've always said, German songs, immortal melodies. Schubert and Mendelssohn are my favourite composers. A person should go to concerts. Why do I never go to concerts? Music and beauty, that makes life worth living. Beethoven was a great composer too. And Wagner. Only too difficult. Music must be easy. Melodies must grab the heart.'

Frau von Zeisel sang, after each of her songs the applause was vigorous, the Counsellor's lady could tell herself she had been right and, while the song about the dream of spring rang out across the packed hall, the Counsellor was saying to himself that the evening could bring only good, the Colonel continued with his reflections and Marion sat in the row with the other girls, her head tilted to one side and her lips slightly parted.

In the interval, Herr Wiesner the banker came up to Herr von Hölty. 'Our krone has been quoted at twenty points down in Zurich today', he said in a low voice, 'where will that lead us?' 'Momentary weakness', said Herr von Hölty, then continued rather more loudly: 'I have the fullest confidence in our High Command.' He was prepared for weaknesses and occurrences which perhaps exceeded the banker's powers of imagination and, so far as the current rate of the krone was concerned, he was able to tell himself he had purchased his raw material advantageously.

Among the people who were now standing round the seats of the Governor and his wife, the Counsellor and the Counsellor's lady were also to be seen. In the foyer, Nikolas went up to the young girls. 'How did you like it?', he asked. He had actually spoken to Marion. He noticed a slight roughness of the skin on her left cheek. She was astonished by the question and after a while said: 'Oh, I enjoyed it very much.' She was looking at a young man who was just coming up to them. The young man said something like 'Beauty and symphony in white', and Marion smiled. But Nikolas remained standing close beside her, he smelled the perfume which emanated from her, while she talked with the young man and laughed frequently. And he thought to himself: 'Who knows? Some time the day will come.' But she was looking up at the other man – for he was somewhat taller even than she was herself – and eventually Nikolas said: 'Excuse me' and went back into the hall. He had time to notice how Marion, the young man and another girl who was standing with them glanced quickly at one another and then laughed.

Whatever mysterious matter Marion might be talking

about with her girlfriend and the unknown young man, her father, the manufacturer, was talking to Colonel Seidel. The Colonel was explaining the military situation to him, and also why final victory was certain. 'The decision', he said, 'will be reached in the south-east. We have Rumania, and the Russians with their internal upheavals are now weaker than ever. Incidentally, we have fresh levies on the way.' The manufacturer had not reckoned so soon on a new levy, and wondered whether it was better to rely upon his rheumatism or upon economic indispensability. But as he was ruminating upon questions of this kind, a bell signalled the end of the interval.

Frau von Zeisel appeared. Greeted by vigorous applause, she smiled amiably and threw her head back a little. Now she sang a Schumann group. 'The Nut-tree', 'With Roses and Myrtles', then came the song 'The Moonlit Night'. It began with a little piano introduction and Nikolas pricked up his ears. Then he heard the melody and the text about the starry sky and the land at night, which as he knew was the land of love. He looked at Marion, she was toying with a little bracelet.

Frau von Zeisel sang three further Schumann lieder, and since the applause was tumultuous several encores followed. It was growing so late that a few of the listeners rose to leave, but many remained; the piano number was coming next, a Chopin sonata. The girl who emerged to seat herself at the concert grand was called Amalie Bronsky.

The Counsellor's lady looked disapprovingly at her badly cut silk dress. Amalie Bronsky played forcefully and soon the critic found himself thinking: 'Talented lassie! Yes, indeed! I've already heard her, very talented! But will she make anything of it? Luck and success, what do they really depend upon? I haven't yet managed to fathom the combination of prerequisites.'

The Counsellor was busy reconstructing in his mind the

conversation with the Governor in all its phases: his opinion about subversive elements and the vigilance which he considered necessary had surely left an excellent impression. Marion's father was thinking about new concessions. Herr von Hölty was calculating the price of cotton at the new rate for the krone. Nikolas did not think much of Chopin.

In one of the back rows sat the director of the piano class, her teacher. 'Bravo', he thought, 'she's really a born concert pianist. How she does attack her instrument, how her playing sparkles, how she exudes music, how her phrases sing! This, precisely this, is my conception of Chopin, just as I taught her. Amalie Bronsky, you have understood me and you can perform it, for you have everything, head and heart and blessed fingers.' And in a spasm of sentimentality, to which he now in the second half of his sixties once in a while found himself liable, he thought: 'Amalie Bronsky, may God protect you!' In each of his eyes, a tear stood, the fat lady beside him noticed and said to herself: 'My God, his heart! If only he wouldn't get excited!'

In the middle of the front row, very close to Amalie Bronsky and so to speak at her feet, sat the Governor and his consort. The Governor sat motionless, his upturned moustache was black, but the skin of his face was pale, displaying many wrinkles and the occasional tiny crater. What did the piano-playing he was listening to mean to him? Did it perhaps take him back to the days of his youth, when at the neighbouring castles young maidens would spend the evening playing the piano and singing; when he, the rich young cavalier, was starting out on his journey round the world; when all the fortune and every possibility in that world lay at his disposal? Now here he sat, the Emperor's representative, as it were the Father of the People in person. Did all not now lie upon his shoulders: the life, the good fortune, the hope of every subject? Was it not his business to concern himself with everything, with the cares and sorrows of everyone? How much sympathy, what measure of help could be expected from him? Could Nikolas Körner, say, count upon it that he, the Emperor's Governor, in a friendly conversation with the girl Marion, would explain the measure of fortune and passion she could expect and shake her to the core? Was it not his duty, as father of the people, to take into his protection young Nikolas's brother, the brother on the Isonzo front? Not his duty at least towards a mother who was sitting a mere two rows behind him, and who – despite committee and concert and despite Amalie Bronsky – had but a single thought? The cares of a governor are multifarious. What was he he thinking in this moment? Certainly not about the boy Nikolas and not at all about his elder brother. What was he planning, considering? Was he a member, or even an actual prime mover, in the group in whose name Prince Sixtus was now negotiating in Paris and discussing the conditions for a separate peace? On his return from the concert, was he expecting news that would herald the turning-point of world history and mean new dawns for the Empire whose end he had still been confidently predicting until a short time ago? Or was it all quite different? Did the Prince believe in Germany and unswerving loyalty? Was he serious, when he spoke of the morality of standing fast and the glory of final victory? Did he pursue whatever opposed it with fire and brimstone? Had he listened to the Counsellor's views with approval? Or was he now, perhaps, sitting secretly smiling over his clerk's zeal and limited powers of discernment? Who knows? Who could tell the thoughts that came to him? Who knows whether there were very many thoughts at all? Who could know it even from the lady who sat on his right hand? She was wearing a pendant with a large emerald. Her bosom was massive; on a little chain, a silver lorgnette hung. She was breathing heavily and each time her chest rose the lorgnette and the jewel knocked together. A faint tinkle, a gentle bell chime could then be heard several places away, despite the piano-playing of Amalie Bronsky.

The concert had come to an end, the Frau Counsellor was congratulated, the Counsellor was ready and waiting, they went home. Herr and Frau von Zeisel accompanied them, as did Frau von Zeisel's mother who actually had come from Graz; they discussed the concert, it was a cheerful gathering and, if the Counsellor and his lady thought about it at all, they must have said to themselves that now and again life does provide fulfilments.

The critic went to his office. When he left the concert hall and emerged onto the street, he found the evening warm. He intended to write only a short review and decided to go on foot. He went past the old Powder Tower, along the winding Zeletnergasse where there was only one track for the tramway, past the familiar portico with its great caryatids; only here and there was a window lit up and he heard the echo of his own footsteps. Even the broad Old Town Square was empty, the hour was already late and furthermore it was wartime. Yes, a war was on! War on the northern, eastern and southern frontiers and war in the west. The critic, whose function it was to uphold artistic standards, who represented principles and ideals, certainly also had his standard for humanity in general – his ideal for the coexistence of all men. Well, measured by this standard, what was the War? How could a critic pronounce upon world affairs? He had his directives. German culture, the music of Bach, Beethoven and Wagner, the noblest flower of the human spirit was threatened in this war. But so far as concertgoing was concerned, it had to be promoted: it strengthened morale on the home front.

The critic entered the newspaper office. In the front

room he found a group of colleagues. 'There, so now we have it', said the deputy chief-editor, 'the American president goes before Congress today to ask for a declaration of war.' The critic felt afraid. To be sure, he had long predicted this development and could only smile at the words of grumblers and patriots. And yet now his heart missed a beat, whether because a fear suddenly took hold of him in the face of the transatlantic colossus – a fear of distress and ill-defined destruction – or whether because words which we hear about us, and use ourselves, nevertheless gain a hold and become embedded in part of our thought system.

'Are we going to report the news?', asked the critic. 'No', said another editor, 'but the order says: "Prepare the public".' The critic went to his room. He lit the lamp with its green glass shade, read a letter, then took a sheet of paper and wrote: 'Under the patronage of Her Highness Princess Reiffenstein, a charity concert took place yesterday in the mirrored hall of the German Institute. The proceeds from the successful and very well attended evening are destined for the starting fund of a newly established association, the War Invalids Relief Society. The noble aim of the enterprise, which was brought into being under the presidency of Frau Anna Klier, was graphically and compellingly expounded in an introductory speech by the spouse of the lady president, Counsellor Alois Klier.'

Here he paused and took a cigarette; in the next room he could hear the leading article being dictated. 'What can our enemies hope for? The Russian army is on the point of disintegrating, the morale of the Italian and French armies has reached an unexpectedly low level. That the English will fight only to the last Frenchman is notorious. Which leaves America. America is in itself not to be underestimated as an economic factor. But what use is America's wealth when the U-boat campaign, so energetically and prudently prosecuted, has definitively cut off all communication with our enemies? Will America continue to supply the troglodytes of the ocean with war materials? If the warmongers in Washington should now gain the upper hand and actually push the United States into a formal declaration of war, what would that mean? Practically speaking, nothing whatsoever. War supplies would not be torpedoed any the less; an American army does not exist; and even if the Americans were to put a few soldiers into the field, those poor devils too would have to journey to the ocean depths along with the guns and ammunition. An American declaration of war can be nothing but an empty gesture.'

The critic began to write again: 'The evening's programme offered delightful solo performances. Herr Bernhard Zimmermann, in the uniform of a one-year volunteer in the artillery, played Mendelssohn's Violin Concerto, accompanied by orchestral director Otto Schwarz. He played it with proficiency and with taste. Frau Alberta von Zeisel's lieder renderings were remarkable. Here we have a singer of real culture, stronger in plastic representation than in pure emotion, stronger in Schubert than in Schumann, but always very accomplished and highly musical. Particular appreciation is due to Amalie Bronsky. She played the extremely difficult "B-minor Sonata" by Chopin with true verve, with unfailing sureness and with melodic magic.' He paused for a moment, then went on: 'Good note must be taken of the name Amalie Bronsky.'

Nikolas returned home with his mother. His father was sitting in an armchair in the bedroom. 'In a bad mood', thought Nikolas.

'It's late, you should go to bed', said his father, and Nikolas went to his room.

'What has happened?', asked Frau Körner. She saw that her husband did not want to speak. 'I see I can't keep it secret', he said and handed her a letter. He added: 'From the colonel of his regiment, a man on leave brought it.' She read the words: 'as an example of fulfilment of duty and heroism, mourned by his superiors and by his comrades' and let the missive drop.

Nikolas, at the other end of the apartment, was pacing up and down his room. Finally he opened the secret drawer, took out his diary and wrote: 'This date, 5 April 1917, is a decisive one in my life. I attended a concert, not expecting anything from it. But I met a girl, and the eyes into which I looked opened up the world for me. Now I understand what poets, I mean the true poets, and musicians, I mean the true musicians, sing of: love, the world of woman. I heard a song, "The Moonlit Night" by Schumann, and it was as if scales fell from my eyes. I feel it all just like the composer, who thinks yearningly of his beloved and who translates his dream into melodies and into harmonies – which spirit us away. O beauty! O life! O thou, my love!' He closed the exercise book quickly and thrust it back into the drawer.

Then he went into the next room, opened the music cupboard and placed the volume containing Schumann lieder on the piano. The song 'The Moonlit Night' was hard to play. He saw four sharps indicated. He played only the melody, which was better anyhow, since in that way he could play really quietly and his parents certainly could not hear it.

Then he went to the window and opened it. The wind was mild. 'Yes', he thought, 'it's spring.' In front of the windows lay the park. By the verge of the main avenue, the gas of a street lamp was glowing. Two soldiers were crossing the park to the station. Nikolas took a deep breath.

The Lawyer's Office

Dedicated to Theodor and Gretel Adorno

I

Sagacity and circumspection established our system of jurisprudence. How could commerce and trade flourish, industry and prosperity bear fruit, had we not the ingeniously and powerfully constructed edifice of our Law? Our judges, equipped with learning and knowledge of men, interpret the statutes; lawyers, with wisdom and skill, mediate between statutes and men. Lawyers study the statutes and the rulings of the Supreme Court.

The Supreme Court rulings were contained in leather volumes with gold letters on the spine, behind glass panes in the Principal's library. A fitted carpet covered the floor, cold cigarette smoke hung habitually in the air. In the summer months the Principal would occasionally keep a window open; then the sound of horns would be heard from the street, the noise of cars braking on the smooth road surface, and sometimes a tepid gust of wind would waft in the aroma of vernal air and petrol fumes. On the desk stood a photograph in a big silver frame. A middle-aged lady in an evening dress: she had on long gloves, wore a row of pearls and carried herself like a queen. She was the wife of Dr Klapp, the lawyer.

The building in which the office occupied part of the

first floor was a former aristocratic residence, the only building of its kind in that narrow, traffic-ridden street in the city centre. When Dr Klapp moved into the premises he had them painted and on the whitewashed ceilings the eighteenth-century stucco-work now stood out with exceptional clarity. Richest of all was the ceiling decoration in the large central room. Here the female employees sat at their typewriters, together with the Assistant, Dr List. A rather more highly placed Assistant was Dr Wieserer. He wore a thin moustache on his upper lip and sat in a small office of his own.

Fräulein Sommer and Frau Kratzenauer used to talk about love – about love, the true motive force of life; about love, which has at some time seized every creature and which even in a lawyer's office kindles all hopes. Fräulein Kleinert did not talk about love, and neither did Fräulein Lange even though she had a fiancé.

Fräulein Sommer had been longest in the service of Dr Klapp, and Frau Kratzenauer maintained that the reddish-blonde colour of her hair was not genuine. Frau Kratzenauer also used to make remarks about Fräulein Sommer's stately though in no way excessive figure, and she used to say of her that she secretly adored their employer. Fräulein Sommer, however, used always to speak only about her postal administrator. The postal administrator was very jealous. He suffered from rheumatism, and when he had to stay in bed for half a year she sacrificed all her free time to him, it could be said she nursed him back to health. To such a healthy condition, at any rate, that he now got attacks only once in a while. Attacks of a minor character and certainly not to be compared with that proper, serious rheumatism of which Fräulein Sommer used to speak with shuddering and awe. The postal administrator had married children. He used to present Fräulein Sommer with opera tickets, and she was thus able to talk in the office about male leads and prima donnas, about *Aïda*, *Othello* and *Rosenkavalier*.

But what was the postal administrator's rheumatism, measured against the tuberculosis from which Frau Kratzenauer's husband had died so young? They had still slept in the same bed during the final year, and Frau Kratzenauer's black eyes shone when she spoke of the joy precisely of that final year, a joy interrupted only by his coughing and eventually ended by his death. Frau Kratzenauer asked Dr List how he handled such joy; she spoke about the world of men and the enjoyment of life. The youngest of her acquaintances was a student: he would visit her on Saturday afternoons, say nothing and after half an hour leave. Dr List had not answered Frau Kratzenauer's question. The typewriters clattered, faint chimes marked the end of a line and when a complete page was torn from the machine a brief whirring noise would be heard. Taking the number of employees into consideration, it was a large and important office.

Dr Klapp's clientele was important, in any case; or, to put it more accurately, it was important as such but at the same time graded internally into different degrees of importance. Fräulein Sommer knew these gradations, long years of experience and the Principal's confidence had given her, the true secretary, a sure hand and the trained eye of the diagnostician. She made the appointments, she announced visitors and showed them in. She would often give the others explanations, since they did not have much knowledge of the higher world. And when she accompanied some visitor or other into the Principal's room, the compliance of her smile and the alacrity of her conduct would often by itself already be an indication of their rank; and she would be satisfied if she observed their discussion going on and on, and if Dr Klapp could be heard through the padded door laughing heartily and with evident approbation.

Fräulein Sommer often used to wonder about Fräulein

Kleinert. She was certainly not more than forty, her pale blonde hair framed a face that many a man must certainly find pleasant; how then did it come about that there were no contenders for Fräulein Kleinert? Or was there, in fact, some special motive for her language lessons, for the evening class which she attended at the Italian Institute? But it happened twice that Frau Kratzenauer ran into Fräulein Kleinert in the street of an evening. It was ten o'clock. She was coming from her class. It was clear that she was returning home alone.

Fräulein Kleinert was in fact studying the Italian language. She had received a thick letter two years before, a letter from the Italian Institute of Culture. In this letter, she was invited to become a member of the Institute and to study Italian. In a few well-chosen words, allusion was made to the advantages that knowledge of a language guarantees in various spheres – in commerce, in the domain of general culture and in social life. The membership fee was also mentioned in the letter, it was not high and, apart from participation in language classes, entry to lectures and other events was included and a discount allowed on group tours. A prospectus from the Italian travel office was enclosed. It showed photographs of Lake Garda, of the autostrada emerging from a rock tunnel between smooth water and oleander bushes; it showed Piazza di Venezia and moonlight over the Bay of Naples.

Fräulein Kleinert only seldom received mail. She read the letter, which – albeit obviously for publicity purposes – had been sent to her personally; she read the missive through a second time; and the printed Italian words in the top left-hand corner, the words *Istituto di Cultura Italiana*, suddenly held an allure: an allure of southern wine, leafy colonnades and the sound of mandolines. Fräulein Kleinert was a solitary lady, and she decided to take instruction in Italian.

The Italian cultural institute, in a quiet street, on the second storey of a modern building, comprised a lecture hall, two classrooms and an administrative office. When Fräulein Kleinert entered, she saw a lady and a young man at two desks near the window, sitting on revolving armchairs; she saw the map of Italy on the wall, a colour print of a seascape and the heads of Mussolini and the King in two larger than life-size photographs. The silence struck her. On a door, a brass plate bore the word: 'Director'. The young man was reading a newspaper. One could scent the aroma of new furniture and the good air of the nearby quay.

Once he had noticed Fräulein Kleinert, the official stood up. He acceded to her wish and filled out a membership card.

Fräulein Kleinert did not miss any of her lessons. How, otherwise, could she have acquired and increased the stock of theory and practice which makes up knowledge of the Italian language and its grammar? She soon learnt the future and the perfect, three alternative forms of the imperative, and when she conjugated a verb she would notice how the word's rhythm and lovely melody altered. Perhaps she completed her exercises all the more diligently and all the more accurately because, as she soon could not help reflecting, she was the only person in the evening class – which was in any case ill attended – who came for enjoyment's sake. One of the male participants was an official in the foreign ministry, the other two were employees of an Italian firm, and the young girl who attended the class recounted before long how she had the intention of marrying an Italian, emigrating with him and establishing an Italian bookshop in New York. It was, therefore, really only Fräulein Kleinert who was left to esteem the congeniality and beauty of the study of Italian as such.

The teacher, in his mid thirties, was of puny build, he

wore a little black moustache and – thanks evidently to an illness – one of his eyelids was half closed. But he was nevertheless extremely impassioned in his explanations. He would often raise his clenched fist and, as he pronounced some new word, open his hand with pistol-shot swiftness and flick his fingers in the air. To Fräulein Kleinert he was always polite.

She was also a really exemplary pupil. She would follow the exposition meticulously and would always volunteer to read out the Italian sentences. At home, if she was preparing herself in the evening for her lessons, she would often say the sentences to herself half aloud; and she would thereby experience something of the joy it always gave in her in the lessons to read out loud to the teacher and the others, when her own lips would form the mysterious speech.

'*Signorina Lucia, ha scritto alla modista che noi desideriamo avere i nostri cappelli per domenica?*' A world of hitherto unknown beauty opened before her in such phrases. For the word *Signorina* held the dignity of southern women and the tenderness of a dark look. And while the melody of the barcarole sounded in the name *Lucia*, the words *ha scritto* showed the writer in a darkened room, lazily dashing off a couple of words in large characters on her writing paper, and the potent accent of the word *domenica* held the light of a Sunday morning. Fräulein Kleinert would often repeat such sentences; and sometimes she would work late into the evening, until the next-door apartment had already fallen quite silent and, through the wall, the pendulum clock could be heard striking the eleventh hour.

But it must be said that Fräulein Kleinert, quite apart from her educational endeavours, proved her worth in the office too. To Dr Klapp and Dr Wieserer it basically made no difference whether Fräulein Sommer – with all her experience and knowledge – or Fräulein Kleinert appeared when they rang, to take dictation.

Dr Klapp's dictation was always clear. 'Write this down, Fräulein', he would say, although it was obvious for what purpose Fräulein Kleinert was sitting beside his desk with notepad unfolded. But then he would pause. Fräulein Kleinert would look at him. Despite his approaching sixtieth year, he still had the appearance of a sportsman. His fair hair interspersed with grey was worn with a parting, his shirts were uncreased, in each of his gold cuff links a small diamond sparkled.

Once he had started, he would dictate in one go and it could not escape notice with what naturalness he held sway in the world of paragraphs: that he made use of this ambiguous and doubtless alarming mystery like a magician; that precisely only in his later years perhaps had he acquired the nimbleness of the master fencer, that ultimate virtuosity. His letters were little models of prose and, even if the same stock phrases of courtesy and respect recurred, this did not detract from the spirit of gallantry that always manifested itself in Dr Klapp's correspondence. If, in a final letter to the debtor of one of his important clients, he announced sequestration and so for ever closed a book of hopes, of business and of domestic happiness, he would not neglect to assure even this addressee of his quite particular esteem. What he used to think about, Fräulein Kleinert did not know: she did not know it when he was dictating the mail with impassive precision or when – the little smile with which he used to dismiss her still on his lips – he had already lain the next document on the desk in front of him and was opening it with the sombre concentration of a scholar.

So far as Dr Wieserer was concerned, he liked to joke with Frau Kratzenauer. He used to say it was a man of the law's prime duty to be a man of the law; but if he did not know the good things in life, the man of the law would not be a man at all – and ergo no man of the law. Of an evening he was often to be seen with his small, blonde wife in the well-known Garden Restaurant in the city centre, where pale beer was served in tall glasses straight from the barrel. Here too he would sometimes sit at a long table, when the companions of his student days held a reunion, the brothers of his fraternity, in which he played the role of an 'elderly gentleman' (even though according to the calendar he was still a very young gentleman). The time of spring madness, of youthful *Sturm und Drang*, had like a plough left behind the long scar on his left cheek. Now he was the owner of a little motor-car. He used to drive his own family to the country on Sundays, they would unpack the food they had brought along at the edge of the forest, while two little boys soiled their new outfits with pickled meat and knocked over the paper cups containing coffee – for such, as he knew, was the way of the world.

Fräulein Kleinert would type faultlessly all the letters, pleadings and other documents dictated by Dr Klapp and Dr Wieserer. She was familiar with legal expressions and their orthography, she knew how to maintain the width of a margin and the pages she used to present for signing at the end of the working day would exhale the purity of new-baked bread, the freshness of a cake.

Only the Assistant, Dr List, usually wrote his own letters.

'He has gone hungry throughout his student days', Fräulein Sommer said of him, 'but you'll see how far he'll go.'

'An odd fellow', Frau Kratzenauer said. 'Why doesn't he talk?'

'A deep one', said Fräulein Lange.

'But he has a head', said Fräulein Sommer. She tapped a finger against her own temple, making clear by this localization what she was talking about.

'I don't like him', said Fräulein Lange. 'Such people are called climbers. And why does he sit here every evening until eight or nine o'clock?'

'The Principal likes him better than that one over there, at any rate', said Fräulein Sommer and pointed to Dr Wieserer's room.

'I don't know', said Fräulein Lange shrugging her shoulders, and her face hardened, here in the middle of the office. She was annoyed, she had the advantage of superior knowledge. Her betrothed often travelled to the Reich.

Her betrothed sometimes remained away over a Sunday. Then Fräulein Lange would ask whether Fräulein Kleinert would like to spend the afternoon with her. They would go to a picture theatre, to a promenade concert or to the big pastry shop. Here they would sit at one of the little gilt tables with their princely ornamentation and, when they had consumed the plump doughnuts with coffee-flavoured or chocolate icing and scraped up every last remnant of whipped cream from their plates, they would watch the families slowly endeavouring to forge a way between the close-packed tables, they would see the Sunday bustle of the waitresses, the impassive faces of the customers who had found a place and the cigarette smoke which hung in the tea-time air. Fräulein Lange always spoke only about her betrothed and his dazzling prospects and, if he were not travelling, Fräulein Kleinert would say she was quite content on a Sunday afternoon to alter a dress, brush her carpet or rearrange her cupboards. In her room in the high-lying suburb, which afforded her fresh air and also a view over a small children's playground, she would hear the occasional radio and sometimes piano-playing too, since, like her, a few families in the building would be spending the afternoon at home.

At about four o'clock there would usually be a short ring at her bell, then the little bespectacled gentleman would be standing at her door. He had only four teeth left, and back at home his wife lay crippled in bed. Fräulein Kleinert gave him her contribution, although she knew the world's suffering was measureless and her salary far from being sufficient to allay it. But she saw the little gentleman, she saw how in his toothless modesty he had been turned away by numerous employers and how in the end, submitting to fate, he put on his little overcoat and left his room to set out on his present round, while his wife, though crippled, followed him with her eyes and begged him to cross the roads carefully.

In the evenings, Fräulein Kleinert would usually still find time to check through her Italian exercise one last time; and since, after six months, she had learnt the use of irregular verbs and was already writing short model letters, it was possible to speak of rapid progress.

II

Fräulein Kleinert had attended her class diligently throughout the winter and during the spring as well, and as her two weeks of vacation drew closer she decided on a trip to Italy. Fräulein Sommer was impressed, as she showed her the programme of the conducted tour. 'Marvellous', she said, 'the Neue Glocknerstrasse, the Dolomites, the North Italian lakes, and Venice into the bargain!' – and she pursed her lips as though she felt pained by the idea of so much beauty and sightseeing. She herself always spent her vacation on the coast of Yugoslavia, and in the little group photos she displayed would appear in a swimming costume. The ladies used to take their holiday trips in turns and both the others had their plans too: Frau Kratzenauer was going only to Karlsbad, she was going to her mother's, and Fräulein Lange had in mind the Bavarian Alps.

It thus came about that Fräulein Kleinert climbed aboard the open coach in Linz and, before she could check where her suitcase and her small umbrella had been loaded, she was already feeling some difficulty in breathing, for the trunk road was straight as a die and they were travelling with unexpected velocity. This continued as far as Wels. But then the hills grew green and a mountain range stretched away in distant vapour. Open fields lay between forest and river, the morning wore on, it did not last long, then they were driving through the narrow streets of a town, they were driving to the bridge, they saw the arcaded houses on the banks and the fortress of Hohen-Salzburg above their heads.

They ate pickled beef, boiled greens and Sachertorte and sat as they did so in a garden, at pleasant, cloth-covered tables; then they were conducted to a square, they listened to the carillon, it was the Magic-Flute melody and Mozart's birthplace was next stop on the programme. The guide repeated that Mozart was the composer of *The Magic Flute*, he pointed out the room with its outdated wall coverings, he pointed out also a tiny piano with black lower keys and white upper keys, at which the composer – inspired, young and assuredly very poor – had sat. Although a warning notice expressly forbade it, one of the travellers attempted to depress a key. A faint, brittle note was audible and, while one of the ladies said: 'You can see with what simple means he was satisfied' and another declared that was true greatness, down in the street the driver for his part sounded his horn, the guide urged them along too, they all climbed aboard and, after a drive through a damp river valley, past meadows and mountains veiled in mist, at suppertime the group came to Zell-am-See.

Here they ate in a large dining-room, at several tables Hungarian was being spoken, through the window-panes one could see the play of lights on the dark water, it was a warm evening. One of the gentlemen from the group, a middle-school teacher, tried his luck with a gambling

machine, the others watched and they all soon went to
bed.

In the early morning, Fräulein Kleinert stepped onto
her balcony. The lake was dark blue. The mountains
framing it were sharply outlined in the clear morning air,
little patches of snow glistened in the sun. She had never
before seen the world of the Alps. A boat lay on the water,
the young man and woman who sat in it were both
dressed in white, the hotel gardens and the bathing
establishments were empty. In the next room someone
cleared their throat, the clink of breakfast crockery made
itself heard from the ground floor.

Fräulein Kleinert dressed and went downstairs. Many
of the hotel guests were already sitting in the dining-room,
the children were being given their usual meals, on her
way to the breakfast table a lady holding her little boy by
the hand had stopped at another table and was discussing
the weather prospects for the day, she wore a dirndl and
her knitting was in a large, open bag. The gentlemen sat
in short lederhosen, many were reading their newspapers
and Fräulein Kleinert saw how the habits of holiday
routine stretched far back into the time before the arrival
of her party and how they would also continue unhampered
after their departure.

The departure was very speedy. The coach was
travelling into the midst of the mountain world. A broad
valley sloped upwards, they saw herds of cows and
wooden dwellings, the coach took the climb at a moderate
pace, the sun was shining. They were now on the famous
Glocknerstrasse. At the tree line, a wind began to blow
and set the great expanse of coniferous growth in
movement. Fräulein Kleinert felt a touch of dizziness, but
the coach travelled deeper into the mountains, took sharp
curves without altering its speed, and she could tell by the
road that lay below them that they were still climbing
higher.

A layer of mist came towards them and they drove right into it. The roof of the coach was drawn shut, it was raining now. They arrived in dense cloud in front of the Glocknerhaus, a damp tingling could be felt in the air.

At lunch, which was taken indoors, it became clear that the group included a wag. He said to the waiter: 'Bring me a schnitzel *à la Holstein*, but with plenty of *à la*, please.' His companions laughed loudly and heartily. When a peddler with various small wares came up to the table, Fräulein Kleinert chose two picture postcards and sent greetings from the Glocknerhaus to Fräulein Sommer and to Fräulein Lange. Outside, the mist had meanwhile begun to move, it swirled in individual swathes over boulders and small snowfields.

While the group was walking to the Pasterzen glacier, the wag said that in such adventures the main thing was not to lose one's sense of humour. He was the manager of a branch bank. 'Carefully, Madam', he said, 'if you have any intention of falling, please let me know.' The path was slippery and the bank manager offered his arm to various ladies in turn. When the clouds parted, they glimpsed other snowfields and snow-clad summits and sometimes a broad valley. Fräulein Kleinert was particularly surprised when she saw the glacier. It terminated in an expanse of scree, the ice wall was greenish and full of dirty fissures.

In the afternoon, as they drove on and the road descended once more, the weather brightened up. In Heiligenblut they found a clear evening. The little church and the valley were bathed in the light of the sun's last rays and behind them, in the middle distance, rose the snow-clad massif of the Gross- and Kleinglockner.

Many hundreds of years ago, long before the old Glocknerstrasse or an Austrian Alpine Club had existed, an adventurous Dane on his journey home had lost his way in the Alps one winter's night. The snow descended upon the dead man and his holy treasure. The emperor of

Byzantium had given him a few drops of the Saviour's blood as payment for important services. He carried the little glass phial in one of his tall boots. It thus came about that some of the peasants, who already in that rough and godly century had settled even far up in the valleys of the High Tauern, discovered the miracle next morning in the snowy landscape. They saw three green ears of wheat growing from the earth. They dug down, and when they found the dead foreigner they wanted to give him a decent burial. But their oxen refused to draw the corpse. The beasts would not budge, so the peasants decided to perform the interment without a ceremony on that very spot. But soon a new miracle appeared and it was now the boot itself which grew from the snow. Now the little holy vessel was found too and the bishop, who for his part had meanwhile already received a report from Byzantium on the departure of the holy substance, naturally had a church built.

The touring party visited the church – it was a new one, erected on the site of the old church destroyed by fire – and they were shown the monstrance in which the holy phial was enclosed. As they emerged from the church, they saw that other touring parties had arrived in long motor-coaches. The new Glocknerstrasse had given the place a powerful boost. They heard foreign languages, saw coach repair shops and numerous hotels in the rustic style.

Fräulein Kleinert had a splitting headache. Frau Wahle, the schoolteacher's wife, declared that it came from rapid and frequent atmospheric changes and gave her an aspirin tablet. It did not help much, and Fräulein Kleinert had to miss the evening meal. She heard on the following day that it had been especially good and that they had all enjoyed themselves famously, thanks in particular to the bank manager's jokes.

Towards noon on this next day the coach came to a halt

in front of a picket of black uniforms. The elegant, laconic
soldiers allowed them to pass and Fräulein Kleinert found
herself in Italy. But the journey continued as before on
mountain roads, over passes and through high valleys.
They saw the red crags of the Dolomites, very jagged and
of medium size, thrown into relief by a pleasant blue sky;
they were taken to newly erected hotels, savoured the
bright, freshly varnished furniture and saw young people
already dancing on the terraces in the morning, while
subdued jazz music spread through the potent, health-
giving mountain air. The cemeteries, whose low wooden
crosses stood in dense ranks, dated from the time of the
battles in the Dolomites. At that time the hotel palaces
had been serviceable fortifications and a little pastry shop
had been a dangerous machine-gun nest. All this had now
been rebuilt, the houses even considerably modernized;
the technology of war, for its part, had in twenty years
made great advances and could now make effective use of the
buildings, the terrain, the network of first-class roads. For
the time being, international summer visitors played golf
on the hilly alpine meadows. A ball would often fly right
in among the soldiers' graves. The air was pure, the view
particularly magical.

Was this then the land of Italy, the land which Fräulein
Kleinert's imagination had portrayed in so many vague
but always colourful pictures, the cradle of that fantastic,
melodious language? She could now hear Italian conversations daily, would hear when the head waiter reminded
one of his subordinate waiters about the potato purée for
this table or the lemonade for that one over there; things
would sometimes even grow turbulent and strong words
fly from waiters to kitchen, from kitchen to head waiter
and from head waiter to waiters. Then, in the flurry, one
would hear the metal lid being clapped over a dish, one
would smell roast poultry, vegetables and pastries.

Fräulein Kleinert also made use herself of her knowledge

of Italian. She did so if she spoke to the porter, to a waiter or to the chambermaid. 'Oh, so Madam speaks Italian?', she would be asked, and if she confirmed it would hear another remark or two about the weather and the lively tourist season. The hotel employees accompanied their communications with vigorous gestures, making sure that the foreign lady understood everything. The touring party too noted Fräulein Kleinert's linguistic proficiency. The bank manager called her 'our fair-haired Italian lady', earning laughter and success with the remark.

From Madonna di Campiglio the party drove to Lake Como. In the valley they were traversing, a heavier, warm air suddenly came to meet them, bringing with it the aroma of leaves, road dust and unknown fruits. A piece of the Italian plain had thrust itself between the mountains. Now they saw chestnut trees against the brighter green of the meadows, and soon already the pale leaves of olives as well. They came then into a marshy region and finally to the lake. The houses here were white, red or yellow in colour, the roofs were flat, occasional palm trees stood in the gardens. The heat was very intense, the members of the touring party had all fallen silent.

In the afternoon they were driven to the gardens of the Villa Carlotta. They walked up hill and down dale, while the guide explained the singularity of the vegetation. He expected they would have heard of the Prussian princess in whose honour the park – which, with oleanders and magnolias and its vista of the Alps, ran down to a brilliant blue expanse of water – was named? It was so hot that Fräulein Kleinert sought a bench in the shade and sat down on it. The next day another lake, other parklands and another royal personage were scheduled as the target of their sightseeing. This time the powerful count was a Borromeo, the guide made the doubled 'r' of the word Borromeo roll like a small thunderclap, thus bringing emphatically to bear the grandeur and awe-inspiring character of the name. This Borromeo owned not just the Isola Bella with its garden and palace, with its cedars and orange trees, but also the Isola Madre and probably everything else in Lake Maggiore and upon its shores – just like that Herr Kanitverstan from our reading book, who owned houses, ships and all the treasures of a city and was still buried in the end.

They spent the night in Stresa, and the hotel was empty. The guests – *clienti* – were now *alla montagna*, in the mountains, said the porter, making a series of upward gestures with the backs of his hands. 'Now it's the dead season, it's *troppo caldo, troppo caldo*, much too hot.' He seemed still to be young, but his head was bald and he wiped the beads of sweat from his pate.

In Milan, where they ate lunch, they were shown the cathedral, which in its time had been the largest cathedral on earth and which was still a very large cathedral. They were shown the famous pictures in the gallery, most of which had a religious content, and finally the touring party was afforded a glimpse of the most famous picture in the world. This was the Last Supper. But Leonardo da Vinci, who was not just the greatest painter but actually the greatest of all as a draughtsman, architect and engineer too, had precisely with this picture tried out a new type of colour. It was now barely perceptible, since the greater and more famous greatness and fame are, the less they no doubt care about what a touring party will see this or that many hundreds of years later – and they nevertheless remain great and very famous. 'Yes', said the bank manager, 'that's just the way it is.'

In Verona, Fräulein Kleinert began to feel the heat particularly badly. She had been given an attic room, you see, and the sun had shone on the roof all day long. The hotelier expressed his regret, it was the season of the open-air performances. At any rate, tickets had been reserved for the whole party. *Lohengrin* was being played. They sat in the arena, which had room for several thousand people, and though the stage was far away they could follow the action quite well. In particular, the water on which the swan glided in – and with the swan the silver-and-blue knight – appeared very natural. The opera was lengthy. Fräulein Kleinert saw the night sky over the arena, it was domed, the stars were countless golden dots. She saw the Great and the Little Bear, the Milky Way and the planet Venus. She knew that since time immemorial, and to this day, many people have connected the image of the stars with destiny. She herself was admittedly not superstitious. But when she thought about the distances which run into millions, about the infinity of space and the path of the stars, and viewed the opera performance on the stage below, then a host of ideas came crowding into her mind for all that.

In Verona they saw a vegetable market enclosed by palaces, they saw tombs, they saw yet another picture gallery and in the afternoon they continued to Padua. On the journey it was a little cooler, the bank manager was in high spirits and he began to hum: 'He lies in a grave in Padua/In the church of Sant'Antonio.'

'Who lies in a tomb in Padua?', one of the ladies asked.

The bank manager was not very sure of his facts. 'Faust, I think', he said.

'Impossible', another lady declared.

Dr Wahle knew the answer. The individual was indeed mentioned in *Faust*, but it was Herr Schwerdtlein, the husband of Widow Schwerdtlein.

At the church of Sant'Antonio, though, they did not find the tomb. But they sat on the stone balustrade of the cloisters, and the morning was so peaceful one could hear the twittering of a bird. Before their eyes the edifice of sacristy and church rose up and with its walls and roofs ascended as if through multiple stage-sets to the bright dome. The journey was already soon coming to an end. Venice was its final stage.

In Venice they were brought to the hotel in gondolas, and as Fräulein Kleinert lay in her room at night and heard the plashing of the canal against the masonry of the building, it really seemed to her then as though with her Italian trip she had granted herself a journey into fairyland.

But next morning she did not feel very well. She asked Frau Wahle for advice and the latter, highly experienced, declared that a digestive complaint was a common occurrence on such journeys and advised her to spend the whole day in bed. A stout, elderly chambermaid brought her broth and tea and a hot-water bottle.

Towards evening, though, Fräulein Kleinert tried to get up; she was weak, she sat down in the lobby. Behind a tall desk stood the porter. Fräulein Kleinert had seen many hotel porters on her journey. But this one here was a mighty man. He wore large, gold-rimmed spectacles, his beard was thick and of deepest black. He answered numerous inquiries and transmitted his bass voice slowly into the telephone like some fearsome deity. He had perforce to be a mysterious, unusual porter, if the hotel management could decide to appoint him, dark and awe-inspiring as he was, actually to preside over the reception rooms. Soon the others came back to the hotel from their sightseeing, and one of the ladies declared that Fräulein Kleinert had not missed very much, it had in any case only been churches, statues and a picture gallery again.

But on the following day – it was the last before the journey home – Fräulein Kleinert, even though not entirely well, was able to go to the Lido with all the others. She saw the pearly-grey sea, the colourful beach huts and the two majestic hotel palaces, which – apart from all pomp – also reserved small ground-floor restaurants for the most easy-going of their guests, who liked to take their midday meal in bathing wrap and swimming costume.

The last evening brought another ride by gondola: a ride over the Canal Grande, upon whose surface the lamps of many other gondolas shone, tiny and festive; a ride through darker canals, under small bridges and round the corners of houses, where the oarsman would let his warning shout die away in the darkness, high and melancholy.

The hour was already late when Fräulein Kleinert returned to the hotel. Her room lay at the end of a corridor, which led round many corners. At one of these corners, by a lamp that stood on a little table, the stout chambermaid was sitting. She was darning stockings and beside her sat the porter. He sat now in his shirt-sleeves and his spectacles had slipped down. Who knows, perhaps they were married. They lived in the city of gondolas and dreamlike canals. Perhaps he was a good husband. He had his day's work behind him, late in the evening he liked to sit beside her and watch her silently.

Fräulein Kleinert went to bed. Her journey was over.

III

After her return, Fräulein Kleinert continued her language classes successfully and with interest. She attended the Institute's events, and if the subject of one of the lectures was Italian art or the Italian landscape, she had a better idea now of how to visualize it.

One of the lectures dealt with labour relations in the new Italy. In the audience at this lecture, Fräulein Kleinert saw a member of her office. It was the Assistant, Dr List.

'So you attend these events?', he asked. They left the premises together. 'Don't you know, then', he went on to ask, 'that it's all just propaganda? And not very clever propaganda either. Do you know what those people really have in mind for us? Today they're fighting as so-called volunteers in Spain, tomorrow they'll be fighting in Austria, the day after tomorrow here and eventually all over the world. They have big plans. In Germany, all the preparations for war are already being made with scientific thoroughness, with gas masks, air-raid shelters and everything else that's needed.'

Fräulein Kleinert was surprised by the Assistant. He noticed this and said: 'But I probably shouldn't be influencing you.'

'Oh, no', said Fräulein Kleinert, 'it doesn't matter at all.' She added, all the same, that she had never concerned herself with either politics or religion.

But now Fräulein Kleinert began to hear more and more about politics and religion. For after the occupation of Austria, hardly anybody was soon speaking any longer about anything else. Fräulein Lange was particularly excited. Her fiancé was now making more and more frequent trips, and each time would stay away for much longer. Fräulein Lange said that conditions in our country had become intolerable and everything was dominated by Jews and Communists. Fräulein Kleinert had noticed no change, but politics precisely had its own ways. Regarding the Jews, however, Fräulein Lange declared that the Principal, with his position, was merely one example of their influence, and Fräulein Sommer too was a Jewish blot on the office. The new Reich had to protect itself against its enemies.

To be sure, Fräulein Kleinert might have asked why just now, when the Reich had become so fortunate and strong, its enemies suddenly appeared so dangerous; but she had once again received a weighty letter from the Italian Institute, a letter which, when she had opened it, with its thick paper, embossed letters and gold insignia radiated a solemn magnificence in her room. The visit of the famous philosopher Antonio Buoninsegna, Professor at the University of Rome, member of the Fascist Grand Council, was announced; a lecture on 'Ethics and Philosophy of Life' had been arranged and, on the following evening, a dinner in his honour at the Hotel Esplanade. Fräulein Kleinert's first thought was: 'I haven't got a dress', but she calculated swiftly, she calculated all her savings over the past three months, and less than a week later she was standing in the dressmaker's salon, the white silk dress was already virtually ready, she was standing between two mirrors, she saw her deep décolletage, the big flower on her left shoulder and her loose blonde hair.

On the evening of the lecture, the hall of the Institute had never before been so full. It was not at all easy to find a place, but Fräulein Kleinert nevertheless by chance found an empty chair. The famous Professor had a little, white goatee beard, his figure was short and plump, his little eyes were lively and so too were his hands. He mentioned a great many names in his lecture, they were unknown to Fräulein Kleinert, but all these great scholars and highly respected colleagues, as the lecturer termed them – they all obviously agreed that Life was an uncertain river, an unpredictable business, and only the moment could determine the right choice. That was the Professor's wisdom and doubtless also the reason why, after the lecture, other gentlemen, probably professors likewise, surrounded him and congratulated him. Professors who obviously put forward the same assertions, since he, the Professor and Councillor of State from Rome, accepted their handshakes with so much pleasure and so many polite bows.

At the dinner, Fräulein Kleinert sat between the ministry official who attended the evening class with her and another gentleman whom she did not know. The gentlemen were very polite. The ministry official asked Fräulein Kleinert about her trip, he himself had spent three weeks in Rimini with his family, it had been very hot there too, but there had always been a breeze from the sea, and his small daughter, of course, had enjoyed the sea-bathing tremendously. He smiled when he spoke about his little daughter, and Fräulein Kleinert smiled approvingly and with appreciation. But the other gentleman had two sons, one of whom was even already studying at the university. Yes, said this table companion and father, time does fly, and so far as Italy was concerned he had certainly long desired just once to see the eternally blue sky above him, but business and duties had invariably shattered all his daydreams. Then, however, he fell silent, and her other neighbour too had nothing to say for a while, so Fräulein Kleinert could not avoid thinking it was now up to her to put an end to this lull in the conversation. But try as she might, the appropriate way of picking up the thread of their discourse afresh did not come to mind. She perceived a whitish-grey mushroom sauce flavoured with wine, which had been poured over her veal cutlet, and she saw that the Italian guest of honour had tucked his napkin into his collar and spread it over his chest. Before the compôte was served, he was honoured in a ceremonial speech.

After the meal, they repaired to another room. Here black coffee was handed round in small cups and this was drunk standing up. The ministry official stood with Fräulein Kleinert, but he soon joined another group and Fräulein Kleinert stood alone with her cup. Somebody offered her a cigarette and she took it, although she did not usually smoke. After a time, she saw an empty armchair and sat down.

Since the Italian mission was holding a reception later that same evening in the philosopher's honour, part of the company was obliged to be thinking already of an early departure and Fräulein Kleinert left the hotel as well. In the evening coat which Fräulein Lange had lent her, she stepped over the marble flags of the hallway, past the gilt chandeliers and the liveried footmen who made haste to open the doors in front of her.

Now she stood in the night air. On the opposite side of the street, the little park lay in darkness. Although Fräulein Kleinert had felt it necessary to drive up to the hotel in a car, on her way home she nevertheless waited for the tram.

In her room, she sat down on the bed and closed her eyes. She was very tired. She could still taste the flavour of the black coffee and the cigarette. What is more, the napkin over the famous professor's chest, the grey sauce, the chandeliers, the exhausting table talk and all the other impressions of the evening long kept her mind in a whirl.

In September it had almost come to war, and on one morning in March German troops occupied our city. A light snow mingled with rain fell upon the troops, and the population stood at the roadside in silence to watch their entry. A few young lads gaped at the great machines of war, the guns and the tanks, which stood on the streets for several days.

Already on the first morning the Assistant, Dr List, had not come in to the office; and when there was still no sight of him the next day either, Frau Kratzenauer was able to tell the whole story. 'He tried to make a run for it, but he didn't succeed. Now he's trapped.' She laughed and added: 'He was another of those Communists.' Fräulein Lange gave Frau Kratzenauer a hard look and she stopped talking at once. Both ladies were now wearing big party badges.

As for Dr Klapp, he told his friends he was an optimist. He had clean hands, no one could say the least thing against him, what should he fear? 'And furthermore', he

added with a wink, 'I have Wieserer sitting beside me.'
Then his acquaintances declared that this had certainly
been a fortunate, indeed prophetic arrangement.

After a while, Fräulein Kleinert had a dream. The
Assistant, Dr List, now in prison, appeared in her dream
and so did the gas masks he had spoken about. It was not
he, however, but Fräulein Lange and Frau Kratzenauer
who were each wearing such a mask. They were dressed
like nurses, the Assistant lay before them on the wooden
prison bed and they were opening the gas cock above his
head. But in addition, on other plank beds in the big hall,
there lay many other Assistants; and over each of their
beds a gas pipe was fixed and the ladies in their nurses'
uniforms were leaping from one pipe to another and
opening the taps. The loud noise of the escaping gas could
be heard. But the young men, including Dr List, all
displayed weeping faces distorted by fear.

Fräulein Kleinert woke up and could still hear the hiss
of the escaping gas. But she collected her thoughts and
realized that somebody in the neighbouring apartment
was running a bath. She arrived late at the office and
heard that Dr Klapp had been arrested during the night.

From now on the whole workload rested upon
Dr Wieserer's shoulders. It was he now who held meetings
and conducted all business. It was a hectic time. There
would often be many clients waiting in the hall, and
Dr Wieserer was so busy that he even had his lunch
brought to the office and sometimes consumed it as he was
dictating. Since he had taken over not just Dr Klapp's
appointment book, but also cases from other colleagues,
he was compelled to take on two new Assistants at once
and was already seeking a third.

Because of the shortage of space, and also in consideration of the increased demands upon him, Dr Wieserer
after a few days already found himself obliged to move
into the Principal's office. Here, moreover, he had the

library handy and in general had more room. An exchange of photographs was also effected, and on the heavy desk Fräulein Kleinert now perceived the pictures of two little boys and a plump, blonde woman.

Soon a large, pale-grey car stood before the office, for Dr Wieserer, with all his new work and responsibilities, obviously required a new car. Soon, too, some bad news arrived. Concerning Dr Klapp. He had hanged himself with his braces in his prison cell.

Fräulein Kleinert went to the funeral. Dr Wieserer granted her permission for this, although only one other employee, namely Fräulein Sommer, wished to attend the interment. He had incidentally informed Fräulein Sommer with regret that she must leave the office at the end of the month.

The funeral took place on the other bank, at an almost forgotten cemetery, since Dr Klapp had arranged many years before for a plot to remain empty beside his parents' grave. Fräulein Kleinert followed the ceremony with interest: it was strange to her, the gentlemen kept their hats on while the Rabbi was making his speech in the funeral hall. It was a very fine speech. He spoke of the man who had lived for justice and law, he spoke also of justice and law in general, and Fräulein Kleinert could not help thinking of the leather volumes which – as the representative of justice and law – Dr Wieserer was now using. Finally the Rabbi spoke of God's law.

The coffin was carried out into the open air and the funeral party followed it. An attendant handed out black-bordered tablets, which could be held comfortably by a wooden handle. They were covered with Hebrew characters. Fräulein Kleinert too took one of these tablets.

Over the grave, there was a metal frame with diagonal leather straps. The coffin was placed on this, then everyone was silent. The Rabbi prayed. Finally he raised his hands and pronounced the benediction: 'The Lord bless thee and keep thee. The Lord make his face shine upon thee, and be gracious unto thee. May the Lord lift up his countenance upon thee and give thee peace.' Meanwhile the straps were loosened and the coffin sank slowly, but with little shudders, into the pit. As nobody yet moved, the moaning of a woman's voice could be heard. Those attending the funeral then stepped one after another up to the opening, and each of them pushed in a clod of earth with a spade. The grave was deep and consequently the lumps of earth struck the wood of the coffin quite noisily as they fell.

Fräulein Sommer's parents were also buried in this spot, she went on to visit the site and Fräulein Kleinert accompanied her. When they reached the cemetery gates, the funeral party had already left. Only the Rabbi could still be seen. By chance he was just removing his head-dress and displayed a bald pate, which was boldly framed by a chaplet of hair.

The ladies climbed aboard the tram, which at this hour was empty. Fräulein Sommer said that the postal administrator had spoken of marriage, but there were still difficulties to be overcome. And all at once she grabbed for her handbag, extracted a handkerchief and began to sob. When Fräulein Kleinert saw this, she took Fräulein Sommer's hands in her own. She was now herself weeping as well.

Because of a procession of Jewish groups that was taking place that afternoon, the electric tram had been diverted and was obliged to make a large detour in order to reach the city centre. It drove past open fields, drove through a residential neighbourhood, then into the district of the Castle and Cathedral, and finally through the avenue of old trees, past the former military academy and the garden wall behind which Queen Anna's hunting chateau was visible, a slender Renaissance building with columns. It arrived at the junction of numerous tramways and, as the road then led uphill, from its winding course a panorama opened over the city. It was an afternoon in May. The river, the spires and many roofs were glistening in the sunlight.

Peace on the Road to Exile

I

The Rossio railway station lies on a small elevation directly above the city centre, and Herr and Frau Ehrlich saw with surprise how steeply the roadway sloped down as, upon their arrival in Lisbon one morning in the second half of June in the year 1940, they climbed into a taxi-cab and explained to the driver that they wished to be taken to one of the hotels. They spent the morning in their beds and – as they then sat, bathed and dressed in clean clothes, in the dining-room which from a raised mezzanine afforded a view over the empty squares, the bright buildings and the rows of little café tables – it seemed to the ageing couple almost as if their journey had about it something of a pleasure trip. They also could not help observing how, in this outermost corner of the continent, the early summer of that memorable year was deploying all its colourful charms and allowing the comfortable habits of the warm season to be enjoyed. In the quiet hotel restaurant a widow sat with her three daughters. The mother and her girls were wearing long black scarves, which fell over their backs from head-dresses resembling birettas. Who knows, perhaps they were visiting relatives in the city, perhaps they were staying there only as transients. Single gentlemen eating at the tables were certainly here in pursuance of business affairs, the meal was unexpectedly sumptuous and choice, and when – after serving them with a plate of cold hors d'oeuvres, a hot fish, two roasts, a dish of fruit and little pastries – the waiter still with courteous insistence offered them soft-boiled eggs, which were to be enjoyed in the Portuguese fashion with sugar as a conclusion to their meal, Herr Ehrlich stretched out his arms and with both hands warded off this excess of hospitality and extravagance.

Travellers who journey to the South are fond of strolling in the afternoon through the streets of a strange city, pausing in front of shop windows, peering into some old alleyway or surveying the ebb and flow of the crowds of people on the piazzas. Lisbon, situated on an ocean bight, the renowned seaport where ships engaged in a modest but profitable trade with the African colonies ride at anchor, undoubtedly offered the opportunity for plenty of sightseeing. When, on their way to the police station, Herr and Frau Ehrlich mounted two precipitous streets and on reaching the top turned into a third, at the end of this no longer ascending thoroughfare – between the straight rows of houses – they spied a patch of blue sea.

They met Herr Kantor at the police station, and the latter at once began to discuss the possibilities of continuing their journey – to Brazil, to Argentina, to the United States. The couple, by now in possession of a hotel room with comfortable beds and a view over the square, were visibly alarmed by Herr Kantor's plans, though it had to be conceded that these were far-sighted and realistic. Meanwhile the police official was handing out the passports, which now contained a visa authorizing a stay of eight days.

It was not so much the thought of their journey's extension, but far more the desire to unburden her heart and report everything, that induced Frau Ehrlich on returning to the hotel to sit down at the little desk in their room and write a long letter: a letter to her friend Frau Wolf, who with shrewd foresight – and after salvaging a considerable fortune – had already over a year before taken up residence in New York. The events of the past week gave wings to Frau Ehrlich's style. In vivid language she wrote of their escape from Paris, the congested streets, the Belgian and Dutch refugees with mattresses tied on their cars (not, as was at first believed, to afford the passengers an opportunity to sleep, but on account of low-flying enemy planes). Then Frau Ehrlich wrote of their arrival in Bordeaux, the mass encampments in railway stations and on open spaces. Here in Bordeaux the government was known to be sitting and deliberating, while in the hotels high sums were being offered merely for the armchairs in the lobby, one of which was precisely available for Herr Ehrlich, a stroke of luck, since a bit of rest at night seemed imperative in view of his notoriously precarious health. As Frau Ehrlich then wrote about Biarritz, the next stopping place for the fleeing couple, there came into her letter something of the clear evening air, the sunset over the rocks and white houses, the deep-blue beauty of the bay. Here, however, the news of the capitulation had reached them, here they had heard through the loudspeakers the voice of the aged Marshal, here they had finally learned – and Frau Ehrlich quoted her favourite poet, Heinrich Heine – that France had foundered.

But France did not allow the victims of the upheaval to move on without further ado, and although in Bordeaux already Herr Ehrlich had, with fortunate prudence, paid the high price for a transit visa via the Negro Republic of Haiti and thereby acquired also permission to travel across Spain and Portugal, the French state machine – in these last days continuing, so to speak, of its own volition – was creating unforeseen difficulties even at the last moment. The great disaster was drawing ever closer, and a crowd numbered in thousands stood for many days in front of the Bayonne prefecture, the crowd clamoured and raged, and Frau Ehrlich was also able to provide a striking description of a thunderstorm which broke over the scene, its lightning bolts striking the open sea, just as she likewise described graphically the indolent conduct of the officials, the slow coming and going of the clerks as they could be seen through the prefecture windows and as, in comfortable conversation and smoking their cigars, they processed the applications for exit visas entirely at their ease.

Now they were in Portugal, in a country that seemed friendly, and although as has already been mentioned it had initially been Frau Ehrlich's intention only to report their experiences, she nevertheless deliberately weighed her words at the end of the letter, she actually said that they were 'stranded' in Portugal and she added that it was a comforting thought to know that, on the other side of the ocean, friends were following the fate of the castaways with sympathy and undoubted interest. Frau Ehrlich read through what she had written and – exhausted as never before after the excitements, the nights in railway carriages, the future so menacing and unknown for a friendly, well-disposed couple with very limited means in the alien land of Portugal – she nevertheless found pleasure in her own writing and told herself the letter was fine.

She sealed the envelope and Herr Ehrlich took it to the post office. With a couple of energetic gestures he made it clear to the clerk that the letter was to be dispatched to America on the recently opened airline. He was an elderly gentleman, but he had the enterprise to utilize the swiftest means; he paid for the stamps and saw the interior of the post office which, with its smooth yellow-ochre marble tiles and its greenish illuminated characters, embodied something of that obviously American promptitude and convenience here in the midst of the land of oranges and sweet wine.

The land of Portugal was an elongated, green patch in the bottom left-hand corner of the map of Europe. How had it ever happened to Herr and Frau Ehrlich to undertake a journey to Portugal, to a country in which travelling conditions unquestionably presented great difficulties, and where the food seemed so uncertain? They had never travelled very far in summer, in spring occasionally to the southern slopes of the Alps. A bank manager whom they knew had indeed undertaken a journey to Spain, but he had come back disappointed.

But soon yet other countries and other names surfaced, countries which had been even farther from the couple's thoughts. Who would ever have thought of Bolivia, Costa Rica or Colombia, regions whose names might indeed be found in a stamp collector's album, but whose inhabitants appeared as faraway and alien as the man in the moon? There was no place to stay in Portugal, that soon became conclusively apparent; and Herr Wohl – a German who had represented Herr Ehrlich's leather goods in Lisbon, and who on one of their very first days in the hotel came to visit his former business associate – asserted, moreover, that after the fall of France the fall of England could be expected within the next two weeks and then a new order for the continent would ensue. Herr Wohl regretted certain personal hardships, but he said these were unavoidable, seeing that revolutionary, world-shattering events were involved.

But who would now call a halt to world affairs at the frontiers of one continent? Who would vouch for it that on the far side of the ocean there could be an existence which, though poor, would at least be peaceful and safe from the threat of new catastrophes? People did not venture to think this through, and they discussed entry and living conditions in Brazil and Peru (since, after all, the paradise of North America was as good as unattainable). Meanwhile the sun shone on the neat facades and the greenery of Avenida Liberdade, one of the cafés ran a section with white-covered tables on the strip of garden dividing the carriageway, here you could sit in the shade of tall trees, eat light doughnuts glazed with sugar, and drink the cold tea which Herr Ehrlich soon learnt to order in the Portuguese language. He would say: '*Cha frio ma sem gelo*' – cold tea but without ice, since the latter would have been injurious to his gall-bladder complaint, while on the other hand a moderately cool drink in the ever more intensely oppressive summer heat afforded agreeable relief.

The visa which entitled Herr and Frau Ehrlich to visit the island of Haiti was only a transit visa, and Herr Kantor warned emphatically against undertaking a journey in reliance upon it. Quite apart from the fact that there was no shipping connection. But other visas too which might perhaps be granted – a visa for San Domingo, for Cuba or for Bolivia – were in Herr Kantor's eyes problematical and dangerous: the poor people who had ventured to attempt it, and who had boarded a ship with their families and movable goods, would in all probability not be allowed ashore. And where to then? Herr Kantor had to concede that on one such point his wisdom ran out. A shipping company was selling tickets for Mexico together with entry permits, but was demanding as guarantee a sum which, as Herr Kantor clearly established, equalled the price of the return ticket.

Herr Kantor revealed himself to be an authority on residence and visa questions. Early in the morning he would already be striding along the pavement of the Rossio, up and down the great square, while Herr Müller, an inventor, listened to him attentively as he walked at his side. Herr Müller wanted to go to the United States. With his marvellous invention he could earn thousands, nay millions of dollars. But Herr Kantor demurred: 'The quota conditions make immigration impossible and a visitor's visa will not be granted. You were born in Hungary? Hopeless. You would have to wait for ten, perhaps twenty years.' And he closed the door to the promised land of limitless possibilities, in which President Roosevelt, who ruled so merrily in New York amid inventors and electricity, needed merely to press a little button in order to reveal to Herr Müller a whole suite of laboratories with workers and undreamed-of equipment. The President, moreover, would already recognize the inventor from afar – were he only to come – and would call out: 'That must be Müller the engineer, whom we've been waiting for all this time.' He would at once get the engineer to initiate him into all his secrets, would instantly promise him to discuss everything with his friend Rockefeller and a dizzying vista of the future would open up. That was America. Herr Müller looked up at Herr Kantor. Herr Kantor shook his head and said: 'Hopeless.'

Herr Ehrlich, domiciled in Vienna but born on the territory of Czechoslovakia, joined them. 'A three-year wait', was Herr Kantor's verdict, but Herr Ehrlich had something new to bring up today.

'What do you think about Brazil?', he asked. 'I shall probably get a recommendation to the ambassador.' And he could not repress a smile, since he was already reckoning in advance on Herr Kantor's approval.

Herr Kantor stood still for a moment. 'Brazil?', he asked and stared in front of him. 'Brazil?', he asked once more and finally delivered the reply himself: 'Brazil is first-rate. Go to the ambassador at once, that's the best advice I can give you.'

Let it be laid to Herr Wohl's credit that he gave Herr Ehrlich an unsealed letter for the Brazilian ambassador, that in the letter he spoke of Herr Ehrlich as *seu amigo*, and that in the letter he also mentioned something of the Ehrlichs' place of origin, of Vienna, city of light and graces. The ambassador remembered Herr Wohl, and he invited Herr Ehrlich to take a seat in front of his desk.

He read the letter, and he leafed through Herr Ehrlich's documents. It was quiet in the room. On the mantelpiece stood an antique clock. An ambassador had short office hours, of course, he had free lodging and he had servants. This particular one wore horn-rimmed spectacles and his skin was smooth and yellowish like a Chinaman's skin. He knew nothing about Hitler. After dispatching current business he could withdraw to his private chambers, he would play bridge or he would spend the evenings with his wife. They would probably sit opposite one another then, in two armchairs, and read their newspapers.

The ambassador looked through the documents, and he took in – without being impressed – the communication which Herr Ehrlich made in his own characteristic French to the effect that he could invest some 3,000 dollars in Brazil. In the hotel, Frau Ehrlich was waiting. She was, it must be admitted, a good wife. After thirty-five years of matrimony she knew all her husband's habits and thoughts. In their childless household, she had looked after him in exemplary fashion. Of an evening, when he arrived home, he would always find everything in perfect order. She had a weakness for long telephone conversations and for her ladies' tea parties. When he got back from the office, he would often be able to hear the buzz of ladies' voices even from the hallway. Occasionally he would go in. Then the ladies would claim to be most delightfully surprised, and he would be very honoured. He was a lovable man, he was the head of the house, he was the breadwinner. It was admittedly no longer easy for him to pay court, since the days of such experiences had long gone – *tempi passati*, he was accustomed to say.

Now the couple were to travel to Brazil. In Portugal,

the immigration authorities had grown impatient, there was talk of concentration camps and repatriation. In Brazil, a new life was to begin. This life depended upon the ambassador.

The ambassador read Herr Wohl's letter a second time and then began to speak. He spoke very rapidly, but Herr Ehrlich understood the crucial point. He said that Brazil was a vast country with wonderful, world-renowned harbours, with wealthy cities and fertile soil. He said that nothing on earth could rival life on a Brazilian country estate. But in recent years circumstances had sometimes become tight – and he demonstrated this tightness by bringing the index finger and thumb of his right hand close together. Nevertheless, he continued, Brazil was a liberal country, it knew no prejudice against creeds or races. It was also willing to grant entry to people without capital, provided it was a question of artists or important scholars and such people as could raise the level of cultural life. This too he demonstrated by raising the palm of his hand.

Herr Ehrlich shrugged his shoulders and for his part was able only to half-raise his hand. He was neither an artist nor was he a scholar. He was an exporter of leather goods – of Viennese leather goods, he added. The ambassador hesitated for a moment, then stood up, intimating that the interview was over.

Frau Ehrlich, in the hotel, was sitting in the small lobby. 'Nothing?', she asked as she saw her spouse coming.

'Nothing, I'm afraid', he said and shook his head.

They did not speak much as they sat at dinner. As residents of the hotel they took this in the restaurant on the first floor, where they were treated as distinguished guests. The silverware gleamed on the tables, on the sideboard stood baskets of large, round fruit. It was really hot, two fans were in operation.

Dinner was almost as important as the midday meal. There was a thick soup with asparagus tips, a white fish then followed, with dark pistachios swimming in the hollandaise sauce. The Spanish rice which was served with the roast fillet had been prepared with particular care, it was mixed with tomato sauce, mild onions and green pepper. Spices of an unknown kind had been added. The waiter put on a final spoonful of Parmesan cheese as well and smiled. Herr Ehrlich smiled likewise. Then followed the salad and then the pastries. The fruit which concluded the meal was refreshing, the waiter bowed as Herr and Frau Ehrlich left the dining-room.

II

Life in the hotel was unfortunately expensive. But after Frau Ehrlich had met Frau Gross, and the latter had told her that she lived in a boarding house in a side street, and that Frau Leonhard too, together with a composer of Viennese operettas, had taken up residence in the same boarding house, the couple inspected the living accommodation.

Herr Ehrlich said: 'What's good enough for Frau Leonhard is quite good enough for me', and they saw an elongated room with the beds set end to end, they saw a lounge in which the furniture was upholstered in canvas and in which there stood a large and evidently very old grand piano, and they saw a dark hallway. They could smell a laundry and the air stagnating in the corridors. 'Fine', said Herr Ehrlich and the move was settled.

Since the beds stood against the wall and Frau Leonhard's room was next door, at night Frau Ehrlich could not help ascertaining details from the private life of a composer of operettas. She had always been a bad sleeper, even before. Now, as she lay awake at night in her room in Lisbon, her thoughts would follow new paths.

Sometimes she would wonder whether it was not all a dream, whether she was not about to wake up in her old home, find the house in perfect order and the business intact. She could hear her husband. She could hear him from the foot of the bed, he was breathing regularly and noisily, as always these past years, you could say he snored. He had become an old man. His thoughts were certainly no longer as fast as might be, but the skin on his hands, which had grown leathery, his cheeks, which now drooped rather flabbily, and above all his kindly eyes were dearer to her than ever before.

What was to become of the couple? Frau Wolf had replied. But what good was her moving, nay impassioned reply? What good was her guarantee, the declaration which she had spontaneously given in writing and in which she had pledged not to abandon her friend, in the event of hardship, to government charity? What good was the document that had arrived with the seal of the American notary and its lengthy, pre-printed text, so impressive and mighty that on the day it came Herr Ehrlich would not even finish his breakfast, but hurried off instantly to Herr Kantor? What good was it? America was barred. The document, which as evidence of American greatness bore the name 'Affidavit', lay on the linen press and Herr Ehrlich would occasionally survey the notary's seal.

Frau Ehrlich, awake in her bed, would hear noises from the next room. The composer of operettas would be enjoying himself. Frau Ehrlich would hear all manner of things at this late hour. On the hot night the window would be open, the Avenida was not far away. The music of a cinema would penetrate the narrow street from a courtyard in the open air. Soon the composer and Frau Leonhard would both be asleep. But outside in the corridor there would still be something to hear. It was the chambermaid Esmeralda. She would come to sweep the floor. Frau Ehrlich would be able to see her watch, which glowed in the dark. It would be past midnight. In Portugal maids have a long working day. Frau Ehrlich would lie and ruminate.

The boarding house was filling up. More and more foreigners were now arriving in Lisbon. They had crossed the Pyrenees on foot. '*Carmen*, Act Three', said the composer of operettas. The venture often did not succeed, then they would attempt it a second or third time, or else they would not attempt it any more. Be that as it may, the boarding house was fully occupied and Herr Carvalho, the owner, would walk up and down the corridor between the kitchen and his little study, he would keep his hands clasped behind his back, probably he was making silent calculations, he surveyed the foreigners, he knew that among the multifarious languages German and Polish predominated, that he had hardly thought ever again to open up the top floor, and that the course of world history was astonishing.

The dining-room had never been so full. The foreigners became excited if they had to wait for the meal. But Herr Carvalho would shrug his shoulders. Things had always gone all right with two waiters, why shouldn't they continue to go all right with two waiters? Nor did it ever cross Herr Carvalho's mind to alter the menu. He himself enjoyed onion sauce and olive oil, the fish and the roast meat too were prepared as his mother in Coimbra and even for that matter his grandmother in Pombal had prepared them, that was how the foreigners would eat, since nobody had asked them to come.

Things were lively in the lounge too, and the circle that used to assemble round the composer of operettas when he played on the old grand piano of an evening grew bigger and bigger. He was called Herr Fuchs, he was not very famous, he was probably only a minor operetta composer, and he spoke with awe of the great operetta composer who had now likewise arrived in Lisbon and had put up in the Avenida Palace Hotel, where great operetta composers naturally stay. Herr Fuchs used to play his own pieces, but he also played familiar melodies: '*Wien, Wien nur Du allein*', he played pieces from the *Waltzertraum* and many by Johann Strauss. Then Herr Ehrlich would smile, he would lean far back in his armchair, he would jiggle the tips of his toes and with his arms suggest the movements of the waltzing dancer.

Then they would talk about their travel prospects. A group of two hundred Poles, it was said, had been allowed into Canada. 'Why shouldn't that happen to us too?', asked Frau Gross.

'Yes', said Herr Dr Winterfeld, a lawyer from Brunn, 'if you want to clear forests in the far North, close to Alaska, then perhaps there's some prospect.'

The composer sprang up and bared his powerful arms. 'Clear forests?', he asked. 'In Alaska? Marvellous.' He laughed, and secretly put his trust in the protective deity of Viennese operetta, who would never permit such a thing.

'Is it true that they'll send us back to Germany?', one of the ladies asked.

'I don't know', said the lawyer.

The others remained silent.

But after a while Herr Fuchs had a sudden inspiration. 'For the time being', he said, 'we're still here in Portugal.'

Then he sat down at the piano again and played.

Herr Dr Winterfeld, the Brunn lawyer, used to go for walks through the various districts of Lisbon. He saw the port, saw the great cranes and the cargoes of cork and bananas. He saw life in the new streets, the mode of greeting of Portuguese men, who would embrace one another, clap one another lengthily on the shoulders and then separate wordlessly. He would take the lift that conveyed him to the upper districts and here walk about everywhere: this was the old town, a muleteer would often come along the lane and the aroma of cheese and olive oil hung in the air.

The lawyer used to think about the world of women. What use could it be expected to make of him – so far from being a charmer, his figure so frail and his short-sightedness so pronounced? Hitherto a devotee of trifling, mercenary enjoyments, in a foreign land he was doubtless even more homeless than the others, he could not but see the future in a yet more uncertain light than those who could at least take with them the objects of a little love. He would sit in the dining-room not far away from Frau Leonhard, he would see her small, curved mouth, he would see, as she ate and breathed, how the lines of her figure could be discerned through her dress, and he would tell himself that such was not destined for him.

He would see her too on the beach at Estoril, when they all bathed together. She would emerge from the water, she would lie down not far away from him and the sea smell of her swimming costume would reach him. He would see the brownish-pink colour of her upper thigh, when she raised herself from the sand and went to the beach cabin where Herr Fuchs and Herr Kantor would be playing cards with one another.

'It's not hard for him, he has means', said Herr Kantor to Herr Fuchs. They were speaking about the lawyer. 'He'll probably succeed in getting to Brazil.'

'Does he have a lot of money?', asked Herr Fuchs.

'I know people who've got more', said Herr Kantor, 'but for Brazil it's more than enough.'

Herr Kantor used to carry about with him in his head a fixed scale, this showed the financial state of everyone and was at the same time a barometer of their travel prospects. Frau Gross, Herr Müller, the Ehrlichs, Frau Wiesenthal and all the others had their place on this sliding scale.

It must be said that Herr and Frau Ehrlich, alas, could

lay claim here only to a very lowly rank, and after Frau Ehrlich had in addition drawn attention to her husband's state of health – and had considered unacceptable in view of the altitude a visa to Ecuador, the possibility of which Herr Kantor was raising – the latter did not know what more to suggest and the couple's prospects were dark.

Nonetheless the circle which now assembled every evening in the lounge of the boarding house treated the couple with kindliness and respect. They were the elders of the company. Frau Ehrlich would often go to her room and fetch sweets which she had prepared herself from sugar and orange peel, she used to ask with great interest about the others' prospects and was delighted if now and again the clouds parted and some new and not unattainable homeland appeared – even if this were only a prairie land – since they were all obviously in agreement that the most important commandment in life was to keep on living.

But if the couple were asked about their own prospects, then Herr Ehrlich would throw his hands apart, smile and say: 'Wait and see, drink some tea.' He obviously relished the old expression, and had no thought that people used really to see him of an afternoon sitting in front of a glass filled with iced tea, under the trees on the Avenida, while he surveyed what passed before him, the natives and the foreigners, the famous and the not so famous, and everyone who met in those weeks in Lisbon, that animated assembly point for fugitives and secret agents.

III

After Herr Fuchs had decided to move to Estoril – where the evenings in the bar, and the afternoons on the terrace with dance music and a view over the blue sea, furnished him with significant stimuli, and where in the excellent

hotel he shared at least his table with a wealthy Parisian
lady – Frau Ehrlich could not fail to detect that the nights
in the next-door room had grown silent.

Frau Leonhard sat alone at one of the café tables on the
Avenida, and when Herr Dr Winterfeld saw her, he
weighed up the possibility of sitting down beside her. She
nodded, and he came over. He would have liked to say
something amiable, but since nothing of the kind came to
mind at that moment, they took up the universal theme,
they spoke of the Western Hemisphere. It appeared that a
Brazilian visa for the lawyer was already virtually assured.
Frau Leonhard looked at him, his forehead culminated in
a bald pate that took up almost half his head, but what
was to be expected of him when, after all, he had
unquestionably passed forty? Frau Leonhard – after the
disappointments of a dramatic divorce; her twelve-year-
old boy in the custody of a father earning his laurels as a
party member – reflected upon a life in Brazil, in a nice
villa with a small, well-tended garden, and she told herself
that one should ask only for what was attainable.

They agreed upon a visit to the exhibition. It was a
jubilee year and the state was organizing a pageant of
Portuguese glory, which had once extended across the
known world. They viewed pictures, they viewed exotic
villages and statistical charts, the exhibition attracted
many visitors. They also boarded the ship in which the
great seafarer had set out upon the ocean. The ship had
been reconstructed, a restaurant on the upper deck and a
bar in the interior were doing lively business. A small
stairway led aloft, the captain's cabin seemed untouched.
They saw the dark wooden panelling, a bed, a chair and
an old pair of compasses. On a table under the port-hole
lay a battered bible, the little window afforded a view of
the sea. 'How beautiful', said Frau Leonhard and the
lawyer would have liked to seize her hand.

Later he hired a car and they drove along the coast to

Cascais. They ate in a restaurant and heard the sea, now choppy, dashing against the rocks. She looked into his eyes and what was impending began to dawn upon him. But since he had already abandoned his pipe dream, he doubted for a little longer.

They arrived back at the boarding house at a late hour, the other guests formed their conjectures and the case was commented upon particularly by the members of the circle which still used to meet in the lounge, even after the composer's departure.

The summer dragged on. People began to understand the newspapers, they listened to a speech by Hitler, his name came as a thunderbolt when he met the Spanish General not far from Portugal, the battle in the skies continued and, while a handful of young sportsmen were defending the countries of the known world and deciding the fate of coming generations, deliverance suddenly came to Lisbon. The American consulate was accepting applications for entry permits.

Herr Kantor was able to explain the miracle. 'Departure from the countries under German domination is virtually impossible', he said, 'the quotas have become almost totally free.' They thought about the victims, to whom they were indebted for their good fortune, and they hurried to the consulate as fast as they could.

Could they have expected that the gates to the land of milk and honey would all at once open theatrically, to allow in the hard-pressed and the frightened in a single long line? The American consulate was an office. In the antechamber an elderly man sat at a desk, not by a long chalk the consul, he wore rimless glasses and his white hair was smoothly brushed. He handed out a form. He wrote the names in a book and shrugged his shoulders if anyone asked him for a definite date.

He sat there without it ever crossing his mind that his

desk stood on the threshold of the promised land. It did not cross his mind of a morning when he took the tram, travelled to the office and began his working day. He would have made the same journey every other day, even in the event of a catastrophe – and who could vouch for it that such a catastrophe was not already in store for the morrow? That, say, Spain would enter the war and Portugal would be occupied – or decide even independently of any external event to expel all foreigners? Even on such a day the clerk of the American consulate would come, he would arrange his papers, fresh faces would doubtless appear before his desk in place of the old ones, but otherwise all would remain as before; and he would officiate, he would think as always about his family in the United States, and the spirit of his mighty country, so tranquil and undisturbed, would as ever be visible on the broad, smooth-shaven surface between his nose and his cheekbones.

Herr Kantor said one should not appear shy. He said one should inquire, go up, hurry the business along. Herr Kantor had flexible tactics and switched as the occasion demanded between offensive and restraint. He knew his craft. As he fetched his form, Herr Ehrlich saw Herr Kantor joking with the secretary. She was a plump girl with a faint moustache on her upper lip, but she was an American. She laughed, Herr Ehrlich observed Herr Kantor and told himself talent was a gift that Nature now and then dispensed.

But the day came for the Ehrlichs too. They waited in the antechamber. They were properly turned out for the interview with the consul. Herr Ehrlich's shoes gleamed, the tie was carefully knotted in his white collar, Frau Ehrlich was wearing a dark printed dress, the impression had to be favourable. The white-haired gentleman at his desk nodded, the couple stood up and went in.

The consul was one of several, but he sat alone in his room and had to decide. He was very young, his hair was blonde, he had grey-blue eyes.

Two armchairs stood beside the desk and the visitors were invited to sit down. Although the chairs were very comfortable chairs, the consul made sure that the gentleman and the lady were really sitting at their ease and displayed the same interest in their momentary convenience that he could be expected to show in dealing with the kindly couple's visa problems, life, happiness and freedom. It may even be that the interview started off with a small misunderstanding. For when the consul looked at Herr Ehrlich and invited him to make himself comfortable, the latter replied: 'It doesn't matter', an utterance that the consul could interpret as meaning that Herr Ehrlich did not hold it against the American consulate that his chair was in fact uncomfortable, whereas in reality Herr Ehrlich was only trying to say that he found the seating accommodation comfortable and that he would gladly have accepted any seating accommodation, indeed any physical discomfort, in order to secure for himself and his wife a little patch of firm ground, a place of refuge.

The consul conducted the interview in the German language. He spoke fluently, although his thoughts were evidently tracing an unknown path and his thin lips gave the vowels their own particular intonation. The tones that came from the young man's mouth were American tones, the tones of a great and faraway continent.

The consul wrote, though, more than he spoke. He looked through the papers, the bank statement, Frau Wolf's guarantee declaration. He asked Herr Ehrlich about his former occupation, he asked whether the couple had ever possessed American citizenship. With his grey-blue eyes he often stared into empty space, Frau Ehrlich smiled at him. Then he stood up and said: 'That's fine.' He smiled too, and Frau Ehrlich told herself he was a good boy.

But the next interview with the consul brought a

surprise. Herr Kantor had been so optimistic, he deemed Frau Wolf's affidavit, indeed the entire state of affairs, so favourable that at his wife's side Herr Ehrlich entered the consul's room, which he already knew, with a light step. He even said: 'How do you do, Mr Davis', since in the meantime he had memorized the name and anticipated that the conversation would pass off cordially as a pure formality and doubtless conclude in the granting of a visa, as had already for instance been faithfully promised to Frau Wiesenthal. But the consul knitted his narrow brow and, from the depths of a field of experience which despite his youth was already his own, equipped with knowledge of the secret workings of state conduct, he let fall his verdict: 'The Affidavit of Support is not adequate', he said. 'It would be sufficient, if Mrs Wolf were a relative of yours, but Mrs Wolf is not a relative of yours.'

Herr Ehrlich's eyes opened wide. 'How's that?', he asked, 'how do you mean?' And as the consul remained silent, Frau Ehrlich had a sudden inspiration. 'Frau Wolf', she said, 'is a cousin of ours, she's a cousin.'

The inspiration had come spontaneously, but it was possibly fateful. The consul in any case paid no attention to this newly disclosed bond of kinship, but somewhat impatiently – yet all the same, so far as one could tell, still ready to help – delivered the following explanation: 'Mrs Wolf must show that she has personal assets larger than can be determined from this bank statement, and she must also lodge a sum specifically under your names.'

That was the end of the conversation, and the couple found themselves back in the antechamber. The white-haired gentleman, who now already knew them, gave them a friendly nod and the secretary too smiled.

This second interview with the consul caused a sensation in the circle of their acquaintances. 'Extraordinary', said Frau Stark, and Herr Kantor could barely compose himself. He made Herr Ehrlich repeat the conversation to him in detail several times, and each time he said: 'I cannot understand it, I'd predicted just the opposite.' That was hardly an encouraging sign for Herr Ehrlich, for when one of the mighty, an authority, has miscalculated and even admits the error, then the ground shakes beneath our feet.

But Frau Ehrlich demonstrated her level-headedness and, although it was no small thing to call once more upon Frau Wolf's readiness to help, although it even seemed conceivable to go too far, she made up her mind to write the necessary letter. She wrote in highly emotive terms, she depicted the couple's grim, even desperate situation and the unforeseen behaviour of a young consul, she promised by all that she held sacred never to touch a cent of the sum provided, then she wrote about their daily bread and of how there was no work from which they would shrink, she wrote of her skills as a seamstress, reminded Frau Wolf of her expertise in all aspects of cookery and especially in the preparation of Viennese pastries, she was also able to place her husband's accounting talents in the right light and she closed the letter with the assurance that a benign God would at the appropriate moment reward magnanimity and human kindness.

Herr Ehrlich took the missive to the post office once more and told himself they must just hope and be patient.

IV

Soon the press at the consulate became so great that it became necessary to queue in the antechamber. Numbers were handed out and one eventually had to make an appointment just to speak with the white-haired gentleman, who in the end was just making appointments himself. The consul general turned to the bureau in

Washington, and the latter had to dispatch new assistants and even new consuls.

The young gentlemen arrived, graduates from the elite universities of Princeton or Yale, and one or other of them must surely have wondered whatever he was supposed to do with the mass of humanity through which he had to thread his way each morning. What was this new deluge of Israel's children supposed to do on the shores of America? Didn't his country have its own, American way of life? What were they supposed to do, all those artists and newspapermen, all those peculiar, strangely dressed people? What were all those tradesmen and lawyers supposed to do? They were all so excited and constantly worried about their lives. And finally, why then had they been turned out of their own countries? The question was certainly legitimate, but what was an individual consul supposed to do, so long as a doctrinaire dreamer sat in the White House. He had ruined his own finances, now he was leading the business life of the entire country to ruin. What else would happen? Would he hurl America into the most costly of all wars? Would he be left at the helm for a third term? The elections were imminent, and in the meantime a consul could only get on with his job.

A few things could already be said about the consuls. It was known that Consul MacFarland lived in a villa at Cascais with his wife and children, it was known that Consul Townsend came to the bar of the Avenida Palace with a beautiful English woman, and it was known lastly that Consul Davis could be seen every evening in the casino at Estoril. He played high and at the same time surveyed the women. He hardly restrained himself, he relied upon his boyish face, his well-built shoulders and perhaps also his position. He looked long and searchingly at Frau Leonhard, and when her companion Dr Winterfeld glanced aside he gave her unequivocal signals. She did not encourage him, but as he played he would repeat this game too, whenever the couple came to the casino of an evening.

They did not come often, only occasionally would Frau Leonhard induce the lawyer to escape from the assemblage in the lounge, from the discussion of visa affairs. They themselves were now provided for, since a Brazilian visa was assured for the couple, whose marriage as everyone now knew was imminent. It was now just a question of formalities, of providing the necessary papers. The granting of the visa had admittedly been delayed by the new situation, but did the lawyer not find himself recompensed for the postponement? He might well marvel at the whims of a destiny which precisely now, when he was homeless and already virtually on the threshold of old age, suddenly no longer withheld from him the joy that it did not begrudge to others. And he experienced that joy manifestly when, say on the Avenida or in the dining-room, Frau Leonhard, slender and in bright colours, came up to him and he knew then that she was his. When they spent the long days of their idleness with one another, there would sometimes be nothing to say, but he would think to himself that doubtless some small imperfection was called for, he would look at her and say to himself then that life was like that.

The wedding itself was a very lively affair. Herr Kantor and Herr Ehrlich were the witnesses, there was a small lunch at the Hotel Bellevue. Frau Gross was present too. Herr and Frau Ehrlich arrived in an elated mood. Frau Wolf had not merely agreed, she had even done so by telegraphic means. She was sending evidence of a previously unmentioned bank balance, her fortune was far greater than had been supposed, a Lisbon establishment had furthermore been instructed to hold a specific sum ready for the couple. Frau Ehrlich spoke with tears in her eyes about her friend across the ocean. But Herr Kantor had some particularly favourable news of his own. He now had not merely his visa, but thanks to special preference even his boat ticket already, he was travelling in two days' time. Herr Kantor could not refrain from praising himself, to have procured the boat ticket so rapidly was an achievement, the visa had been child's play. 'Consul Townsend', he said, 'was wonderful to me.'

So they talked, they ate, and after the second roast Herr Ehrlich tapped his knife against a wine glass. The others fell silent. Herr Ehrlich made a speech. He spoke first of a certain gentleman, whose noisy goings-on they could thank for the fact that they had been driven from their homes. He smiled when he spoke of this gentleman and the others understood the allusion. However, Herr Ehrlich continued, every cloud has a silver lining. He spoke then of the bonds of friendship which had been knotted on alien shores, and he spoke of the bonds of love. It was a lengthy speech, and Frau Ehrlich, who had already wept at every mention of her friend, wept again as her husband concluded his speech. She saw that he was content, they all stood up, they clinked their glasses together, then they sat down again.

After the meal they went back to the boarding house together with the newly-weds. No honeymoon had been planned, understandably, a sufficiently long journey was impending in any case. The boarding house was so overcrowded that Herr Carvalho, strive as he might, was not in any position to make a double room available, so the lawyer and Frau Edith Leonhard, now Frau Edith Winterfeld, remained in their former accommodation.

Two days after, they went to the harbour to bid Herr Kantor farewell. It was a fine afternoon, no longer hot, the small ship of the American export line lay in bright sunlight, its paintwork was white, its metal parts glittered, the water had a fresh smell and a light breeze was blowing. They were allowed to go aboard the ship. 'Say hello to the Statue of Liberty for me', said Herr Ehrlich to

Herr Kantor. Herr Kantor was wearing a peaked cap and shook Herr Ehrlich's hands vigorously.

But then Herr Ehrlich decided upon a tour of the ship. 'I'm carrying out an inspection', he said, and he looked at everything, from the topmost deck to the kitchen, and then a lot more things aloft. Frau Ehrlich did not approve of the many stairways, but her husband would not be restrained. He saw the clean cabins, each with its armchair and bunk beds, he saw the lifeboats, the dining-room and the saloon, in which there was even a baby grand. He returned home in a state of high excitement and looked forward confidently to the next interview at the consulate.

But what use was his confidence, what use was Frau Wolf's awe-inspiring wealth, whose statistics were shown to the consul with a certain pride when Herr Ehrlich, with pressed trousers and glossy boots, and Frau Ehrlich in her beautiful print dress appeared once more before him? The young man now had other ideas.

'Well that's all fine, then', he said, 'but now you must demonstrate necessity.'

Herr Ehrlich could not have been more astounded. 'How's that, necessity?', he asked, while his wife interrupted him: 'Of course, it's a necessity for us to get across, indeed it's a vital necessity.'

That was a very good answer, however the consul cleared up the misunderstanding. 'I understand', he said, 'but the question is not whether it is a necessity for you, the question is whether it is a necessity for the United States that you should come. You must show that you are necessary in the United States', he added. 'We must know whether you are needed.'

Now nobody could say anything. The consul remained silent. He stared in front of him with his blue eyes, and soon his glances began to roam around the room, for he was perhaps already thinking about his evening's entertainment in Estoril, about the journey he would take along the coast in his sedan, about the highway upon which in this autumnal season the streetlamps would already be shining through the twilight of the early evening hour, and he was perhaps also thinking about some girl. But Frau Ehrlich knew that the minutes of this silence, however meaningless they might be in the life of the young man, nevertheless contained all conceivable decisions concerning the life of the elderly couple. Her heart was beating very hard, and since it was high time to say something, she asked a question: 'Have all the others had to bring evidence of that kind too, then?', she asked.

How was she to know the proper way to deal with an official of the American foreign ministry? Her kind parents had certainly not made her attend the consular academy, they had sent her to a girls' high school, provided her with literature courses and music and all that seemed needful as a preparation for life. How could anyone have foreseen today's situation? But the consul smiled. He said: 'You must just see what you can do', and his thoughts had already moved away once and for all from those two people there.

In their misfortune, it was certainly a further misfortune of a particular kind that Herr Kantor had gone away and could no longer give advice. Now the lawyer had to express an opinion, as best he could. He said he had already heard of similar cases, and advised Herr Ehrlich to write to New York. This was done, Frau Ehrlich wrote once more to Frau Wolf, she described the situation, she pleaded for help, she pleaded with Frau Wolf to pull strings, to entreat her acquaintances and, as she wrote, she could not help wondering whether their friendship was really great enough to withstand a fresh and so insistent plea. Had there not just in the last years been a slight cooling? Must one not remind oneself that the case of a cook who came from Frau Wolf's household had not been clarified entirely? And one felt quite considerable alarm when one saw old sins from bygone years appearing suddenly on the scene again and turning against one.

In the meantime one could only wait again, and while further friends left, the boarding house filled up with Poles and Frenchmen, and of the old circle only the lawyer and Frau Edith were left. They were getting into the winter months now, a steady rainfall inundated the streets, the rain often beat against the window-panes and the palm trees on the Avenida bent in the wind. The chambermaid Esmeralda sometimes placed a metal bucket full of glowing coals in the middle of the room, it was not much help and the nights in particular were bitterly cold. Esmeralda was a friendly girl and in the morning would always have a chat with Herr Ehrlich. He did not speak Portuguese, to be sure, but they still carried on the conversation in Esmeralda's language. Her skin was ash-grey, but her eyes were young. When the sun occasionally did shine, they would talk about the fine weather; if it was wet outside, they would talk about the rain.

Esmeralda helped in the laundry, which exhaled the smell of drying materials into the corridor; she tidied up the rooms on two floors; she helped in the kitchen; and until late at night she scrubbed the floors. She worked like the Portuguese girls working in the fields and in factories; like the girls who carry fish through the streets in baskets on their heads; she worked like all those who were born so poor beneath that kindly southern sun, only to grow old and die in the same poverty.

Esmeralda sometimes endeavoured to fan the glowing coals into a blaze. Herr Ehrlich would look at her, he would see how the feeble glow faded after her departure and would abandon himself to his own thoughts.

But though he was now beginning to have grave doubts about the future and even already about Frau Wolf's readiness to help, Frau Wolf in fact did what had been asked of her. A letter arrived from a firm calling itself the Standard Industrial Corporation, and in the letter Herr Ehrlich was highly lauded as an expert on the Viennese leather business and especially on ladies' handbag accessories. The letter was taken to the consulate, it was given to the white-haired gentleman, and at the next interview with the consul it lay uppermost in the file.

Whatever might now be threatening, Frau Ehrlich smiled at the consul. He shook his head and said that the evidence was insufficient. Frau Ehrlich was already prepared for this, and she began to spin a yarn: 'Frau Wolf', she said, 'is a major shareholder in the Standard Industrial Corporation. She will, of course, employ my husband, as soon as we are in America. We are as close to one another as two sisters, and she knows what to think of my husband.' And since everything was now at stake, she added: 'If you want, Mr Consul, we can bring you evidence of this future employment too.'

But now the consul looked up. 'If you bring me that', he said, 'then I can't give you a visa. It is forbidden to give a visa to anyone who has a work contract in America.'

Frau Ehrlich had not been prepared for anything like this. Her head bowed and she began to sob. She sobbed so much that her shoulders heaved. The consul stood and looked at her. At the university in Princeton, he had not learnt what he should do when an elderly woman sits in front of his desk and sobs so bitterly.

She sobbed that evening too, when she sat on her bed in her room at the boarding house. Frau Edith sat beside her. The gentlemen had gone to the dining-room, where the lawyer ordered a coffee. Since all hopes for North America must now obviously be abandoned forthwith, the lawyer spoke to Herr Ehrlich about a visa for Brazil. However nebulous that might seem, however hazardous the financial situation of the elderly couple also made the undertaking, he nevertheless promised to put everything he possibly could in train as soon as he arrived.

But Frau Edith, sitting on Frau Ehrlich's bed, was striving to comfort her. And suddenly an idea came to her. The gentlemen came back from the dining-room, she said she had a strong migraine after the exciting day, she asked her husband to allow her to go to sleep, and she also advised the Ehrlichs to go up soon for a good long rest.

She went to her room, she changed her clothes, she waited until all was quiet, then she slipped out of the house in her long dress and evening coat. She hailed a taxi-cab, the driver saw that the lady was in a hurry, her destination was the casino at Estoril.

Frau Ehrlich lay awake in her bed. She heard the other guests returning home, she heard French and Polish conversations and occasional laughter. The music from the open-air theatre no longer made itself heard at this time of year, later on Esmeralda came and scrubbed the floor. Then she too left and the night was still.

In his bed, Herr Ehrlich turned onto his side. He changed his position a second and a third time, she asked softly whether he was awake. He said he had a headache, and also said that he could not raise his right hand. All was clear to her now, she jumped up, she laid her hand on his forehead, he could no longer speak clearly. She knew that she needed help. She knocked on the door of the next room. Frau Edith gave no answer. She opened the door, she found the room empty, Frau Edith must be in the other room. She ran across, she knocked, and the lawyer came out, he came in his nightwear and without glasses. He too realized what had happened, he saw too the open door of the adjoining room and his wife's empty bedchamber.

But he went to the telephone to call a doctor for Herr Ehrlich. He closed the door, which was standing open, then waited for the doctor. Herr Ehrlich was now evidently unconscious, the lawyer waited in the corridor. A Frenchman opened the door of his room, looked out then closed it again. Roughly half an hour went by. Then the doctor came and confirmed that death had already occurred.

Two days later they buried Herr Ehrlich. The Winterfelds attended the funeral, and so did the chambermaid Esmeralda. At the last moment Herr Carvalho came along. During the simple ceremony he stood, solemn and massive in his dark suit and with his uptwirled moustache. After it was all over, he made a speech to Frau Ehrlich in Portuguese.

When they returned to the boarding house, they found a letter from the American consulate. The letter was addressed to Herr and Frau Ehrlich. They were invited to submit to a medical examination, since the appropriate numbers for the granting of an immigration visa were now at the consulate's disposal.

Without the efforts of Frau Edith, who was now looking after her from morning to night, who sat beside her, kept her company and even helped her to dress and undress – without the encouragement of her capable younger friend, the elderly lady would never have decided to go for the medical examination, to fetch her visa or even to board a steamer. Frau Edith did more than Frau Ehrlich was allowed to know, managing to arrange things so that she would not be left behind on her own in Lisbon. She took care of the boat ticket and, in order to ensure her timely departure, paid the necessary bribe from the remainder of her own money. Frau Edith and the lawyer finally took Frau Ehrlich to the ship, and they also had a few words with the captain.

The ship, a Portuguese steamer, was actually designed for trade with the African colonies. But it was seaworthy, it had pleasant saloons and the captain, who treated his human freight with courtesy, opened all the first-class saloons to second- and third-class passengers too. Not many people ventured to speak to the lady dressed all in black, whose veils blew in the wind and often became entangled, so that she soon found herself obliged to take them off. She sometimes lay in a deckchair or she would sit inside, she would leaf through a magazine, but mostly she sat doing nothing at all.

The great composer of operettas, who had for some reason or other also obtained his visa very late and had hence been detained for so long in the Avenida Palace Hotel, was likewise making the crossing on this ship. He complained to the captain because the latter had proletarianized the first class, and could be seen pacing slowly and bad-temperedly up and down the upper deck. Often he would stand still, stand at the rail, his tall form and aquiline nose in massive and famous relief against the cloudy sky over the Atlantic.

The Private Ball (fragment)

Certain details concerning the Theresienstadt camp had become known to me through my correspondence with the O.s, two old friends who in May 1945, to the relief of us all – we had almost given up hope for them – had been discovered after three years of confinement in the camp. Of course, even with these letters to go by my impressions could be only vague and, whatever else may have been told us in the meantime by eyewitnesses, I am well aware that we cannot get any real idea of those living conditions: the dirt, the privations, the lack of dignity of that existence, the sickness and the hunger. But the worst thing seems to have been the fact that, dreadful as everything was, the inmates were always afraid of something still more dreadful; the fact that no one knew when this might befall them; the fact that the fearful word *Osttransport* was always on their lips in the final years. We know today what that word meant, and many of the camp inmates suspected it even at the time. I asked the O.s about the fate of many of my friends, and Frau O. gave me a detailed report. She wrote to say that almost every one of those about whom I had asked had been transported to the East, where in most cases all trace of them had been lost.

Well, in the past few days I had an encounter in New

York which brought rather vividly to mind a particular passage from one of Frau O.'s letters, by now two years old – a passage no more noteworthy in itself than all her other information. The passage to which I am referring concerned a schoolmate of my sister's, a middle-aged spinster named Margit Stark, daughter of the former Professor of Criminal Law at our German university. Margit Stark too had not escaped being transported to the East; about her too nothing more had been heard. The hope that one of her late father's colleagues – many of whom, with secret and public advocacy to the student body, had rendered outstanding service to the German cause long before the occupation of our country, indeed it was said of many a one that his passport, the document of a then still-sovereign state, was inscribed with the symbols *i.d.D.* ('in German service') – the hope that one of those gentlemen might prevent Margit's internment proved illusory, nor could there even be any question of averting the final tragedy. Today those academic gentlemen probably say that they could do nothing. But however that may be, Frau O. wrote to me that Margit, before her transportation to Poland, had performed extraordinary feats for the old and sick of Theresienstadt. Indeed she portrayed her as a kind of heroine, and this description caused me a certain astonishment. For I knew my sister's schoolmate, recalled her over-agitated way of speaking, knew that she suffered from migraine and every conceivable complaint of a nervous order (had she belonged to the previous century, she would have been the lady with the smelling salts and the sudden fainting fits), she was often to be seen in doctors' waiting rooms and ever more often as the years went by. I must, alas, also say that she did not belong to the type in whom some form of spiritual alertness, wit or creativity affords a congenial reverse side to this kind of frailty and to the trouble it causes both to itself and to its environment. As the years went by, she was merely found somewhat eccentric, occasionally even called egotistical, a development which, if one considers the whole person and her life's course, is not entirely surprising, but which contrasts strangely with Frau O.'s words. Since Frau O. obviously could not praise her too highly, she wrote one further detail, wrote that Margit had been particularly devoted in her care of old Frau von Lauffer, that she had sat beside her for hours on end, far beyond the call of duty, and had done everything imaginable to alleviate the death of the old lady, who incidentally, according to Frau O.'s report, accepted her situation with a certain dignity.

This passage from the letter came to my mind again recently, when here in New York I met Frau von Lauffer's daughter, who spoke to me about her mother's death and said that nothing could persuade the old woman to leave her house or – when she had to dispose of the latter – our city, until eventually it had been too late to emigrate. Frau von Lauffer's daughter Eugenie – herself, by the way, already the mother of a son who had spent a year in the American navy during the Second World War – Eugenie told me that the last sign of life from her mother had been a postcard that had arrived via Sweden and, as it later turned out, reached its destination several months after its sender's death. In this card, one of the very few items of mail from the camp to have found its way to the outside world, Frau von Lauffer had written that there was no need to worry. Thanks to the care and the kindly exertions of Margit Stark, she was quite all right.

However vague my impressions may be of the prisoners' existence, I could not help picturing the scene. I saw Frau von Lauffer in the room with many other women; saw Margit at her bedside or, since the shortage of space probably did not allow that, sitting on her cot; and I wondered what it really was that had brought the two women together there. What was it that occupied Frau von Lauffer's mind, since the realm of thought which we all knew to be hers had definitively perished and her concerns – concerns about the smooth functioning of her household, the disposition of her domestic staff, the seating arrangements at a dinner party, the problem of which ambassador should as senior in rank be allocated the place on her right hand, the problem of whether a room should be reserved at the Carlton or the Palace in St Moritz, at Claridge's or the Berkeley in London, concerns finally about a decent marriage for her two daughters (a problem, as I recall, whose resolution did not please her any too well) – since all such thoughts were now quite out of place here? Had she – who had been known in her circle as a 'wicked tongue', feared as a guest since she could heap such devastating criticism upon the conduct of another house, but who for no obvious reason would also manifest a sudden, intense predilection for this or that person, thus distributing praise and censure in accordance with quite impenetrable principles, yet in her censure always showed a certain humour, a pronounced talent for mimicry and caricature (a celebrated performance was her impersonation of the stout, lisping Countess F. speaking about Tagore) – had she then preserved something of this humour, perhaps as her sole possession? But a sense of humour is precisely something Margit Stark, throughout the time I knew her, never displayed, and the question is whether the place in which she now found herself was the place to generate a previously lacking appreciation of the humorous. So what was it that brought her and Frau von Lauffer together? We knew how Frau von Lauffer would put in an appearance at the opening of an exhibition or in the concert hall, in full and manifest possession of her advantageous looks, satisfied with the results of haute couture; but had she perhaps in her time shown towards her amiable spouse an unsuspected docility, a natural modesty which he, the spouse, could not help but find touching in his beautiful wife? And was it perhaps this same natural modesty which now, among the prisoners in the concentration camp – where, so I am informed, unprecedented instances of human generosity, self-sacrifice and community spirit went together, alas, with many cases of pettiness and insistence upon paltry privileges – was it, then, this same modesty which now manifested itself anew and equally touchingly to Margit Stark? I do not know. Nor do I know what Frau von Lauffer saw in the girl, who even if not young was at least of a younger generation, or what drew her to Margit, immediately after her own arrival in the camp when she was ailing and needed her help. Perhaps it was simply one of her sudden, inexplicable predilections, but perhaps also the fact that among the 30,000 inmates who were living crammed together in that confined space, Margit Stark was the only one of them all to have seen her house and her carpets, the pictures and the tapestries.

Eugenie, Frau von Lauffer's daughter, spoke with emotion of Margit Stark. I saw tears in her eyes, and I thought of the time when Eugenie attended the German high school for girls in our city, together with Margit and my sister, and when Eugenie too was thus a schoolmate of Margit's; I thought, in particular, of the winter following the War's end – which had surprised and so thoroughly shaken the lives of those girls, with its sudden onset of dancing engagements, parties and evening balls.

It was not enough to know Eugenie's mother, one had to know Margit's mother too, the Professor's wife, since she came from a family of repute. Not of such high repute as the Lauffers, the Wesselys or the Gombergs, naturally, but all the same she was born a Kahn, the Kahn and Zifferer distillery was renowned, and even though a person might not have any direct contact with the above-named – had received no invitations and so could return no invitations either – nevertheless the Professor's wife met the ladies on numerous committees and charitable bodies, met Frau Lobau, Frau Körner, Frau von Lauffer, Frau von Greinz, they all knew her, of course, and their behaviour was always friendly, indeed often cordial. The fact that her paid-up share in the distillery was insignificant, and that the greater portion of this in itself trifling portion was invested in Austrian war loans, did not diminish the standing of the Professor's wife. She knew what was due to her upbringing and her position, and the women of her own circle did not regret it when they joined her company for tea. Everything was immaculate, starting with the chambermaid, the celebrated and elegant Anna, who opened the door and who used to wear a white lace cap for her afternoon gatherings.

During the winter I was thinking about, a printed invitation arrived for Margit. The invitation came from Herr and Frau Oskar von Lauffer, and since it read: 'For Tea at 9 p.m.', the Professor's wife knew this meant Margit's first ball. She checked through the document, Margit too read it several times, she saw that her mother was nodding solemnly, and the ball at Eugenie Lauffer's house – at the palazzo with the two heavy gates and the lace curtains at the windows on the first floor – stood before her in unknown splendour. The Professor too was shown the invitation, when he arrived home that evening. He straightened his pince-nez as he read the card and even he, the man of learning, was slightly surprised. Margit noticed when she went to bed that evening how her mother's glance accompanied her lovingly and how the Professor too was nodding. Who knows? They were making their plans. This invitation was perhaps only a beginning. That evening they doubtless saw with joy the sheen on their only child's reddish-blonde hair, studied the lines of her indisputably fine countenance and thought of her sweet nature.

The fact that Margit went to the apartment of Fräulein Pohl, the dancing mistress, for two private lessons – in which Fräulein Pohl took the gentleman's role, to the strains of her gramophone – this was something no one was to know. But in the meantime Fräulein Vosatka, the private dressmaker, was working away at a pink silk dress. When nine o'clock struck on the evening that preceded the ball, Margit told herself there were only twenty-four hours to go; and when her mother urged her to go to sleep now, so as to be fresh and look fresh the next day, there were only twenty-three hours left. She lay down on her bed, she told herself that a fresh appearance and a fresh demeanour were important at a private ball, but on just that evening sleep would not come. She told herself she must sleep, she saw the impending evening ahead of her, and as the hours passed she saw herself tired and ugly at the ball, saw everything ruined, she tossed about in her bed and eventually pummelled the pillow with her fists. She heard the clock on the tower of St Heinrich's strike two, three and four as well.

She sat in school next day with a headache, she saw Eugenie in her usual good spirits and perceived that, to her, this day meant no more than any other. Even when upon her mother's advice she lay down again in the afternoon, she did not sleep, she had never been so tired, and only when evening came and Fräulein Vosatka herself appeared to fit her dress, and also a girl from the hairdressing establishment of Wagner and Vogel – a significant financial outlay – did she feel that her limbs had come to life.

The Professor sent for a carriage, Margit received a kiss from her mother, then she left the house and the one-horse conveyance moved off promptly. She felt a slight nausea in her stomach, the carriage clattered over the cobbled surface of the Old Town, then drove onto one of the bridges. High above the other bank rose the silhouettes of Castle and Cathedral, they drove across, a few lights were visible, it was the hour of the palazzo and the evening's festivity. A porter directed the vehicle through one of the gateways, a footman opened the carriage door, she accompanied him up a flight of stairs, on the landing above another footman showed her the way.

But when she entered the great drawing-room, she found the lights dimmed, a few conversations in hushed progress, and did not know where to turn. Finally she was noticed by Eugenie. Eugenie was friendly – perhaps somewhat less friendly than usual – and led her across to her mother. Frau von Lauffer was standing in a glittering, silvery dress, around her on the little tables and on the mantelpiece a number of glass and silver objects gleamed in the room's dim light, two strings of pearls hung down almost to her knees, she gave Margit her hand and said: 'Delighted to meet you.' She said it even though she was certainly not delighted and probably regarded Margit's dress with disapproval. She was standing in a group with her husband, whose tall stature and carefully groomed moustache Margit noticed, and with two young men, young men of an evidently somewhat older generation, they were laughing with her, they were doubtless frequent and welcome guests there. Then Margit stood alone. She saw that the room was very large, and that the furnishings were covered in dark yellow silk. Everyone was talking and many of the girls were laughing.

But soon folding doors were opened, the adjoining room was white and brightly lit, it was the celebrated ballroom of the house, the dance had begun. It took a while, but then Eugenie came and with her came a young man. Eugenie introduced him, his mouth was wide, he made a bow, he invited Margit to dance. He did not dance well, he remained silent throughout. Margit saw the other couples. The tailcoats and white shirts, the brightly coloured evening dresses, all were moving to the rhythm of the music, Paula Greinz had thrown back her head as she danced, her black tresses falling over her neck, she was laughing in response to her partner, she seemed to press her body against his.

'Do you like dancing?', asked Margit's partner. 'Oh, yes', she replied. Then they danced on. They danced a second dance and then several more. In the intervals, the young man wiped the sweat from his forehead with a silk handkerchief. 'It's hot', he said. They sat down on one of the red-upholstered benches which stood along the bare walls. Five small chandeliers – they held wax candles with yellowish flames – hung from the ceiling of the long room. Later Margit was led back to the drawing-room by her young man, and in a group of others he soon disappeared. Once the room where the buffet stood had been opened up, people moved to and fro between buffet and ballroom.

Eugenie had introduced Margit to another young man. He smiled in a friendly way, he too asked whether she liked dancing, he held her close, then he spoke of other dancing parties, he had many invitations. Margit heard the music, she felt how her own body and the body of her partner were moving in time, she looked at him, soon other young men arrived. From then on she danced a great deal, and one of her partners said she had a charming figure. He himself had steel-blue eyes, the preparation with which his hair was smoothed down had an exceedingly pleasant aroma, he squeezed her hand, as they danced she could feel his white shirt-front, she kept her eyes half-closed, what this moment gave her she would have found it hard to describe – and probably never even attempted to describe such a thing.

The ball continued, her partners came and went, people sat in the drawing-room, in a small room two card games

were in progress, later on portions of ice cream were
served, people went back to the ballroom, the whole night
long an elderly man in evening tails stood there and
watched the young folk, his eyes open wide.

Margit left the ball with others, they went on foot, and
when she arrived home her parents called her into their
bedroom. The Professor lit the lamp on his bedside table,
opened his gold pocket watch, it showed five o'clock in the
morning. A few hours later, in school, Margit was not
tired at all.

Hardly ten days had passed when a second invitation
came through the post. It came from Paula Greinz, once
again it said nine p.m. This time too the Professor sent for
a carriage, in this house too there was a buffet and
dancing, now Margit already knew many of those present.
People greeted one another almost like old friends, they
danced, the music, the young men, the aroma of their hair
preparations, now and again a stronger hand clasp,
towards morning ice cream – it was already familiar to
her. And when a third invitation came that winter – this
time from Marion Rotter – then Fräulein Vosatka hastily
made a new dress, it was a blue one, the procedure was
already so well known now to Margit that it seemed as if
she found a certain enjoyment in violating its laws slightly,
in being ready somewhat later with her dressing, letting
the carriage wait, it seemed she was coolly taking a chance
by appearing somewhat later at the party, so that her
parents were able to believe that she was already so much
a part of this new, festive life that she could afford to treat
it with a certain indifference when she strode unhurriedly
down the stairs on her way to the ball, with her new dress
and her dark coat thrown over it. The Professor's wife
would speak of Margit at her ladies' tea parties, she would
occasionally mention in passing the houses where her
daughter was invited to private dances, she would mention
it and then pause for a moment in her conversation.

Next winter came, Fräulein Vosatka received in good time the instructions to make a new dress, and in the Lauffer house too plans were being made. Three supper parties had been given – parties for the grown-ups – now it was time to think about Eugenie. One evening after dinner they were sitting in the library, Herr von Lauffer was leafing through his stamp collection, Eugenie and her mother had laid out the guest lists in front of them. They saw that these had grown, especially under the heading of girls. The new American ambassador had two daughters, the Hungarian likewise. And since they had just recently come to be on quite intimate terms with Baron Ettweiler, the number of girls was raised by a further three. Frau von Lauffer picked up the list once more and read the names in an undertone. 'Franzi Lobau', she read and nodded. 'Marion Rotter', she read and nodded likewise. 'Margit Stark', she read and looked at her daughter: 'Margit Stark. Do you really have to?'

Eugenie reflected. She knew she must now deliver a verdict and that the verdict was fateful. When we think about later verdicts, of course, and about the lists on which twenty years later Margit's name was included but alongside the name of Frau von Lauffer, then it must indeed seem to us as though Eugenie overrated the importance of her verdict. Neither she nor her mother had any inkling of the victories which the joy of destruction, the joy of refusal where desire is most urgent, that human joy about which we cannot think without turning pale – they had no inkling of what victories that strange joy would one day celebrate. But it cannot unfortunately be denied that it was, indeed, a certain joy which shone in the eyes of the then seventeen-year-old girl, when she mustered her verdict and said: 'Margit Stark, no, I don't really have to.'

Herr von Lauffer behind his stamp collection had not really listened to the conversation. He told himself that the conduct of his household was in good hands. But would he have told himself that – would he not, on this occasion, have made a highly unexpected intervention as head of the family – had he known about the new dress that Fräulein Vosatka had already sewn and about the joy with which the Professor used to think of his daughter, sometimes even in the middle of a lecture? Many used to say of Herr von Lauffer that he was not excessively clever. Others would say that he was merely reserved, that he always knew what he wanted. But all were agreed that he had the most fervent admiration for his wife. He leaned back and looked at her. Considering that she had already long since passed forty, her looks were truly amazing, the lines of her throat, her smooth skin, her beautifully curved nose, Herr von Lauffer could not turn away his gaze.

Eventually he stood up, they went to bed. He entered his room, it overlooked the tranquil courtyard. His family, his house, the business, he could consider everything to be in perfect order. A bright window in the porter's lodge cast a little light upon the courtyard. Even in the layout of the courtyard, the sparse ornamentation of the inner facades and the lines of the roof he saw the virtues of the architecture of the eighteenth century. In bed, he looked through an illustrated paper for a while before extinguishing the light.

'The ball at Eugenie Lauffer's will certainly be only a small affair this year', one of Margit's friends told her, but Margit did not believe it. On the evening – she knew the date – she sat with her parents. She looked at the clock, it was nine now, she could tell what was going on at half past nine and what at ten. But only when the Professor said: 'I know Margit, she doesn't take a thing like that seriously', when she saw him nod at her and try to smile behind his beard, only at that moment did she begin to weep.

'You didn't invite Margit Stark', Paula Greinz said to Eugenie. 'Oh', Eugenie declared, 'one doesn't really have to.' And since Paula Greinz now said the same thing, namely that one did not have to, Marion Rotter too was of the same opinion when she wrote her invitations.

But the following year, so it was reported to Margit, the ball at the Lauffer residence was particularly splendid. The older generation and the young people were invited on the same evening. The Professor's wife heard that Frau von Lauffer had had a chef brought in from the Hotel Bristol in Berlin. Margit knew the date of the event, she knew likewise the evenings when Eugenie's girlfriends gave their private balls, but as the years went by she stopped keeping track of these dates.

Frau von Lauffer used to be seen at all the important concerts. Her dress would be universally admired, her taste, however well known it may have been, was always the object of the keenest interest. She would sit with her head tilted back and, whatever it may have been – Cortot, Huberman's annual concert, a song recital by Lotte Lehmann – would listen with an intent expression. At home she would sing many of the melodies to her chambermaid, who would have waited up for her and be helping her to undress. She would sing them out of tune, at least so Eugenie maintained. Eugenie too had a certain talent for mimicry, admittedly to a lesser degree than her mother, but she could amuse her girlfriends greatly by showing them how Frau von Lauffer would sing to her chambermaid and then let fall disparaging remarks about first one, then another of the concertgoers. But in the concert hall Margit, sitting with her mother, would see Eugenie's mother in the front rows. Depending on the movements of the heads which Margit saw in front of her, Frau von Lauffer's head would vanish and reappear. Her hair became grey, and in the final years it was white, but it would always be arranged very ingeniously yet simply,

the two diamonds in her ear pendants would sparkle in
the light of the hall.

Wedding in Brooklyn

My arrival in New York was favoured by propitious circumstances. I travelled with relatives who are close to me and with good friends, I was awaited by other dear friends. Already during the crossing I was picturing to myself our reunion: from the first evening they would speak of their American experiences, I of my European vicissitudes. The latter then seemed to me adventurous enough, for the date was December 1940 and the terror from which I had escaped was not yet visible in its ultimate consequences, the unimaginable things of which human nature was showing itself capable had not yet been demonstrated to the full, the hitherto unimaginable daring of a solitary flight or the miracle of a solitary escape were not yet known. So my own escape struck me in those days as entirely miraculous, I told myself I would celebrate it with my friends at the moment of our long-awaited and joyful reunion.

And so it indeed turned out. My friends the A.s were admittedly not waiting for me on the quay, but I was handed a letter informing me that they were just returning to New York that very day from a journey, indeed their train was apparently arriving at the very hour that I was leaving the ship. It was afternoon, I was able to communicate with them from my hotel and we fixed an appointment for the evening.

The fact that when changing trains in the subway station I did not board the train I had been told to, but instead embarked on a journey to Harlem and so arrived well and truly late at my friends' apartment, I could look at as a mild tribute to all the threatening contingencies to which the foreigner is exposed on his first day in the unfamiliar metropolis. I also remember especially the astonishment I felt when I entered the building which had been indicated to me as the right address, one of the large apartment buildings on Riverside Drive. I found myself in a luxurious room with marble floor tiles, rugs and gold stucco-work, found myself received by a crowd of liveried footmen and thought I had ended up by mistake in some elegant club or perhaps in some railway magnate's reception room. I had to make sure that the address was the right one, and could not understand how my friend managed to live in such pomp. I soon concluded, however, that the magnificence of this first impression, with its expense shared out among countless tenants, represented nothing but an (incidentally quite harmless) case of those many outward splendours which at every step illuminate the life I was just entering upon – though admittedly without changing it.

My first evening in New York, at any rate, went as expected. What I might do in the foreign country, what the next day might bring – that was certainly quite unclear and I could not predict how it would turn out. But thoughts of such a kind were far from my mind that evening, I found myself at my destination, found myself with my friends, found them warmer than ever, indeed after the months that had just gone by it meant a lot even to find myself in the home that now surrounded me, in that middle-class residence. My friend led me to the window. Far below, along the river, the car lights were moving, a few lights on the opposite shore were, I was told, the lights of New Jersey, from the harbour we could hear a foghorn. New York – from the height of this apartment on Riverside Drive – seemed to me on that evening a mighty and silent city.

How often in the following years have I been obliged to think of that evening! How deeply is every detail, almost every turn of phrase, embedded in my memory! But I have also often wondered how things went for all the others, the hundreds of thousands – and many have no friends and relations, or their relations would have done better not to have invited them over at all – often I have not been able to help wondering how things went for all of them on their first evening in New York. Certainly the Committees have accomplished a great deal. But have we not been taught by the subsequent itinerary of so many that even the best committee can achieve only a very limited amount?

So I have often imagined the following: I have arrived, I have travelled alone, I know of no house where I can go, no friend whom I could notify, what do I do on this first evening? My new life is just beginning, how do I make a start? Do I decide, since it is after all my first evening, to celebrate it and despite my limited means go for once to an expensive restaurant? It would be a melancholy undertaking. I should bring out my best suit; sit down nonchalantly at one of the tables; while ordering, allow the waiter to believe me to be a stockbroker, an industrialist or a successful actor: a New Yorker, for whom his visit to this hostelry is nothing but part of his daily habits. The guests would have the same impression; they arrive, a young man with a pretty wife, perhaps it is her birthday, they have theatre tickets, they have long planned this evening. But however that may be – and whatever likewise may be the meaning of the tête-à-tête between the two elderly gentlemen at the other adjoining table – the guests sit here, they have their lives, they are thinking about yesterday and about tomorrow. No, it would be a mistake to go to such a restaurant, and I think I should emerge from such an adventure truly despondent. Yet even the cheap hostelry that would be far more appropriate to my means would in many respects be no better. Indeed, it would perhaps even be worse, since one would be sitting closer together, the conversations about business and children would buzz around me, and I should even perhaps be obliged to take part in the discussion.

Sometimes – and, as I have said, I have often meditated upon the circumstances of a first evening in America – sometimes I have thought to myself it would be best to jump head over heels into the new life: simply to appear in some closed society, for example at a funeral service, there to sit down on a bench as one of the bereaved, to receive condolences and, since life must now be begun, simply to begin it, be it even by mourning some man I never knew. It would, of course, also have been conceivable to attempt it with a wedding reception; possibly a rewarding experience, two hours after one's arrival, to sit unobtrusively at the table, to watch, to take part in the jokes, and only in certain circumstances, perhaps right at the end, casually to mention: 'Yes, I have just got away from Europe.'

I must confess that the idea of the wedding party, like that of the funeral service, would probably not have occurred to me, had I not been told about the arrival and death of Dr Walter Korn, former music critic on the *Tagesboten*, the widely read paper from my home town. The tragic occurrence, about which even the American papers published detailed accounts together with a photograph and obituary, took place only a few days before my arrival. If now, impelled by the news concerning Dr Korn, I attempt in what follows to describe something of the course of his so brief sojourn – it lasted only two days,

alas – in this great country, people will perhaps expostulate
that it is risky to seek to guess the thoughts of a lonely
man who died a lonely death. The dead, people will say,
should be left in peace. The fact that I knew Dr Korn (at
our concerts, the short, rather plump man wearing black
horn-rimmed glasses and already bald despite his youth
was a familiar sight); the fact that I had many pleasant
conversations with him and that I read his reviews in
which the same, somewhat academic turns of phrase
would often recur, but which in general demonstrated
knowledge and solid worth; the fact that I could even
remember his father and the time when the latter, a textile
wholesaler, changed the 'h' in his name to an 'r' – all that
cannot serve as an excuse. The excuse can only be a
summary one, a summary one for the writer's craft as
such – for the occupation which, to many, seems so
indiscreet and intrusive. But if we cannot seek the assent
of the dead, from whose protests we know we are safe, we
can nevertheless at least turn to the living and feel
ourselves a little encouraged if they tell us they have
experienced this or that in a similar way.

The ship on which Dr Korn reached New York harbour
did not like mine arrive at midday, it arrived in the
morning. The morning, so far as I know, was clear and on
such a morning the passengers stand on the open deck.
Many friendships had been formed but, as at least
Fräulein X. noticed, one could already see people flying
apart – each of them already busy with his own concerns,
the fathers already looking anxious lest their families be
separated – but meanwhile to the left, on her island, one
could actually see the famous Statue of Liberty, only
clumsier and smaller than one had thought, and opposite
stood the buildings of Manhattan, one was travelling
straight towards them and the huge towers grew, black
and white and sharply outlined against the morning sun.

Yes, that is a great moment, but Fräulein X. was nevertheless also looking around her and, so far as Dr Korn was concerned, she saw that instead of his travelling cap he was now already wearing a hat on his head and looked entirely solemn, whereas on the evening before in the bar he had still been quite talkative and had even sat down at the piano to play the American anthem when, late at night, the first light of the new continent became visible, no doubt a lighthouse far out at sea.

Does this great moment constrain travellers to a swift consciousness? Does it constrain them, when on entering New York's harbour they find themselves so unexpectedly confronted by those colossal buildings, to measure themselves against this new world and to encompass hopes, possibilities and projects all in one single, rapid flight of thought? Dr Korn certainly knew what this moment meant, and perhaps he even saw before him the torrent of millions, the torrent of Dutch, Scottish, Irish, German and Eastern Jewish immigrants who stood on the deck of the ship with hopes and projects, with projects for the country whose mute facades now rose so massively in the blue winter air. Certainly without hope, without the idea of a happy tomorrow, there is no life, and the man who often wrote pertinent things in the *Tagesboten* about our theatre and its operatic performances, he too no doubt had his hopes. But perhaps it was the case that preoccupation with such requirements of the moment as his luggage and his umbrella, thoughts concerning his papers and the impending interview with the immigration officials, all this and nothing else was engrossing his mind.

The officers of the immigration department carried out their duties in the second-class restaurant, and Walter Korn – promptly and with the respect which an official evidently expected of him – gave his answers. His fortune totalled 400 dollars, he showed four hundred-dollar bills (smaller bills do not have to be declared), and he

explained that his sponsor, Abraham Schiffman, fur
dealer, of 130 West 28 Street, was the husband of his
cousin Else Schiffman. Şoon afterwards he stepped ashore.

He stepped onto the quay and as he now, after more
than two years – and we knew that thanks to his
membership of the Amicitia freemason's lodge he had not
actually been in a camp, but had all the same been under
arrest for three weeks; we were aware of the hardships of
his flight from the country, the hardships of his sojourn in
France and the hardships of a fresh flight – as he now, I
say, after more than two years breathed the air of freedom,
a young man with a reddish-blonde moustache stepped up
to him and said that Frau Schiffman was sorry not to have
come herself. 'Yes', said Herr Katz, an employee of Herr
Schiffman's, certainly a competent employee since he had
found our Dr Korn with such rapidity and assurance,
'yes', he said, 'great preparations are being made.'

'What for, preparations?', asked Dr Korn, of whom it
certainly was not to be expected that he should know
about everything that was being prepared in the land of
freedom. 'What for, preparations?', he asked and wondered
whether his spoken English was not an over-literal
translation from the German.

'Oh, don't you know then?', said Herr Katz. 'Miss June
Schiffman', he declared, 'is getting married tomorrow. I'm
supposed to give you an invitation to the wedding.'

'Many thanks', said Dr Korn and did not mention that
he had known nothing till this moment of a Fräulein
Schiffman; that even Herr Abraham was a stranger, a
shadow on the furthest horizon of his consciousness
throughout the years; and that only just recently, when
world history had begun to move, had Abraham's shadow
too begun to stir, to take on physical roundness, the
roundness of the American businessman, clean-shaven
and smiling, who had signed his sponsorship affidavit.

'Fräulein Schiffman', said Herr Katz – they were now

sitting in a taxi, had left behind the press and crawling progress of motor-cars and trucks and now found themselves travelling more swiftly on the elevated highway, to the left they saw the river with the harbour installations, the fat-bellied, black and dazzling-white ships, to the right at regular intervals the street openings and Dr Korn observed the flat roofs and in the distance here and there a tower or tall rectangular construction – 'Fräulein Schiffman', said Herr Katz, 'is marrying a law student. They got to know each other at Cornell University. Here young people get to know each other at college and then they often get married.' He smiled and Dr Korn, now on his first journey along the Hudson, noticed a few freckles on Herr Katz's forehead and a gold tooth in the left-hand corner of his mouth.

'Hitler', Herr Katz next declared, 'is a devil.' He made this observation perhaps on the occasion of some mention of Europe, perhaps he would have made it anyway for the foreign visitor's sake. But whether the American people would decide to go to war for that, Herr Katz was not prepared to say. He remained silent. Concerning the nature of the decision – which affected the fate of Europe, the fate of the world and in all likelihood Dr Korn's fate too – nothing could be gleaned from the wrinkles on his forehead or his knitted eyebrows. Meanwhile, the car was driving past a park, high up behind it a row of smooth house-fronts could now be discerned and on the other side of the carriageway – since they had already left the harbour – the broad river, which gleamed whitely and lost itself in the distance like a silent lake.

The car stopped in a quiet street in front of a three-storied house. 'We have taken a room for you here', said Herr Katz. 'This West Side was once the most elegant neighbourhood in New York. The room costs seven dollars a week, I assume that will be all right for you.'

'Oh, excellent, excellent', said Dr Korn and with a faint

bow thanked Herr Katz (I well remember that kind of bow, his gesture of thanks); with his slightly protruding eyeballs he looked at the other almost as if intimidated and, since he was anyway so short in stature, he now looked up at him all the more: he was the very embodiment of friendliness and even Mrs O'Connor, the landlady who conducted him to his first and, alas, only New York room, said that he was an amiable gentleman.

The room was situated on the top floor. Dr Korn saw a rust-brown armchair, a rust-brown cover on the bed and on the wall a small picture. It portrayed two dwarfs, they were toasting one another with beer mugs, and when she originally hung the picture on the wall Mrs O'Connor had certainly had the laudable intention of providing a little cheerfulness, though without thinking in particular of the critic of our morning paper, who after Herr Katz's departure would one day sit alone in this room and perhaps be really glad to see some cheerfulness around him, be it even, as here, only that of two dwarfs.

He stood up and looked out into the corridor. A middle-aged man was emerging from the bathroom in his underclothes, even though the morning was already far advanced. His arms were white and displayed copious tattooings. When Dr Korn had sat down again in his room, he listened. The house was silent. Apart from the unknown man, who probably had a night job, the residents seemed not to be at home.

Is it not our duty, since we have arrived in the new continent, since so much life and industry surrounds us here, to plunge in, grasp our briefcases, hurry from meeting to meeting – ought we not to know that in America hours, even minutes count? Dr Korn too had his portfolio, the contents of which were: a little text on Johann Stamitz, leader of the Mannheim School; then an offprint from the *Zeitschrift für Musikwissenschaft*, dealing with an opera by Franz Schubert; and in addition a selection of his newspaper reviews. Schubert's opera had its charms, and it would indubitably be a service to make the piece known in America. Did he, therefore, perhaps see himself as initiator of a performance, did he see himself in the end surrounded by interviewers, plied with questions, treated with honour, offering enlightenment, eventually even fending off the excess of public interest – since after all he was not the composer, but only the critic, the authority? Or did he not see himself rather with his portfolio under his arm, in the office of one man of power after another, the latter pronouncing a few kind words but nevertheless sitting quite absent-mindedly at his desk while he, Dr Korn, as best he could in the English language, would summon up all his eloquence to make Franz Schubert's work interesting, to argue the case for music?

Music (so much is certain) was his love, and if as a critic he was perhaps sometimes called pedantic – and undoubtedly the artists with whose performances he was obliged to find fault contributed most to the dissemination of such a view – it should not be forgotten that in earlier years, after many concerts, after many opera nights, after listening in a state akin to intoxication to some work then new, he had seen a life and future ahead of him. And so far as later years are concerned, certainly nobody would be there when he – who in conversations would often not do much more than correct some pronouncement concerning the date of a composition or the register of a part – when he sat alone in his room of an evening. Who knows with what curiosity and with what delight he perhaps – and perhaps even till late into the night – perused his scores?

Now, though, he is sitting in the room in New York. And if he is now thinking about music, we for our part cannot resist a strange thought. For is it not a strange idea that the success of Franz Schubert's music is now amalgamated with the physical well-being of Dr Korn, indeed with his physical survival as such, with his capacity to rent a room and to eat in New York? However curious this amalgamation may be, however painful it may appear even to himself, one thing is certain: the man who arrived at the harbour with his knowledge of Schubert and with his findings in regard to Johann Stamitz has to eat; and we shall not be satisfied until we see him sitting in front of a full plate at the cafeteria, his eyes behind his spectacle lenses fixed upon his portion, and his cheeks, somewhat rounder than usual, crammed with food. And the question is whether that will suffice for us. For anyone who has known Dr Korn will confirm that in his life he knew other pleasures too. It is hard to say what place belonged to music among those pleasures, but unquestionably after eating he loved a good cigarette, unquestionably he felt good in cheerful company, laughed often and even made his own contribution to the conversation, recounting Saxon anecdotes with a first-rate command of the dialect. But we are making plans for Dr Korn, considering his future, without giving any thought to what was in store for him in America.

In any case, for the moment eating was not a subject of concern. The critic, after a certain time in his room, felt hungry and went out. The advertising sign on a shop selling pharmaceutical goods and cosmetic products also invited people in for a meal. Dr Korn entered the room, behind the counter a fat man in chef's apparel was preparing two fried eggs. Dr Korn too sat down at the high counter, he likewise asked for two fried eggs and saw about him the bottles of toilet water, the chocolate boxes and the fountain pens. The shop was incidentally none too busy, the fat chef was talking to two other customers about some sporting event. After consuming the fried eggs Dr Korn drank a cup of coffee, and after this too had been accomplished he went back to his room.

He had now perhaps already been ashore long enough to make a start and be up and doing. His former editorial colleague Kettner had been in New York for two years; he also had a recommendation to Professor Schneider who, it was said, had considerable influence even in America, even after his emigration. So he made two telephone calls, and that evening his former colleague came to collect him.

'Well, old buddy!', said Kettner and slapped him on the shoulder. Did Kettner, the news reporter, still think that music was an admittedly necessary, but because of its seriousness somewhat ridiculous section of the paper? Did he still see the critic as the unworldly little man, the pitiful art enthusiast? He, Kettner, was now domiciled in America, already he could almost be called an American, and with the proper nonchalance he conducted his newly arrived colleague along Broadway, through the crush, past the brightly lit shop windows and the illuminated signs over the movie theatres, and conducted him finally to a big cafeteria whose metal fittings glittered like silver and where the foods on display, the pastries and the large fruits, were likewise exposed in a flood of light. He explained to him how one was supposed to serve oneself here, how to use the tray and the paper napkins. 'It's all done in a particular way, you see', Kettner said, then they sat down opposite one another.

Dr Korn noticed that Kettner's reddish hair had grown sparser and his neck somewhat thicker. 'Do you work for a newspaper?', he asked him.

'Heavens, no', said Kettner with a laugh, 'there are no bucks in that.' He was marketing glass buttons and costume jewellery. 'Salesman', he said, 'that's what they call it. I go to firms and I get percentages from my own firm. It's really great.'

He consumed a pea soup, then spoke about America in general. 'The Americans, you see, mean well. You have to take them as they come. After all, everyone can do what he wants here, it's marvellous. You can be a dishwasher tomorrow and operate an elevator the day after, it doesn't matter a bit. Most of my friends do that kind of thing.' He seemed in really good spirits because of the possibilities he was disclosing to his old colleague, while at the same time thinking with great satisfaction about the sale of glass buttons and costume-jewellery items, an opportunity that was naturally offered only to a few.

But life had its dark sides even for Kettner. He now ate a slice of roast beef with potatoes and spinach and spoke about his mother. He had brought his mother with him to America, and now she was ill. 'Cancer', he said, 'everything I make goes on her illness.' He took a large mouthful and added: 'It's absolutely hopeless.'

Dr Korn remained silent, while Kettner emptied his loaded plate. Through the clamour of shouts and conversations in the crowded cafeteria, telephone bells regularly made themselves heard and the clatter of crockery.

But next day Professor Schneider was to assess the situation in America less cheerfully than Kettner. Dr Korn found himself in a spacious room and through the broad window saw the park below, the bare trees and a pond, upon which a thin sheet of ice was just forming. 'Yes, it's difficult', said the man of learning. He sat in his armchair, fingered his rimless spectacles and with a faint sigh said once again: 'It's difficult. What have you published?'

Dr Korn grasped the portfolio which stood beside his chair. Then the Professor leafed through the printed sheets and at length stared wordlessly in front of him. 'Very difficult', he repeated after a brief pause. 'You see, even my pupils have a difficult time.'

Dr Korn could have replied that the difficulties were perhaps not insurmountable, since the Professor had an evidently spacious apartment, in a building with a doorman and a clear view, while he himself, Dr Korn, did not need a doorman, nor did he have to follow from his desk the flight of solitary birds across the wintry park, that indeed he did not want to have anything more than a little room; he could have said that if the well-furnished and large apartment was assuredly an appropriate counterpart to the Professor's achievement, he too had a certain achievement to show and a modest room, measured by his own achievement, did not seem to be too much. But I knew Dr Korn. To say anything like that was not his way.

The Professor incidentally had a suggestion to make. 'You must just let people know that you're there. Show yourself in various places, show yourself in libraries, and in time something may perhaps come your way.'

What answer could Dr Korn give? He undoubtedly expressed his thanks before leaving the Professor's apartment, travelling down in the elevator and finding himself in the street again.

He took a turn in the park. It was a Sunday. He saw families as they walked in the park, the women in their fur coats, several fathers with cameras and the children running ahead as they played with their balls. But there were not many whom the park had enticed and who liked to see the gloomy sky over the city on one of the last Sundays of the year.

The wedding took place in the evening. The hotel in which the ceremony was being held lay in Brooklyn, and Dr Korn made a long subway journey. As the train travelled through the subterranean tunnels he was thinking about the extent of the city, thinking about the families who on a Sunday would be spending the late afternoon in their apartments, their number ran into millions, many would perhaps be sitting together wordlessly, waiting for the day to be over. One went directly from the subway station into the hotel without going out onto the street, and Dr Korn saw everything in one place here: not just the subway station and the hotel, he saw also the entrance to a movie theatre, saw a bookstore, a flower shop and a hat salon – and so far as the wedding was concerned, there were even several weddings. The lift deposited him on the floor containing the premises, several doors stood open, one could see rooms at the end of which a canopy had been erected and one could see other, larger rooms with long, covered tables. Many of the ceremonies were evidently in progress, others were still in preparation, the groups were standing in the lobby, among them a number of brides in bright dresses with big bouquets of flowers.

Dr Korn looked around him and soon recognized his cousin, their greetings were warm. Thanks for the affidavit and congratulations on the family event were expressed all at once, while Else Schiffman had a reunion with a kinsman to add to the emotion of the hour. Dr Korn had recognized her, of course, her figure with its powerful hips now resembled her mother's figure, even the lachrymal sacs beneath her eyes were already almost the same; but Cousin Abraham's massive frame was as expected, except perhaps for the two front teeth which had grown apart and protruded slightly and for the fat white flower in his left buttonhole. Yes, it was an astonishing coincidence, the daughter's wedding and this reunion, and the friends who were already present, Herr and Frau Rosenbaum, Herr and Frau Blum, Frau Cutler and also the bridegroom's parents, Herr and Frau Meier, were all very impressed. But they did not have much time to talk, and however much Herr Blum would have liked to converse with the critic, however much he might stress how he had to know everything about Nazi Germany, Herr Schiffman admonished them, they sat down in the chapel-like room and the ceremony began.

It began with a musical offering. A girl sang, accompanied on the harmonium. She sang a song about love, and she sang it at a pitch somewhat lower than that for which the harmonium had been tuned. The critic noticed that the gentleman who sat in front of him was very corpulent, saw two rolls of fat on his neck beneath the hat which he was wearing in consideration of the religious ceremony. The lady beside him was nodding rhythmically to the melody of the song, a young mother was endeavouring to restrain her child from interrupting.

Then the harmonium played the wedding music from *Lohengrin* and, led by her father, the bride entered the room. All the guests turned their heads to see her, and all appeared very satisfied. Her white dress had a slight shimmer, the veil surrounded a face with well-formed, rosy cheeks. Her eyes were extremely dark and at the same time contained two shining points of light. The bridegroom led in Else Schiffman, he was slender and he too had flushed cheeks. When he stood beneath the canopy and turned his gaze towards her, the onlookers said to themselves that the couple was truly one to gladden the eyes.

The Rabbi followed, in a vestment of dark material and gold. As he paced through the rows he was saying a prayer in the Hebrew language. He prayed beneath the canopy as well, then switched into English. He spoke about love and family, about the future and faith in God. Then he put his questions to the couple, the bride's 'Yes' was a bare whisper, the bridegroom strove to enunciate his more powerfully, finally the Rabbi took the bride's hand and put the wedding ring in place.

Dr Korn, in one of the middle rows, was following the solemn rite. Was he perhaps thinking about the morning? About his conversation with the Professor? Was he calculating that his 400 dollars – he was carrying them with him in his wallet, since the banks had been closed since his arrival – was he calculating that the money would be just enough for four months? Or were such

thoughts not appropriate at a moment as solemn as this?
Could he not help but be ashamed of them, when after all
he could see Else Schiffman weeping; when he saw before
him the newly-wed couple, the charming and charmingly
smiling bride, the bridegroom in whose face one could
read such a quantity of youthful hope and shining life
prospects; and when he saw how they had just formed
their life's bond? Many kisses were exchanged, and then
the well-wishers surrounded the family. Dr Korn – it is he,
after all, whom we have accompanied here – seized the
bride's hand and looked into her eyes.

'Thank you, thank you very much', she said. She held
his hand, what did she know about him? Has her mother
in a surge of family vanity built up the foreign cousin's
reputation far too much? Has she perhaps told her dear
ones of a famous man of learning, a great authority? Does
the young bride, therefore, picture her mother's cousin in
a first-class hotel, economic questions irrelevant, the
American authorities honoured and delighted on the
occasion of his presence? Does she have that picture, and
is she not aware of the room in which an emigrant spends
his afternoon? Is she not aware of the problems and
anxieties that beset him when he sits alone at his meal?
And does she have any idea whatsoever of how his heart
used to pound at the consulate, of the sleepless nights he
spent before his journey to her country was allowed? And
does she, above all, have any idea about the Other Side?
Is she aware of what it means to leave one's country and
become a refugee? Can she imagine how, behind the
French fortifications, behind the lines that had been
considered impregnable, the tidal wave – the nightmare of
concentration camp and prison, death and torture – how it
all burst in anew? Does she have any idea, as she accepts
the congratulations so amiably in her bright, tasteful
dress, does she have any idea what it means when the
name of Hitler appears in gigantic black letters on the

horizon? She probably does not have any idea. But out of all those here, why should we torment just her with our visions? It is her wedding day. She looks rapturously at her young husband, her life, her little apartment, her happiness, it is enough to keep her busy for this evening.

The wedding dinner was served in another room and it was carefully planned. For Dr Korn sat beside Fräulein Wolfner, a lady from Berlin, a relative of Else Schiffman's – only very distantly related to himself, as was established at this first encounter – but on the other side sat Mrs Cutler, and Mrs Cutler displayed a great interest in music. She said that Toscanini was a great conductor and she attended afternoon occasions at which a famous lady educationalist discussed and explained musical works. 'She shows us everything', she said, 'how the themes come and go. She shows the themes with a projector too. It's very interesting.' Mrs Cutler also went to the opera, and her likes and dislikes were very definite. She loved *Don Giovanni* and she said: 'I hate *Figaro*.' She loved *Die Valkyrie*, she hated *Tristan*, and *Fidelio* she simply found bad.

'Do you mean', asked Dr Korn – and he looked up from his plate and interrupted his meal, since the question was so to speak a question of principle – 'do you mean it happens just like that, then, that a master writes a good work today and a bad one tomorrow? Do you mean, if we are not in the mood to find pleasure in a master's work, that we should not first search our hearts and seek to blame ourselves?'

His English was deficient, but Mrs Cutler had understood him. Now she too saw it as a question of principle, and although she had really come to a wedding celebration – and could see quite clearly that Else Schiffman had not over-exerted herself upon the menu – she defended her musical standpoint. 'Look, isn't music written to give us pleasure, to enrich our lives? So don't I have the right to say: "I want this and not that, this pleases me and this doesn't"? People are always talking about the masters. Were they demigods? Weren't they humans? Could they really not produce anything bad, then? Just think of Mozart, how badly he conducted his affairs, how wretched his end was. And Beethoven was no model either, after all.'

Poor Dr Korn! Was Mrs Cutler perhaps an important patroness of music? Did she have influence? Could she be helpful? In seeking to make his own viewpoint clear and convince her, had he been able to catch her out in a patently demonstrable error – explained to her that so far as Beethoven was concerned many false legends were in circulation, that Beethoven had precisely understood very well how to manage his affairs and, for the public opinion of his time, was the greatest composer – then it would perhaps have been possible to get at her in her own ways of thinking and thereby bring her to a revision of her views. But Dr Korn could quite see that this would not have been easy, and he refrained from it. A conversation about Verdi was a failure likewise, and Mrs Cutler soon turned to her other neighbour.

The lady from Berlin, Fräulein Wolfner, to Dr Korn's left, proved to be a lively conversational partner, she spoke of her business experiences, of her pastry shop in the Bronx. It was very hard for her as an immigrant, she said, but in five years she had built up something. And so she spoke about apple pie and lemon meringue, about coffee-ring, marshmallows and cupcakes. The talk of all these pastries came at the proper time, for soon the wedding cake was served – a large, white tower construction – Fräulein Wolfner was able to give expert explanations and the bride, accompanied by applause from the guests, started to cut the cake.

'I don't understand the German people', said Mr Blum – and he had to make an effort to speak to Dr Korn, for he was sitting on the opposite side of the table, not near him at all – 'the fact that nobody has turned up, no hero, no liberator!' 'That wouldn't be so easy', said Dr Korn, and he too had to talk loudly across the table. 'Not so easy', he repeated and considered how he could explain it all. Mr Blum seemed really disappointed.

Soon the seating order was dissolved, though, soon too the bridal pair had disappeared, they were known to be taking a night train to Florida. The guests remained for another two hours. Herr Blum persisted with his question, Frau Rosenbaum agreed with the critic, saying that President Roosevelt would certainly have done whatever there was to be done. Herr Kaplan said that the President was a manifest disaster, the only result would be taxation and war. Frau Rosenbaum replied that Willkie too would have been for a strong policy – and the excitement of this conversation soon abated. They then all talked a great deal longer about the bride, her dress, her charming behaviour and, at half-past eleven, it was time for a general departure. Else Schiffman said she hoped to see her cousin some time soon, and Fräulein Wolfner invited him to visit the pastry shop in the Bronx.

Then the critic took the subway. During the journey it must have happened that someone gave him wrong information. For in Manhattan, when he mounted to the surface at 96th Street, he found himself not as expected on Broadway but on the East Side of the city. The fact that it was not far to his room on the West Side, he certainly knew. But whether he did not know about the bus which crosses the park on 97th Street, or whether he wanted to save the money for his fare; whether the danger in Central Park at night, for it was already past twelve o'clock, whether this risk was unknown to him – all of that is impossible to establish. The police report said only that he was proceeding on foot and that he was evidently held up by a single man approximately halfway across. The police report also concluded that he was carrying on his person the 400 dollars in cash which he had brought over with him; that this was his entire fortune; and that this was why he had resorted to physical means to defend himself and engaged in the struggle in which he was overpowered. So much for the police report. The question could still be posed of whether, in his decision to cross Central Park on foot, there had not been a certain wantonness, a frivolous gambling with the danger of which he was perhaps after all conscious, indeed of which perhaps even some passer-by on the East Side may have warned him. One might even wonder whether it was not precisely also some definite inner state that tempted him to engage in a struggle whose outcome, by all natural reckonings – even without knowing his adversary – could not but appear exceedingly doubtful. But such reflections operate in the domain of speculation; the police report mentioned nothing like that.

Abraham Schiffman did not know that his words were prophetic when – already at home, long after the end of the wedding celebration, already in his sleeping attire – he remarked to his wife: 'This cousin of yours, he may be very nice, perhaps he is a great connoisseur of music, but I don't think he'll get very far in this hemisphere.' 'Don't you think so?', asked Else Schiffman and her thoughts moved into other channels.

   She thought – how could it be otherwise – of her little June. She saw her in the arms of a strange young man, carried off, on the threshold of life, a new being, but nevertheless more loved than ever. And she thought back, twenty-four years it was, to when she had left her own mother, and Abraham, full of life-defying courage, had taken her with him. Yes, that was Abraham, the young man with his laughter and with those unpredictable moods for which he had to be forgiven each time,

Abraham for whom she had to tremble in the night when that war had swept him off to Europe, to France. And now little June! Was the same thing in store for her?

She lies now – at the hour when her foreign cousin lies on the ground in Central Park and has already ceased to breathe – she lies now in the sleeping car, on the train that travels swiftly and almost soundlessly through the night in a southward direction. At this late hour she is already asleep. A strand of her black hair has fallen across her forehead, she seems to be smiling as she dreams. Is she dreaming about her dear boy and the years that lie ahead? To be sure, he too will go off, and this time it will last longer and the news will be so uncertain that June, brave and level-headed though she is, will be obliged occasionally to believe the worst has happened. But we shall not think about this possibility. Probably he will come back, safe and sound and cheerful as ever, a new life will be begun, it is to be hoped his career too will move forward, the beginnings will certainly be modest but later, who knows? perhaps an office in Wall Street, high up in one of the skyscrapers with a view over the harbour, the wide, grey expanse of water and the ocean steamers which appear on the distant horizon. Meanwhile the children will be brought up, with little anxieties and joys, dental fillings, measles, school, summer camp, they will go to junior high school, do sport and music – wait! seeing that this cousin Walter Korn has arrived, can't he teach the children music? – then they will be sent to college, and perhaps one night the girl will travel to Florida on this very train. Who knows?

Professor Schneider – at the hour of which we are speaking – was still sitting at his desk. He often worked late and today particularly late, for he was just on the point of completing a long paper. The calm of the night was conducive to his work, the silence of the building and the park below, one often heard distant shots, gangsters, police, some drama of jealousy, that kind of thing was not uncommon in Central Park, one paid no attention.

The paper that the Professor was just finishing was a contribution on the great theme whose commencement he had reserved for his maturest years. After wide-ranging works on the music of the baroque, on lieder, on the piano, on Mozart's operas, he now felt himself in a position to tackle the theme that would doubtless engage his attention for the remainder of his creative span and represent the crowning of his life's work: the theme of Beethoven. Philosophical experiences, the experiences of a rich life and now in his vintage years the experience of America, this change of scene which had it is true arrived unintentionally, but which had nevertheless considerably extended his horizon, enriching his experiential universe – all this equipped him finally to tackle this intellectually most arduous, humanly most moving realm of musical history. In his style, moreover – he wrote in the German language, but his writings were at once translated into excellent English – in his style, I say, he had now achieved that superior clarity and composure, that detached beauty, which distinguishes the magisterial performance; but simultaneously also achieved a directness and warmth that raised his writings as documents of true humanity high above the level of the general spirit of research. He read through the last sentences of the conclusion, 'Beethoven and the concept of humanity'.

'We thus note', he read, 'how those artistically un-occupied, ruthlessly ascetic, so to speak blank areas in Beethoven's work come to life, see how the light of the great, new, world concept illuminates them: the concept of humanity, of fraternization, of immediate language, the language in which the blessed path from Man to Man opened up. The path from Man to Man! Does that not sound like a promise? The voice of a new and happy century? We ourselves, the grandchildren, the great-grandsons, we are still ever and anew looking about us, lost and intimidated. When will the voice reach our ear? When will it set our hearts in motion?'

He read the sentences through once more, then he stood up. He went to the window and saw that it had begun to snow. He saw some snow on the narrow sill and noticed the flakes falling slowly in the light of the street lamp below. The snow fell upon the park, upon the broad surfaces from its northern to its southern end, it settled upon the flat roofs and the squares of the midtown district and further down among the giant buildings of finance, in the narrow streets in which the silence of the night was now disturbed by no single vehicle, it settled upon the spacious Battery Square close beside the ocean and out on the islands, Ellis Island, Governors Island, Bedlow Island, collected round the feet of the Statue of Liberty and remained lying until the morning hours in little hollows upon her head and shoulders, while in that pearl-grey and white landscape she held aloft her electrically illuminated torch to arriving travellers.

Afterword

by Peter Staengle

With Kafka, Rilke and Werfel, the case was rested long ago – it is commonplace to lay particular emphasis on Prague's significance for modern German literature. A high degree of recognition, however, obscures the view. What else was going on? Who were the comets in the Kafka galaxy? What fate befell the younger generation? Even a cursory glance at Max Brod's volume of memoirs *Der Prager Kreis* (*The Prague Circle*) will detect a shimmering diversity, descry jewels still to be salvaged. It will also hit upon the name of Hermann Grab. In dictionaries of writers or literary histories, this may be sought in vain: 'Even the dead will not be safe from the enemy, if he is victorious. And this enemy has not stopped winning' (Walter Benjamin). Grab left behind him a literary oeuvre of small dimensions: a few stories and the novel *The Town Park*, published in Vienna and Leipzig in 1935. The minimal impact of the (new) editions arranged shortly after the War's end by Ernst Schönwiese, a friend of Grab, confirmed Benjamin's dictum with melancholy emphasis.

The work of Hermann Grab is concentrated in two thematic areas, which present autobiographical material without confessional importunity. These are his Prague childhood, in the sanctuary of a high bourgeois milieu around 1916, and his flight and exile. A compilation of details furnished in letters to his publisher Schönwiese throws light on this background:

> Biography scandalously uninteresting. Born 6 May 1903 in Prague, studied philosophy and music in Prague, Vienna, Berlin, Heidelberg, D.Phil. in Heidelberg. (No mention need be made of the fact that, in order unlike my father to have a free hand in choosing a profession, I took a law degree on the side for the sake of a 'secure future' and for a year worked part-time in the 'lawyer's office' about which you know.) Then a few years as a journalist (music critic) and music teacher in Prague. *Town Park* written 1932, published New Year 1935. Also many unpublished poems, novel and stories. (All this should not be published and has, moreover, for the most part vanished; there is just one bundle of short stories, mislaid in Paris during my flight, that I am still hunting for.)

With respect to the latter, Grab hoped that the manuscript would be found among Walter Benjamin's papers. But Kurt Hobi, who followed up this trail in his valuable dissertation on Grab, unfortunately had no success.

> I left Prague in February 1939, not in order to emigrate for good, but just to take a look around. I gave a concert in Paris which gave me the chance to bring out my three historic keyboard instruments (as you know, music is my daily bread). After 15 March, I naturally did not go back to Prague, I stayed in France. When France collapsed I had the most incredible difficulties in making my escape, but I managed and by the end of June was already in Portugal . . . I came here [to the United States] from Portugal five months later, by the

normal route. Through the most unfortunate con-
catenation of circumstances my mother remained in
Prague, was deported to Poland and died there – a
natural death, so I was told, but everyone knows
how greatly natural death was hastened under such
conditions.

Working in New York as a music teacher, piano-
teaching post in a conservatory. Since becoming an
émigré, have only published a couple of small musical
pieces, written a few novellas and worked on a novel.

But this became true only in the period from 1944 on,
since in another passage he writes: 'To my shame I must
confess that in the first five years of emigration I have
written nothing.' On 2 August 1949 Hermann Grab died
in New York, after a protracted serious illness.

Grab's activity as a musician, and in particular as a
theorist and teacher of music, can be gone into only
sketchily here. But if, under the strain of exile, he
complained about music as a livelihood, this disguises the
fact that he accomplished a considerable amount in it. For
example, as Theodor Adorno writes, only Grab managed
to contribute 'something authentic on the relationship
between individual and oeuvre' in the case of Richard
Strauss.

It is also striking what supreme importance music had
for his literary work. First in terms of content, through the
ever-recurring succession of concerts and piano lessons, of
music critics and piano instructresses. Perhaps more
fundamentally – as H.G. Adler has emphasized – in a
formal and stylistic sense, when advanced musical methods
are utilized in part: 'The comparison with music is . . .
legitimate: it holds good for his thematic direction which,
multi-meaninged like a system of musical motives, is
elaborated and picked up anew; it holds good for his

melodically rhythmic sentence construction, which reveals itself when read aloud.'

How could it have been otherwise with this refined music lover, who was intimately connected with the circle round Arnold Schönberg and from early on fostered close bonds of friendship with George Szell and Rudolf Serkin.

In the winter of 1934 (the edition itself states 1935) *The Town Park* appeared. Grab had already finished his only novel – which Hermann Broch in a letter called 'an extraordinarily talented book' – three years earlier. The book introduced readers to that high-bourgeois world which had given birth not just to himself, but also for example to Franz Werfel (compare the latter's portrayal of this milieu in the story *Kleine Verhältnisse* [*Humble Origins*]). The blurb on the flap of the Vienna edition confirmed the material authenticity: 'My home town Prague, and the memory of a bourgeois childhood with its hopes and its shadowy areas, provide me with the outward occasion for the fable.' A certain identification of the author with his hero may be supposed (the fact that both were able to celebrate their thirteenth birthdays in 1916 is merely the most conspicuous feature they had in common).

The method was not unknown. Klaus Mann, one of Grab's first admirers, had already named the source accurately in his review for the exile journal *Die Sammlung*: 'He has learnt much from Proust . . . Proust . . . invented the technique by means of which a new sensibility, a new experience can be expressed in the smallest and most intricate things. Grab possesses this technique, together with his well-preserved experiential stock of psychic and sensuous impressions. He can thus afford to devote only a minimal place to action.'

There are even parallels of content which another admirer, Peter Hartling, finds traced in a series of motifs (young girl – park – mysterious world of Frau Gérard).

Clearly inspired by Proust are likewise the constantly recurring reflections upon time and the modes whereby it operates and is experienced, and finally the evocation of involuntary remembrance (*mémoire involontaire*) which structures the novel and gives it coherence.

This is what is said in a kind of programmatic passage: 'But Renato was nevertheless to remember this little scene of the first encounter between Felix and Marianne for a long while and even many years later. It had been preserved in the form of one of those snapshots which our mind produces perhaps quite at random, but which when strung together yield the album we leaf through from time to time and see as our life.'

Proust's crucial role for Grab is evident also from the fact that Grab styled himself his first reader in Prague – he could recite long passages of the French original from memory. Furthermore, while *The Town Park* was in gestation, he composed a highly regarded essay on the occasion of the tenth anniversary of Proust's death and a lecture on his life and works.

Other favourite authors: Hofmannsthal and Stefan George come to mind. Special mention should be made of Kafka, about whom more will be said, and Thomas Mann, for the novel was once rightly alluded to as the 'kernel of the Prague Buddenbrooks'. Echoes of Katherine Mansfield and Virginia Woolf are also perceptible. Thus Renato (like Mrs Dalloway before him) had to find out that behind the appearance so laboriously maintained by conventions, the death sentence had long ago been pronounced over the old bourgeois society: ' . . . and as the uncles told their war jokes and even laughed a bit about poor, dead Aunt Melanie, Renato in fact seemed to glimpse – through the damaged places in the scenery and the gaps left where it was badly positioned – the vista of a backstage laid bare: a backstage which extended into the gloom and whose presence took his breath away, as he observed Aunt Melanie in her black casket journeying alone into this darkness.'

The collapse of the bourgeois world, which a (still) functioning surface concealed: that led to the reflections which, in his essay 'On the Beauty of Ugly Images' (1934), Grab devoted to the early work of Max Brod. These can be seen as Grab's *aesthetica in nuce*.

While speaking of Brod, he developed his own creative principles. When, for example, the metaphoric system of the theatre (scenery, background, curtain) is used with special frequency, on the grounds that it can 'indicate most clearly the illusory nature of life' – it shows the 'facade of everyday existence'. This was emphasized and amplified through the image level (equally essential for the novel) of the mechanical (automatic machines), which served to make visible 'the antagonism between real powers and puppet-like life'.

To endure this antagonism and give it literary form was the criterion for Grab's poetic objectivity; his intensive experiential aptitude, his 'retina sensitivity' (Carl Seelig), were based upon it. Moreover, it allows a decisive differentiation from Kafka's method, if one passage in the essay on Brod is slightly amended: 'For whereas in Kafka the surface, the medium, has become transparent to the point of invisibility', in Grab 'the medium [is] of constitutive significance. The most precise artistic sense and the most delicate irony cause the particularity of the time and place to rise up before us . . . From invisible backgrounds the aroma of a city seeps in through the cracks of this world, the air of the lead-steepled dream city Prague.' False reality thus achieves poetic dignity without Biedermeier transfiguration.

Grab did well to define his relationship to Kafka. In their forced allegoricality, the works of the early thirties betray a further clear dependence; the literary loner chose the most natural model (not ultimately even in the geographical sense).

The short story *The Taxi-driver* executes variations on central Kafkaesque motifs. There is the threat from an inaccessible power which has the ability to alter its personifications, a power which is unclean and yet at the same time pure; music degenerates into din, speech becomes unbounded: 'the sounds . . . were not in the least like our customary ones. Those sounds are quite impossible to reproduce' (compare, here, Kafka's animal kingdom or the unsuccessful communication in *Metamorphosis*). Finally, in the end, the (by contrast with Kafka) at best dim remaining knowledge of the origin of guiltless guilt, the irrevocability of the verdict and the permanence of its execution: 'Whatever am I to do? The thing should just never have occurred. It would have been less trouble to bring up my own suitcase.' The symbolic function of the concluding passages in Grab's stories, and of the chapter endings in the novel, should be emphasized particularly.

Only *The Taxi-driver* was preserved in its earlier version. The other stories inspired by Kafka vanished, Hermann Grab reconstructed them later from memory in his New York exile. They are: *The Murderer, What the Dead Man Said* and *Disarray in the Spectre Kingdom* (original title *Spectres*).

In retrospect, however, these first works prove to be not just literary studies; from a distance their temporal relevance is revealed. They can precisely also be read as allegories of the Nazi terror as it approaches and establishes itself. Thus *Disarray in the Spectre Kingdom* symbolizes – as Ernst Schönwiese has shown – the 'collapse of values' diagnosed by Broch: 'Now, alas, there is great disarray in our spectre kingdom. Formerly, as we know, times were different. One could . . . ask and receive a very precise reply.' Now people only smile soothingly. 'In the place to which the spectre folk have vanished, however, there nothing at all is known.' By custom, Count Abelard still roams about, but it seems to be merely a habit. Nothing has happened yet, 'but that is certainly just an accident. On average he comes more and more rarely, soon no more will be heard of him.'

It is still clearer when, in the other story, the murderer with the black moustache (!) forces his way into a family – for which, read 'bourgeois society': 'No one dared move. Eventually it was Monsieur who broke the silence: "Sit down then", he said.' The murderer's cynical affability reminds one dreadfully of that of concentration camp thugs, as documented by the transcripts of war crime trials: 'The murderer had incidentally become very companionable. He pulled out his wallet and took from it a couple of photos. "You must take a look at my lad's pictures", he said to Madame. "The little rascal's five now, look, here he is, sitting in a boat, and here he's standing on his little skis."'

The Nanny, Hermann Grab's first literary text to appear in print, reveals a detachment from Kafka. Though the lodgers may still distantly recall *Metamorphosis*, the material and atmosphere are rather those of *The Town Park*: the nanny is a close relation of the 'willing helpers' Miss Florence and Fräulein Konrad.

The literary works between the novel and the stories produced after 1944 in America should be regarded as probably lost. Unfortunately. For it would have been possible to reconstruct from them an authorial development which Hermann Grab hints at in one passage of a letter referring to *The Lawyer's Office*: 'You will see' this text 'as doubtless equally far removed from the Proustian *Town Park* as from the Kafkaesque *Taxi-driver*.' The generic designation 'novella' exactly catches the character of these stories. The command of plot is clear and taut, without digressions and rigorously outlined. Ideological excursions, which do indeed constitute the paratactic coherence of the novel – its mnemonic structure – but at the same time endow it with a certain breadth, are now entirely dispensed with. To this corresponds the simple language, all the more intensified by its graphic precision, which through its sparseness achieves a lively narrative tempo. Perhaps the finest example of this is furnished by the hectic Italian trip of the secretary so avid for culture in *The Lawyer's Office*.

That there was any fundamental turn in Grab's aesthetic outlook, however, cannot be maintained – at most, a consistent reorientation of his perceptive apparatus. The material is once again remembrance, the self-inflicted fate. But now the connection between the author and what is represented remains unspoken. In the object lens of the autobiographical, fellow sufferers appear: Grab's personal presence in his figures increases in proportion to his withdrawal behind them as their creator. This is shown by a passage from *Peace on the Road to Exile*, of which he said he 'set most store precisely by this novella'. It is said there of Frau Ehrlich's first letter, among other things: 'In vivid language she wrote of their escape from Paris, the congested streets, the Belgian and Dutch refugees', then 'of their arrival in Bordeaux, the mass encampments in railway stations and on open spaces.' In Biarritz, 'however, the news of the capitulation had reached them, here they had heard through the loudspeakers the voice of the aged Marshal': in Bordeaux already 'Herr Ehrlich had, with fortunate prudence, paid the high price for a transit visa via the Negro Republic of Haiti and thereby acquired also permission to travel across Spain and Portugal.' Hermann Grab too, when he escaped from France, passed through the same stopping places on the road to exile.

Peace on the Road to Exile is, as Grab wrote, 'a portrait in miniature' of his sojourn in Portugal. He considered it his most important work. He was nonetheless afraid 'that difficulties stand in the way of its publication, since this story presupposes a maturity on the part of the reading public with which it is perhaps not generally endowed'. His fears, as may be conjectured, affected the presentation, since perhaps nowhere in testimony of similar content is the quest for sanctuary pursued with such nightmarish relentlessness, nowhere is it contrasted with so jarring an atmosphere, which reminds the elderly couple of a holiday trip. The irritation of the reader derives from this contradiction.

To depict the unity of the contradictory, the whole constituted by different layers of reality, was Grab's fundamental poetological principle and the one which can be observed throughout his entire work (allusion has already been made to his treatment of the contradiction between essence and appearance). This principle makes possible a realism which, albeit impressionistically conveyed, never falls slave to the surface appearance. Grab's literary evolution should be seen in the attempt to wrest ever new techniques from this principle.

The Moonlit Night and *Wedding in Brooklyn* achieve complexity through the conjunction of happiness and death. The representational method in *The Lawyer's Office* and the fragment *The Private Ball*, on the other hand, renders transitory the identity of the present. Thus Fräulein Kleinert's dream turns into grisly reality in the concentration camp killers disguised as medical orderlies. The parallel passage in *The Private Ball* speaks for itself: 'Eugenie reflected. She knew she must now deliver a verdict and the verdict was fateful. When we think about later verdicts, of course, and about the lists on which twenty years later Margit's name was included but alongside that of Frau von Lauffer, then it must indeed seem to us as though Eugenie was overrating the importance of her verdict.'

If one surveys all stages of Grab's narrative work, one is tempted to indicate a material unity of the single texts even beyond their autobiographical substance. This is also suggested by the information according to which, only just before his death, Grab was thinking of a novel which was to encompass the period of time marked out by the stories; its hero was to be Felix Bruchhagen.

Like his single works, Hermann Grab's oeuvre as a whole is made up of those snapshots whose inner coherence is established by his principle of dissonant harmonies, as he formulated it in *The Town Park*: 'Even later on, if we may perhaps succeed in drawing a little closer to the truth, even then we are certainly still a long way from having the full truth, which causes all things to harmonize with one another. The world is obviously presented to human vision only in sections and only insofar as these sections are at variance with one another.'

After the Second World War, Hermann Grab's work suffered the same fate that essentially befell all exile literature: for a long while, it found no reception. Entry to the as it were aristocratic precincts of literary history was guarded by its trustees with a zeal brought to mind by the anecdote that Theodor Adorno recounts in his *Ohne Leitbild* [*Without a Model*]: 'In the spring of 1936, Hermann Grab and I were sitting in the Löwenstein Park at Klein-Heubach. My friend was then under the influence of Max Scheler and was speaking enthusiastically about feudalism, which was able to such a degree to harmonize castle and grounds with one another. At that very moment, an attendant appeared and roughly shooed us away: "The benches are reserved for their Noble Highnesses".'

Peter Staengle
Heidelberg, Summer 1984